DEWITCHED

WITCHLESS IN SEATTLE

DAKOTA CASSIDY

COPYRIGHT

ISBN: 9781720113768

Imprint: Independently published

ACKNOWLEDGMENTS

Darling readers,

If you're joining me for the first time, welcome to Ebenezer Falls, Washington! A fictional suburb of Seattle, where my heroine and amateur sleuth, Stevie Cartwright, has gone to lick her witchless wounds.

This cozy mystery is a spinoff of my Paris, Texas, romance series. If you've not visited the whacky happenings in Paris, fear not, darling readers! This series is completely stand-alone. If you've read Paris, expect to see some familiar faces dropping in from time to time.

Though, please note, the Witchless in Seattle Cozy Mysteries series is best read in order, to understand the back story and history of each character, as well as their journeys, which develop and continue from one book to the next.

And lastly, I so hope you'll join me for *The Old*

Witcheroo, book 4 in this series, releasing in August 2016!!

DEWITCHED

BY DAKOTA CASSIDY

CHAPTER 1

"*A*re you Stevie Cartwright?"

A really good-looking older man dressed in a black suit with a lavender shirt and deep-purple tie stood at the opening of my door, where, just behind him, chaos ensued on my front lawn.

In the middle of the swirl of activity, I couldn't help but notice he stood out like a bright plate from Pier One in a sea of Corningware. Not that Corningware isn't perfectly lovely. It is. It's reliable and functional. But it's not exactly Waterford—which is what Win informs me is the best of the best, in his snobby opinion.

Me personally? I'm just fine with a paper plate, but Win (he's my dead British spy ghost) insisted I at least consider upping my taste game and contemplate a more refined set of dinnerware.

Looking up at the stranger decorating my doorway,

his good looks so devastatingly handsome, I forgot the question.

"So you *are* Stevie Cartwright, correct?"

I scanned him from head to toe once again. Wow, the caterers didn't just dip into the handsome lottery pool when they hired the help, they dove in head first.

"You must be the greeter, right?" I stuck out my hand and he took it, though he looked a little confused.

But no worries. My house was enormous and there was more activity going on than at a beehive convention, as everyone prepared for my housewarming party. I was just as confused as him, to be honest. So I waved him in distractedly. What was one more person in the madness?

I scanned him from head to toe again, noting his outfit didn't match the rest of the caterer's staff, but then, his job was to address the guests as they arrived. He should be showier.

Sticking out my hand, I smiled. "It's nice to meet you. Gosh, I hope you don't mind me saying, but you're really good looking. So I'd better warn you now. The mature ladies of Ebenezer Falls are going to have to be herded like cattle or you'll have a backup at this door worse than anything you've ever seen on the I-5. Just a head's up for efficiency's sake."

At first he stood up straight and appeared to preen a little, but then he cocked his head, a head with just enough gray at the temples to be dangerously delicious. "I'm sorry, say again?"

I winced, tightening the belt on my bathrobe. "Did I

2

offend you? Sorry. Sometimes I say things before I think them through thoroughly. It's a curse, I tell you."

"No. No, I'm not offended. Not at all. In fact, I'd quite agree," he said on a velvety chuckle, smoothing his full head of thick black hair. "But I think we have our signals crossed—"

"Stevie!" Win, my ghost I mentioned earlier, yelped in my ear, his distress crystal clear.

I winced and held up a finger to the man who was still talking, his words muffled due to Win.

Dollars to donuts my spy was all up in arms over some minor detail that wouldn't make a hill o' beans difference after tonight was through, but that didn't stop him from nitpicking me to death anyway.

We'd only been planning this housewarming party for a month. Yep, that's right. It had been almost thirty full days of torturous choices—dinnerware, cutlery, silk or rustic-themed napkins, colors, ice sculptures, flowers, lighting, entertainment, and so on. Hence my analogies to Corningware.

Torture, I tell you.

I pressed my fingertips to the Bluetooth I used as my beard for communicating with Win when others were around. I'd been caught a couple of times talking to him as though he were in the room with me, not just in my ear, and it always proved awkward.

So I wore the Bluetooth almost as an accessory nowadays.

"What now? Swear, Winterbottom, if you're inter-rupting me when I'm with the staff—the staff you insisted we hire for this housewarming—just to tell me some Cirque du Soleil member with a fancy, unpronounceable one-letter name is stuck at the airport with her leotard and satin rope again, I'm going to kill you!"

"Now that's simply impossible, isn't it, Cheeky One?"

I bobbed my head, turning around to attack the next problem in the kitchen, when I distractedly noted that the handsome man followed. "Fair point. But I'll think of some way to make you wish you'd never met me if you throw one more problem on my plate. This housewarming was your idea, International Man of Mystery. I would have been fine just inviting everyone from town over for some Cheese Whiz and Triscuits— maybe even pizza or weenies in a blanket if ambition really struck. I've never hosted a party of this size before—let alone with fancy dishes, a string quartet, and some guy hanging from the ceiling in the parlor by a ruffled sheet! Give me a break, would you? It's been Stevie, Stevie, Stevie all day long!"

"Your husband, I presume?" the debonair man asked with a smile.

"I'd rather eat toxic waste," I replied. Curious as to why he was following me around.

Petula, from Parties By Petula, the catering service we'd hired, said her people were go-getters, initiators. She must've said that a hundred times while we planned this party. As handsome as he was, he needed to go take some of that initiative.

"Toxic waste, Dove? Really? Why do you have to be

so curmudgeonly?"

"Are we going to get into the million reasons? After you just finished asking me to shine the handle on the fridge with a cloth made of cashmere?"

"Bah! I didn't. I just said it had a lot of fingerprints and it should be freshened. Be careful not to scratch it, use a soft cloth. A mere suggestion, nothing more."

"Okay, fine. Let's get to the point. I still have to dress and do my makeup before my mother arrives. I've told you about Dita, haven't I? She makes me unreasonable, surly even. I want everything in place before I have to locate her world and make it revolve around her. So what's the problem *this* time?"

"Your mother's attending the party?" the stranger asked, catching a glimpse of himself in the freshly shined fridge. He stopped for a moment in front of the French doors and smiled at his distorted image.

No, he really did. It was exactly like you'd see on a cartoon where the character catches a glimpse of himself in the mirror, smiles, and his teeth sparkle. He flashed a million watts while he lifted his chin and checked each angle with a tilt of his head. Then he gave himself a thumb's up—two, if I'm to be precise.

Healthy self-esteem is a good quality for sure.

But I had things to do. So I tapped him on the shoulder and pointed to the entryway. "Listen, er… really great-looking guy. I have five hundred million things to do before this shindig starts. So if you'd just go wait by the front door for instructions from Petula, I'm pretty sure you won't lack for company."

I didn't bother to wait for his answer of compliance; I had a dress to squeeze into. Waving to the chef in our amazing new white and Italian marble gourmet kitchen before grabbing a blob of cheese with some brown thing under it, I zipped out of the kitchen and up the gorgeous new staircase, alight with twinkling fairy lights.

Racing down the wide hall, I didn't even take the time to admire the smooth, creamy-colored walls or the pictures of scenic cottages Win had personally picked out.

Skidding around the corner, I fell into my bedroom where my familiar, Belfry, napped on the furry back of our rescue dog, Whiskey.

Setting my blob of cheese on the nightstand, I did take the time to appreciate my bedroom.

Gosh, I loved this room. It was every dream I'd ever had as a teenager. Especially my bed, literally built against the tall windows facing the Puget Sound. Framed with wainscoting in pale lemon and a bookcase built into the headboard, and blue and white chintz bedding with tons of fluffy French country pillows. It was, in a word, magnificent.

A hanging chandelier cast a warm glow over the room, the sparkly multi-shaped jewels making shadows on the walls. A white brick fireplace—which I wasn't able to take for a test drive right now at the end of May—sat on the far wall, and would keep me toasty come December. A matching wingback blue chintz chair with a warm cashmere pale lemon throw draped over its back sat by yet another set of windows over-looking the front lawn. To top it off, a big braided rug lay in the center of it all.

It was heaven.

And I really wanted to crawl back into that heaven and forget this whole party thing.

But I'd promised Win I'd get involved with my fellow Ebenezer Fall-ers, and he told me this was the best way to do it. Good food, expensive wine, and ridiculous ice fountains were the way to reintroduce myself to the people I'd grown up with and forge new adult friendships.

He'd said this was how to welcome everyone into my life again after having left when I was just out of high school to move to Paris, Texas, for training as a paranormal 9-1-1 operator for my coven of witches. Who were no longer my coven, by the by.

This party was a friendly way to say "howdy neigh-bor." For some reason, probably because not so long ago I'd lost everyone in my life, Win felt it important to thrust me into the face of anyone who crossed my path because he never wanted me to be alone.

Which I mostly never was. Not with him in my ear, our new dog Whiskey and my bat familiar Belfry. This particular worry of his made *me* worry about Win's future on what we laughingly called the place he was spending his afterlife—Plane Limbo.

Where spirits who aren't yet sure they're ready to cross hang out and linger. Or in Win's case, turn their afterlife into one big party, conga line included. I wondered if all this getting-me-involved meant he was considering crossing over for the first time since I'd met him.

Win had refused to cross over from the start, but I wasn't pushing him to, either. He was one of the reasons I'd been able to keep my head above water after I lost my witch powers. But I worried someday he might not have a choice, and as selfish as it seems, he was my tether these days. My glue. I needed him, and I'd mourn his loss for a very long time if he left.

Whiskey, our St. Bernard, stretched on the bed, his mahogany and white fur rippling as he groaned his pleasure, rolling over for tummy scratches.

"Duuude!" Belfry chirped his discontent. "A little warning before you do that, huh, buddy? You could crush me and then what? Who would you have to pretend-throw the ball to you when these lugs are too busy solving murders?"

I giggled. Belfy is a cotton ball bat. Two inches of snarky, snarly, snow-white, loveable, forever-napping bat, and I'd have never made it this far without him after being kicked out of my coven and losing my powers. He remained steadfast in his loyalty to me as my familiar, the coven be damned.

Plucking him from the bed before Whiskey crushed him, I held him up and looked him in the eye, his yellow snout and ears twitching as he asked, "You ready for tonight, Cinderella?"

"I'm afraid of tonight," I replied, eyeing my glittering red designer dress. A *brand-new* designer dress

Win insisted I purchase, rather than dig into my stash of secondhand vintage clothing.

I love the coup of finding a designer label in a secondhand store. There's nothing more fulfilling when it comes to shopping for clothes. Win insisted I could more than afford all new designer clothing, but he missed the point entirely. If I can just buy whatever I want, it takes the fun out of the hunt. Also, there was a time when I *couldn't* just buy what I wanted—before Win gave me all his worldly possessions.

"You're not nervous, are you, Stevie?" Bel asked. "You know all these people, for cripes sake. What's the big hullabaloo?"

"They've never met me this way, Bel. I used to be just Stevie Cartwright, brooding, pouty, Goth-black-makeup lover. And when we moved back here, I was thrown into the position of Madam Zoltar, medium to the heavens, before anyone really had a chance to see all this. But no one knows *this* Stevie. The one with all the money for a champagne fountain and Italian marble countertops. It feels kinda showy, don't you think?"

Belfry twittered his wings. "If I were you, I'd worry less about that and more about the fact that I have something to tell you. So get dressed. It'll keep your hands busy so you can't grab something and throw it at me."

My eyes narrowed. If Win had put him up to something—like, say, I dunno...elephants arriving at any second—I'd kill him. He and Win were always in cahoots these days.

"Bel…" I said with clear warning.

But he flapped his wings. "Go! Shoo. Put that snazzy dress on and I'll talk."

I set him back on Whiskey's fur and grabbed my amazing dress. Even if it *had* cost the earth, and I hadn't hunted it down myself, it was gorgeous. A long-sleeved turtle neck of glittering red, it cinched at the waist and had a flared skirt that just grazed the middle of my thighs. Paired with silver-strapped heels and shiny silver hoop earrings, I fell in love with it the minute Win pointed it out in an expensive boutique in Seattle.

I made my way into my equally fabulous bathroom with a real cast-iron claw-foot tub and said, "Okay, Bel. What's on your mind?"

"Are you near the soap dish?"

"Why?"

"I don't want you to throw it at me."

I couldn't hold back my laughter. "Just spit it out."

"My parents are coming."

Sweet Pete on a carousel.

I pulled my dress over my head and let it fall to my waist, brushing it past my hips without saying a word.

"Boss? You still upright?"

Grabbing the brush, I ran it through my hair, happy with the caramel highlights I'd had added just yesterday. My chestnut hair was rather drab, in my opinion, and now that it was growing out, I needed a change.

"Boss?" Bel repeated with a tentative tone.

"I'm still upright. When?"

"Well, that's the thing…"

"*When*, Bel?"

"Tonight. Oh, crud, I might as well just spit it all out. They're bringing—"

"Not Com and Wom. Please say the twins are off in familiar boot camp or something." I almost moaned, biting the inside of my cheek. *Pleasepleaseplease-pleaseplease.*

Bel snorted. "You're joking, right? What witch in even her half-right mind would want one of those two hooligans for a familiar? They couldn't guide a pet rock, let alone a fully grown witch with fully grown powers."

I loved Belfry. He was my family, always—but *his* family?

The Bats (yes. That's really their last name. Bat) were a firestorm of crashing, sticky fruit drippings and mayhem.

His twin brothers Com and Wom were like toddlers on a continual sugar rush, always into something. And Mom Bat? Mostly as adorable as Bel but not exactly on top of things, if you know what I mean. She turned a blind eye to her sons' shenanigans more often than not.

And Dad Bat, well, he was of the mind that boys will be boys. The translation of that? Win's house and all the beautiful things he'd filled it with were going to crumble around our ears by the time they left.

But wait…

I gripped the white porcelain sink and closed my

eyes as a shiver of dread slithered up my spine.

"Belfry? Is Uncle Ding coming, too?" Then I winced and said a silent prayer.

"Yes…?" he replied in a hesitant squeak.

My head fell to my chest and I took deep breaths. Uncle Ding Bat (again, yes. That's his real name) was a feisty senior—all wings and snout in all the wrong places. Mostly *my* wrong places.

But okay. I could do this. If I could handle a houseful of two hundred guests or so, people spinning from sheets in the living room, and a testy French chef in the kitchen, I could handle the Bats coming for a visit. They deserved to see their son as much as the next parents.

"Are we still speaking?" he asked, flying into the bathroom as I quickly applied some lipstick and mascara.

"Don't be silly. Of course we are. Just remember to keep them away from Dita. You know how much she loathes the twins."

He settled on my loofah on the sink. "I'm on it, Boss. By the way, have I told ya how proud I am of you for inviting Momster?"

Nodding, I jabbed my earrings into the holes in my ears and slipped on my sandals. "You have. She'd have found out about the party anyway, because she and Bart are traveling through Seattle to Ebenezer Falls to pick up some things she has in storage. So it was an easy decision."

In truth, it wasn't an easy decision. Sharing my life

and all the new things in it with my mother wasn't something I was doing lightly. I'd thought a lot about this. But over the last couple of months, I'd seen people torn apart who'd never be able to make things right. Not until they met somewhere else again—if they met somewhere else at all.

I didn't want to leave this plane motivated by disharmony and anger.

"You're a good egg, Stevie. I know Dita's not exactly Donna Reed, but maybe you can make lemonade. Or at least martinis. Booze has helped less get through far worse."

The moment my mother Dita heard I'd been booted from my coven—after a powerful warlock accused me of meddling with his family and slapped the witch out of me from the great beyond (yep. He literally slapped the witch right out of me)—she'd shut down all communication. Probably for fear our leader, Baba Yaga, would punish her for consorting with the shunned.

It didn't matter that when it came to your child, nothing should prevent you from supporting her— short of murder, that is. And even then, you can hate the crime and still love the criminal.

But my mother wasn't that sort of mother. She was shallow, vain, and went through boyfriends and husbands like I went through Pop-Tarts. Nurturing wasn't part of the plan with my mother. Sometimes I wondered how I'd survived my childhood, as distant as she'd been…as caught up in her own life as she'd been.

But over the past couple of months, with the changes in my life being what they were, I'd realized I'd be in my grave long before her immortality would run out.

I'd seen a lot of death these past couple of months, and even if we didn't get along, I didn't want to leave this world angry with her. Mildly irritated might be the only way, but harboring all this leftover childhood anger with her was not. I was going to accept her for who she was and not hope she'd miraculously turn into Carol Brady.

Because that would never happen. Plus, *The Brady Bunch* had way more kids than my mother would ever be able to handle.

Taking one last look at my reflection, I smoothed my hands over my dress and blew out a breath of pent-up air. Everything would be okay. It was going to be a great night.

"You look beautiful, Stevie," Belfry said on a whistle. "Never prettier."

I curtsied and smiled, stroking his head with my fingertip. "Why thank you, kind bat."

As I headed back into my bedroom, my stomach rumbled, reminding me I hadn't had the chance to eat all day. Scooping up the blob of cheese and brown stuff, I shoveled it into my mouth.

I regretted that the moment it hit my tongue. "Oh my goddess!" I spit it out, wiping my tongue with my finger as I gagged. "What is that?"

"I'll have you know, it's goat cheese from the finest

stock. A herd raised by monks, thank you. And fig, grown and shipped straight from the trees in California," Win chided.

"It tastes like sweat and airplane fuel," I said, gagging again.

"You've eaten sweat and airplane fuel, I gather?"

"No. I'm only guessing, but if you'd like, I'll go drain Sea-Tac before I'll eat any more of that."

"You have the taste buds of a five-year-old, Stevie Cartwright. If it's not a Pop-Tart or a box of Cheez-its, you can't process it on that undeveloped palate of yours."

I held my hand out to Whiskey and offered him the snack. "Here, buddy. You have airplane fuel and sweat. It's on me."

But Whiskey took one sniff and whined, turning his nose up at it and making me laugh. "See? Not even our dog will eat it. Now, I need to move it because the alarm on my phone is bound to go off any second, telling me something else is arriving. I just can't remember what. Clowns?"

"Perish the thought. Mimes, Stevie. We've hired mimes. They're the silent, *refined* entertainers."

I did my best impression of a mime stuck in a box.

"Thank goodness we hired professionals," Win drawled in his uppity British accent. But then he paused just as I started toward the door to join the chaos downstairs.

"Stevie?"

"Uh-huh?"

His aura wrapped me in a warm bubble. "You look stunning tonight. Positively, beautifully glowing," Win said, his voice husky and silken in my ear.

I swallowed the lump in my throat, unsure why his compliment made me choke up. "Thanks, Win," I whispered before I scurried back down the hall and toward the stairs.

As I zoomed down the steps as fast as I could in heels, I inhaled at the sight of that man again, still at the front door. He was smiling his movie-star smile. Chatting amicably with some of the quartet and signing a napkin.

Curious indeed, but I had no time for investigating.

Still, I couldn't get over how good looking he was, and from this distance, maybe even a little familiar? Nah. Where would I know a guy like him from?

I stopped at the bottom of the steps, my hands wrapped around the thick square of the banister cap, and caught my breath before entering the melee of activity.

That was when he approached me, his movie-star smile on point. "Stevie? May I speak with you?"

"Oh, of course."

"Privately?" He swept his arm in the direction of the parlor like he was introducing royalty.

"Well, it's not exactly private. I mean, there's a guy hanging from a sheet in there." I pointed to where, moments ago, the Cirque acrobat had been checking the pulleys the engineers had installed especially for his performance.

He turned up the wattage on his smile of persuasion. "He's gone on a quick bathroom break."

"Then sure," I mumbled. What was so important he had to talk to me in private? He was a door greeter—or something fancy Win had given a label to, but I'd never heard of.

He held out his arm and offered an escort.

I gave him a strange look but reminded myself, he was older. Chivalry wasn't dead for him. So I slipped arm through his and let him lead me into the living room, er…parlor. Win called it a parlor.

White calla lilies and hydrangeas filled tall vases scattered about the room, on end tables and atop a chest of drawers, all created at the local florist shop owned by Adele Perkins. The sheet still hung from a beam spanning the ceiling, the soft silk cascading to the floor in a pool of lavender.

"So how can I help you?" I looked up at him, drawn by his compelling gaze.

"My name is Hugh Granite, and—"

I think my shoulders shook a little with laughter when I heard him say his name, making him stop speaking. I didn't mean to almost laugh, but c'mon. Hugh Granite? You have to admit, it's comedy gold.

Yet, he still gazed down at me as though confused, giving me the impression no one laughed at him or his name, and if they did, they were of no importance.

So I covered my almost laugh with a cough and rubbed my nose. "Sorry. Allergies. Nice to meet you…

er, Hugh…Granite." I spit his name out, stuttering and coughing some more to hide further snickers.

Hugh Granite. Priceless, I tell you. I hoped Win was hearing this.

"Yes. That's correct. I am *the* Hugh Granite. International star of stage, screen and film. In Japan, of course."

Of course. *The* Hugh Granite. Big, big star. In *Japan*.

I fought another laugh, holding my breath to keep from snorting because his face said he wasn't joking around. His title meant something to him, and he was looking at me like I was just shy of the cuckoo's nest for not acknowledging as much.

But he was so endearing in the most overblown way, I couldn't mock him. Though, I'm sure Win was having a field day in his head right now.

"Well, it's nice to meet you, but if we could just get to the point? My mother's coming, and if you knew my mother, you'd want time to gather your wits and put them somewhere you can find them so they're handy when she starts poking you with her big stick. Mothers, right? Sheesh."

Now his face changed, but only for a blip of a second before he was smiling again, catching his reflection in the big picture window to his left and straightening his shoulders. "Of course, I understand. My mother is nothing like yours. *Nothing*. But still, I understand." He patted my shoulder with his impeccably manicured fingers as though he were soothing me.

Okey-doke, then. I bit my lower lip and scrunched

my eyebrows together in a frown. I couldn't help it. I was missing something here. "Okay, so what was it you wanted to talk to me about?"

Now he nodded again, his dark, perfectly groomed hair never moving. "I, Hugh Granite, have come to tell you something. Something wonderful," he said in his game-show announcer's voice, each word over-enunciated.

Did all stars of stage, screen, and film use third-person narrative when they talked about themselves? Maybe it was a Japanese thing...

Scratching my head, I sighed and glanced up at him. "Okay. Well could you do that, please? I have tons of guests coming and if you only knew the kind of crazy chaos happening in my kitchen right now, with that wood-fire pizza oven, you'd see why I want to move this along. So, Hugh Granite, talk to me."

"As requested, then..." He paused, rather grandly for emphasis, if I do say so myself, and held out two hands to me as though he were offering me a gift.

But I didn't take them because this was getting weirder by the second.

"Mr. Granite, you were saying?"

He let his hands fall to his sides and puffed out his chest as though preparing for an important speech. And then he let 'er rip.

"I'm pleased to announce that I am your father."

Then he gave me a thumb's-up sign and grinned wider still—and I'd swear I saw his teeth sparkle.

CHAPTER 2

"*Y*our mouth is open, Dove." Win whispered the gentle reminder.

"So you're not the doorman who works for Petula?" I squeaked.

"It's *herald*, Stevie. If he weren't an international star of stage, screen and film, he'd be the herald. A herald announces the guests with flourish," Win admonished on a grating sigh of frustration.

Right. That was the fancy word Win had used when he'd decided to have each person announced as they arrived.

But Hugh smiled again, his dark eyes twinkling. "No. But I understand your confusion. I once played a maître d' in one of my earliest Japanese films. A pivotal role for me, if I do say so myself. A young, handsome devil of a man, seeking his fortune in sushi. That must be where you recognize me from."

"Stevie? Close your mouth again, Dove."

I did as I was told, but I still wasn't able to think of a single thing to say.

"Now answer *the* Hugh Granite, international star of stage, screen and film, and the man who claims he's your father, Dove. It's impolite to ignore a guest."

But I couldn't form words. So I just kept staring at Hugh.

Hugh sighed, his wide shoulders lifting upward. "You're in shock. A wonderful shock, I'm sure. This happens to me all the time when people first meet me, and it's delightful. It isn't every day you find out Hugh Granite is your father, is it?" he asked, his words bloated like his ego. But I couldn't even be angry at him for thrusting himself upon me like he was the Gift of The Magi.

Because he was so dang *cute*. No, really, aside from his incredible good looks, perfect hair, even more perfect teeth, he was darn well adorable.

There was no denying his voice was gentle and warm, and matched the look in his eyes as he stared down at me tenderly—almost hesitantly, waiting for me to react.

"Stevie? We have things to deal with promptly. So for now, say these words," Win ordered in his concise British take-charge tone. "It's a pleasure to meet you, Hugh Granite, international star of stage, screen, and film, but as you can see, I'm very busy right now. Can we have a nice long chat about where you've been for the last thirty-two years of my life after I deal with the acrobats and mimes and my party has gone off without a hitch?"

I frowned, but I attempted to repeat the words anyway, because they sounded like they might get me out of the frying pan for the time being and stall the flaming fire.

"It's nice to meet you, Mr...er, stage, screen, and Japanese film star, but party...and thirty-two years, actually almost thirty-three now. And um, stuff...to do... So, talk later. I mean, you and me. M'kay? Gotta go." I pointed in the direction of the hall outside the parlor.

And with that, I pivoted on my heel and ran from the room like the devil himself had shown up for the party.

I'd hoped to find shelter in the bathroom just off the kitchen so I could process what had just happened, but was intercepted by Petula, who had that needy look on her face. The one that said there was a problem. It didn't happen often, and she was a stickler for perfection. So when she came running, I asked how high I should jump.

She raced toward me, her wide hazel eyes glassy, her sandy-blonde hair piled on top of her head in haphazard fashion with a clip. "There you are!" she drawled on a sigh of relief, gripping my arm with her pudgy hand. "We need someone to make a decision about the ice sculpture of the dragon. Apparently there's been some kind of mix-up on placement. Can you come with me?"

I liked Petula. She was a crackerjack of sound and motion. Chubby, which—she declared with a warm smile that made her eyes crinkle around the outer corners—was from sampling her vendors' foods. She was warm and friendly and she always smelled like a pastry store with a hint of sage.

I let her lead me away mostly because I didn't have a choice, stumbling in my heels as we headed back down the hallway to the front door and out onto the porch.

Petula pointed to the amazingly gorgeous round tables covered in pale-pink silk tablecloths that dotted my front lawn, set up in a circular fashion to encourage mingling. "Do you want the sculpture on the dessert table, or the table where the Bustamante boys will make made-to-order fajitas and tacos?"

Win had insisted we utilize the talents of some of the food truck owners, and the Bustamantes were high on his list, as was Carlito, now an honorary Bustamante, according to Maggie and her boys. Her daughter Bianca was still warming to him.

Long story short, Tito Bustamante was murdered last month, and he'd owned a taco truck—the best-ever taco truck. My favorite dining experience in all of Ebenezer Falls. Tito's son, Carlito—a son he went to his grave unaware of—had come to town to locate his biological father in the middle of the investigation into Tito's death.

Tito's adopted sons, Mateo and Juan Felipe, now ran the taco truck in their father's stead, and they'd included Carlito in every way possible.

But I didn't even have time to consider how proud Tito would have been if he could see his adopted children, born to Maggie from her first marriage, and his newly found biological son working so well together, before Win said, "Oh, definitely tell her the dessert table. Dragons breathe fire—we don't want to evoke images of heartburn mixed with our Mexican food, do we?"

Clearly he'd read my lack of focus, and likely the blank expression on my face, the way he always does. And he always knows exactly what to do.

I nodded distractedly. I don't know why I hadn't made the correlation between fire and spicy tacos. Duh. It was so obvious.

Not.

"The Mexican table. So we don't inspire an OD on antacids—or something. Does that work, Petula?"

Petula clapped her work-worn hands. "Of course. You're so clever! And now I'm off. The quartet should arrive at any second and I'd like them warmed up and playing before the guests begin to arrive, which should be in about twenty minutes."

She hopped down the wide front steps of the house in her sensible shoes, all energy and motion, and threw herself into the fray of activity, leaving me to continue staring blankly, unable to move.

"Stevie?"

"Uh-huh?"

"Maybe you should take a moment?" Win suggested.

"Or a lot of moments," I mumbled as the lights, strategically mapped out by Win, began to turn on, turning my front yard into a twinkling mint-green and soft white fairy garden. The evening was cool, but not uncomfortably so, and the chance we'd taken by having an outdoor party in May, in Seattle, looked like it wouldn't end up the risk I'd envisioned.

The newly planted hydrangeas in blue and white, their fat blooms drooping from their stems, added to the aura of an English cottage garden. Lavender and purple salvia surrounded them, accented by pink tea roses, the flowers all aglow with specifically chosen lighting to best accent their beauty.

Chester, the man I secretly considered my surrogate grandfather—and the real grandfather of the man I was dating casually—had helped me meticulously plan this particular garden, and it was as beautiful as I'd hoped.

But I couldn't enjoy it right now, or take pride in it, because my *father*, Hugh Granite, was somewhere inside my house, certain I was thrilled to bits he'd made an appearance after almost thirty-three years.

How did I even know he was telling the truth?

"Dove, please take a moment to gather your thoughts."

"Do you really think he's…" I couldn't finish the sentence. It sounded ludicrous in my head. I couldn't imagine what it would sound like out loud.

"Your father? I will admit, there's a resemblance. It's

in the line of your jaw and the set of your pretty eyes. What I'd like to know is how and why?"

"Why now and how did he find me?"

"Exactly. We must protect you from frauds, Stevie. You're a very rich woman. Now, I'm going to stress once again, please take a moment to gather your thoughts. Have a glass of wine. I want this to be an enjoyable evening for you. As good as it possibly can be, after Hugh's admission. I don't want you frazzled and upset. I'll have Belfry call Petula, if need be, and give him instructions to pass on to her if we run into any more problems."

Petula, as well as Liza, the college student and friend I'd hired to handle the Madam Zoltar shop in town, both thought Belfry was my virtual assistant from Connecticut. It helped tremendously to fall back on Bel and Win.

But I shook my head. If I didn't think about what had just happened, I could compartmentalize it for now. But there was just one thing I had to ask myself.

If Hugh Granite, international star in Asia or wherever, really was my father, how had two such vain people made *me*? Given, Hugh was certainly sweetly egotistical, but my mother? Not so much.

Maybe I should ask him to leave and come back another day when I was more prepared to find out if he was just messing with my head? Was he dangerous? He sure didn't look dangerous. But there were plenty of madmen out there who looked as gentle as newborn kittens. I didn't know what to do. So many decisions, so few brain cells not already eaten up by party matters.

Yes. Wine. I needed wine. Maybe that would help me loosen up enough to parse through all this new information.

"Stevie? Wow! You look beautiful," Forrest called before he let a whistle go, thus, ending my dilemma.

As he climbed the porch steps, I had to admit, he looked pretty impressive, too. He'd worn a tux, the crisp lines and smooth material accentuating his chiseled face and sandy-brown hair.

I reached up and tweaked his bow tie with a grin. I liked Forrest. I liked him a great deal. He was easy to talk to, made killer coffee at his shop, the Strange Brew, and he was even easier on the eyes.

We'd had a few dates now, coffee, dinner, sometimes lunch. But nothing serious.

I forced myself to look as relaxed as possible even as my eyes scanned the lawn for Hugh. "You look pretty great yourself. I was just going to grab a glass of wine. You want one, too?"

"Sure," he said with one of his devastatingly handsome smiles. "The house looks amazing, Stevie. I can't believe you pulled this and a housewarming party together in so little time." Putting his hand at my waist, he ushered me back inside the house.

"Me either, but we did it."

"We?"

"Oh, I meant me and Enzo and his crack team of

subcontractors. Never could have done it without him. He's a miracle worker for sure."

Forrest stopped just as we stepped into the entry-way, where I gave a cautious peek around for Hugh.

"Did you hear that?"

I paused to listen. "Hear what? The string quartet? They're warming up."

He shook his head and cocked his ear. "No, that wasn't the sound of violins I heard."

And then I heard it, too.

A shrill scream.

Turning back toward the wide-open front door, I shot Forrest an apologetic smile before I ran to see what was going on.

It was one of the Cirque du Soleil members. I'd name-dropped Win's name in order to entice her to come perform. Of course, *after* I'd done all my name-dropping, I asked Win how a spy comes to know an entire troupe of acrobats. To which he answered, who doesn't appreciate women who could twist themselves into every position in the Kama Sutra without a single grunt?

Short answer to my question? None of your beeswax, lady.

Anyway, the long-limbed, graceful goddess in a soft-pink leotard was screaming and swatting at her hair.

"Get eet off!" she screamed in a pretty French accent. "Eet's in my haaair!"

And that's when I saw it—a tiny white bat wing

poking out from the troupe member's long blonde locks.

Aw, heck. The Bats had arrived. Let the games begin.

I zipped down the steps as fast as my heels would allow, making a dash across the lawn as the petite woman screamed in terror again. "Kill eet! Get eet out!"

A crowd had begun to form and someone, also in a leotard, with a pair of scissors, pushed their way through the gathering performers.

"Noooo!" I bellowed, diving into the throng of people, pushing my way past them to get to the acrobat. "Wait! I can help!"

The slender woman trembled, her hair a nest of tangles as she shook her arms out, bouncing oh so gracefully in a circle. "Get eet out! Get zis beast out of my hair!"

I latched onto her arm and turned her to face me before eyeing the man with the scissors. "You! Put the scissors away, *please*. Now, just hold still. It's probably just a bat, as scared as you are. They're common in these parts, and I know it's freaking you out, but we need bats as part of our ecosystem so please try *not* to hurt it. I promise, if you just hold still...er, what's your name?"

"K," she said on a violent shiver. "Just the letter, notheeng else."

"Just one letter?" I asked for the sake of Win, because I couldn't stop laughing over their one-letter names.

"*Oui, mademoiselle,*" she said on another shiver

"Before you say anything else, mostly everyone in the troupe *does* have one-letter names, Stevie. Save the crass jokes for later," Win chastised before I'd even had the chance to crack a joke.

I fought a smirk and gripped K's arm. "Right, K. Just hold still and I promise I can get him out of your hair without you losing any."

I began to spread her lush locks and ramble on about the plusses of bats, plucking until I identified Ding, Bel's uncle. Of course it was Ding. The old adage "blind as a bat" definitely applied in his case.

"You are not frightened?" K asked, calmer now as I untangled Ding.

"Nah. It's just a bat." I pulled him out and held him up briefly while everyone's eyes widened and they made horrified faces. "See? Aren't they cute?"

Pushing her hair from her face, K's slight body shuddered in revulsion. "Eet's deesgusting. Ack!"

"You oughtta tell the broad to eat somethin' before she starts usin' words like—"

I coughed—loudly, to cover Uncle Ding's retort. "I'll just take him out back and set him free. I'm sorry you were frightened." I tucked Uncle Ding into the palm of my hand as the performers rallied 'round K to soothe her, hoping they hadn't heard his response.

When I reached the steps, I opened my hand and gave Ding a stern look. "Uncle Ding, what were you told about flying without an escort?" I whisper-yelled.

"Well, hello gorgeous!" he chirped, his sweet aging

face a total deception. Uncle Ding was a letch. An utter and total tiny ball of letch. All tiny hands, all the time. "Long time no see, hottie. I had an escort, but I left his butt in my dust somewhere around Eugene, the slowpoke."

"Oh, you did not," I admonished, pointing a finger at him. "I know you, Uncle Ding. You sonar-ed her boobs from way up there, didn't you?"

He shrugged his wings before giving me a guilty look, his wrinkly white face scrunching up. "Okay, so my aim's a little off."

"You're such a fibber. Uncle Ding, you cannot accost the women attending this party. Understand? It's unacceptable, and if you'll be staying here, we have to have rules."

"Fine, fine. Everybody's always with the rules, so serious and everything. Bats just wanna have fun."

"But you can't have fun in an unsuspecting woman's boobs. Now, I'll take you up to see Belfry, and you must stay in my bedroom during this party. But above all, behave, please? There are a ton of humans down there who'd become unhinged if they knew you could talk. Hear me?"

"Like you need to ask twice. Who *wouldn't* want to stay in your bedroom?"

"Ah, charming old goat, isn't he?" Win cracked.

Uncle Ding bristled in my hand. "Who the flippity-flop was that?"

I held him at eye-level. "You can hear him? How?"

"Sonar, honey. Yeah, I can hear him."

How interesting. "That's my British ghost, Uncle Ding. An ex-spy from the afterlife."

"Oh yeah?" he croaked. "I thought you couldn't talk to dead people anymore? Rumors all over the place in Familiar-ville goin' around about ya. What gives, hot stuff?"

With a sigh, I made my way up the stairs and ran for my bedroom to bring Uncle Ding to Bel. "It's a long story. Hey, where's the rest of the family?"

And then I heard another scream from outside, and someone's panic-riddled yelp. "Look! There's more of them!"

"Uncle Ding? Rev up the old sonar and tell the family to fly into the open bedroom window on the second floor, please. And you all need to stay hidden. No one knows I'm an ex-witch. This isn't like Paris, where you can freely fly around wherever you want," I said, referring to my old hometown in Texas where everyone was paranormal.

"Do ya think I just checked out of the crib at the maternity ward, girlie? I know the score. Keep your fancy dress on, I'll send 'em a message."

Carrying him to my bedroom, I set him on the bed next to Whiskey and Bel and ran to the window to open it, just before the rest of the Bats flew inside in a cloud of white.

They tackle-hugged Belfry, rolling him over the surface of the bed and making him squeal with feigned reproach. "Stop, you guys! Com, quit drooling! It hasn't been that long!"

"You c'mere to mama, my squishy love muffin," Mom Bat—or Deloris, as I called her—squeaked with warmth.

"Son, good to see you, boy!" Bel's father, otherwise known as Melvin—or more lovingly, Bat Dad—nudged Belfry.

The twins, Com and Wom, lunged for Belfry again, knocking him over with their roughhousing. A tumble of white cotton rolled across my pillow, making Whiskey groan his displeasure.

The scene made me smile. They might be a handful, but they loved Bel, and he loved them. That was all I really cared about.

Plunking down on the bed, I stroked Whiskey's fur. "Okay, so guys, I need you to listen, please. Stay put tonight. You can get plenty of exercise once the party's over, but if I hear another scream of sheer terror because one of you crash-landed in the punch bowl, it's curtains for you. Got it?"

"I got this, Boss," Bel assured. "You go enjoy your party and tell me all about it when you're done."

I stroked his head and smiled. "Thanks, buddy. Enjoy your visit."

Scratching Whiskey on the head, I'd turned to make my way out of the bedroom when I heard an all-too-familiar voice call out with enthusiasm, "Stephania! Where's my girl?"

Ugh. Momster in the house.

"$\mathcal{W}$hat was all the commotion with Hardy Clemmons?" Win asked in my ear as I skirted running into my mother for the third time tonight, ducking behind an ice sculpture of a castle and peering around it to see which way she'd gone.

"A commotion? I missed the commotion. Is everything all right?"

"You missed the commotion because you're hiding. And I imagine everything worked itself out. I only came in on the tail end of Hardy stomping off in a huff. Seems calm enough now. Why do you hide from your mother, Stephania?" Win asked as I crouched lower.

"Why does a chicken hide from a fox? Or a more current analogy, Taylor Swift from Kanye West?"

"Now, Stevie. She can't be *all* bad, can she? Stop ducking around corners and trying to make yourself small so she won't see you, because we *can* see you. The invisible game doesn't work in real life like it does when there are monsters under your bed."

I pressed my finger to my Bluetooth and whispered, "I'm not hiding. I said hello to both she and Bart."

"Yes. Indeed you did. Then you gave her the warmest air-kiss ever."

"You hush. Who do you think taught me to air-kiss? My mother. That's right. She taught me to do that so I wouldn't muss her hair or her lipstick."

Or her clothes or whatever else was important to her nab-a-man ensemble.

"You're still hiding from her," he accused.

Yeah, I really was. After the good talking to I'd given myself, I still wasn't able to just pretend nothing had gone wrong with us—I wasn't able to hide the hurt over her not at least checking on me to see if I was okay after losing my powers. "Well, have you seen her?"

"Oh, indeed I have. She's quite lovely. Breathtaking. Just like you."

I'd warm to that compliment if it meant anything, but Win thought every woman with a pulse was breathtaking. "Yes, she's beautiful, isn't she?" I asked, rising and slipping past the crowd gathered at the Cirque exhibit, where women in tasteful bathing suits were acrobatically slipping in and out of a life-sized champagne glass full of water. "But that's not what I meant. Or did you miss how she eyeballed every available man on the lawn like they were candy in a candy store?"

"I didn't see that at all. I saw her glance, maybe even peruse, yes. But eye? No. That's too strong a word."

My mother was always on the hunt for a new husband on the off chance the old one died or divorced her. She'd once told me it never hurt to keep your options open.

And she was doing just that, making quite a splash as she wove her way through the partygoers, reintroducing herself, with the handsome Bart on her arm.

I tried to focus on how beautiful everything was, how it was all running like the clockwork Win had said it would. How everyone was dancing and laughing and eating the amazing food. But I felt edgy and snappish while my mother held court.

Some might call that jealousy, but it's not that at all. I used to be overjoyed with pride when all my little friends said my mother was the prettiest mom ever. Because she was. She still was. Her skin was like peachy porcelain, smooth and creamy, her blue-gray eyes wide and shiny with a thick fringe of lashes that were all hers.

She didn't look her age, not even a little. Her body was firm beneath her backless gold lamé dress, her tanned legs toned, her arms sculpted. A crown of her gorgeous chestnut hair was strategically placed high on her head, artfully dyed with red lowlights, the rest falling to the middle of her back, which might look ridiculous on some women her age, but not my mother.

Like I said, I was once very proud about having the prettiest mom in Ebenezer Falls.

Until she stole one of my friends' fathers right out from under that friend's mother's nose. Needless to say, sixth grade ended up a hellish year, where I sat alone on the playground at lunchtime and recess.

"Well, you have to admit, she seems happy with your stepfather. Maybe true love has changed her?"

That she did. She smiled and laughed up at him, cooed over his every word. Bart was as handsome as Dita was beautiful, his dark suit expensive, his cufflinks like shiny jewels at his wrists. Everything about him screamed money—just the way mom liked her men. He was totally snow white, which was unusual for my mother. She typically liked them darker, but I guess it didn't matter what color their hair was if they had a fat bank account.

Bart held himself with a regal air, his wide shoulders making my mother's look diminutive and delicate. And I'm sure he was an awesome guy. A guy who'd no doubt have his heart broken before Dita was through with him.

Had she broken Hugh Granite's heart?

And where was my sperm-donating Japanese star of stage and screen, anyway? Why was he just now popping into my life? Was he paranormal—a warlock, maybe? And what would he say when he and my mother finally met up again after thirty-two years? Should I warn her that he was here? *Was* he even still here? Had they already run into each other? I shuddered at the thought.

As always, Win read my mind. "Do you think you should mention to your mother your alleged father is here? Won't it be awkward for all involved that he just popped in after all this time, after she never told you who he was to begin with? Wouldn't she be the person to ask if *the* Hugh Granite is really your father?"

"I don't even know where he is, and we don't even know if he's telling the truth, Win. I gave a lot of thought to what you said about people trying to con me for my money. Maybe that's all this is?"

"I know you have a lot on your plate tonight, but giving your mother fair warning is the very least you can do, con man or not."

Win was right. He was always right. "You're right. I don't like it, but you're right. If you see her, shoot me the memo, okay?"

"Dove? I thought you were going to try to get past all the baggage with your mother and move forward. Circumstances in your life being what they are right now."

I bobbed my head. That was fair. I *had* said that. This was all part of turning over a new leaf. I'd better get turning.

"You're right again. I promise I'll go find her and we'll chat."

But Forrest grabbed me from behind, wrapping his arm around my waist, and I didn't stop him. "Dance, milady?" he whispered in my ear.

I giggled and let him spin me around before leading me to the dance floor set up in the middle of the lawn, surrounded by dreamy globe lights. The quartet was on a break and the small orchestra had begun a zippy tune.

Smiling, I said, "Just for a minute and then I have to find my mother."

"Color me intrigued. *The* Dita Cartwright, back in Ebenezer Falls after all this time," he teased.

Even more intriguing—that everyone prefaced my parents' names with a preposition—or was that an article? Again, another decision I was incapable of making.

"Live and in the flesh," I remarked dryly. I hadn't shared much with Forrest about my mother, not in the way I had with Win. It was too personal; too embarrassing for someone I was just getting to know.

Forrest twirled me, pulling me close and swaying. "Did I already say you look amazing tonight?"

I grinned, my cheeks flushing hot. "You did. But I don't mind hearing it again."

"Then you look amazing tonight," he whispered once more before brushing his lips over mine.

I didn't even have time to process Forrest's kiss or how it made me feel before, Ginger Jenkins, tapped me on the shoulder, sliding in beside us to sway in sync with our movements.

"There you are, Stevie! We've been looking all over for you! How's our favorite medium these days?" Ginger smiled broadly, her petite height shadowed by the linebacker frame of her husband, Ronald Terrence Jenkins, the presiding mayor of Ebenezer Falls.

"I'm good, Mrs. Jenkins. Glad you could make it."

I knew why her smile was so bright and what she was angling for. It was an election year, and Win had been right: since I'd come into all this money, everyone wanted a piece of me.

"Stevie, wonderful to see you—terrific party. And you look lovely," Ron said, his fake politician grin firmly in place as he tipped his glass of champagne in my direction.

"You, too, Mr. Mayor. Funny how things change, huh? I remember when you used to be my seventh-grade science teacher and now look. You're the mayor!"

Ron brightened his smile as Ginger patted him on his barrel chest with affection and rocked with him. "We'd love to talk to you about our upcoming campaign if you have time this week."

I smiled and nodded distractedly before Forrest whisked me away again, saving me from putting my foot in my mouth—which I was often wont to do.

I sighed in relief against him, patting him on the back. "Thank you. I never know what to say when people start talking about money. I just inherited it. I don't know the first thing about campaign donations."

The story I told everyone who wondered how I was making it rain cash was simple. I told them a dear friend left it to me—and that wasn't far from the truth.

I'd heard a rumor or two about me and some torrid

affair with an older man (or "just like her mother"), but for the most part, everyone just took me at my word.

Forrest laughed, gripping my hand while his other rested at my waist. "Me either, but Ron's campaigning hard, so look out. Though, if I'm honest, someday I'd like to hear all about how you came into all this."

I looked around at all the things money bought. The mimes, slipping in and out of the clusters of people in their black-and-white striped shirts and white face paint. The orchestra, sitting in a pit in front of the dance floor with the garden as their backdrop, playing Sinatra tunes.

The Cirque acrobats, twisting and arabesque-ing with colorful sheets and hula-hoops, arcing in graceful leaps beneath the fairy lights. My amazing front lawn, high on a cliff, overlooking the Puget with tables dotting the landscape, bright lanterns glowing atop them. The endless array of expensive food and ice sculptures on tables with candelabras, leaving the horizon with a soft glow.

And the house. The most beautiful place I'd ever lived, big, sprawling, with every amenity known to man. And looking at it, the wide front porch, the lantern lights lining the cobblestone walkway, the stained-glass door, the beautiful white brick exterior with steel-blue shutters, was when I realized—these things were all awesome. I loved every one of them.

I won't lie and tell you life isn't easier with some cash. Because it is. I no longer worry about the light bill or paying my rent on time. I didn't even have to work as Madam Zoltar 2.0 if I didn't want to.

But I'd give all of it up if I could meet Win. *Just once.*

I'd go back to that fleabag hotel where I'd started when I first came back to Ebenezer Falls and eat one-dollar tacos for the rest of my life if I could just *see* him.

If I could sit next to the handsome man I'd seen in that picture I found in the back of my closet. The picture of Win and a woman named Miranda. The woman he claims murdered him. Who I came to find out was a fellow spy and his former lover.

The picture I still have in my room—still mostly unexplained because Win claimed he wasn't quite ready to tell me the details.

It was the people *in* my house who made me happiest, who fulfilled me, and Win was a huge part of that, even without knowing the full story of his life or death.

"I ask you, Dove, how did that mime get in the mix? He looks like he's kung-fu fighting his way out of a trash receptacle."

I fought laughing out loud at Win's comment while still in Forrest's arms as I looked in the direction of the mime he referred to and wrinkled my nose. In the middle of a group of several of the shop owners from town, his black-and-white striped shirt and white face paint glowing in the semi-dark, he attempted to tip his hat and dropped it into Sandy McNally's plate of shrimp.

Ooo, he really was bad. He'd moved on to another trick, but he didn't look like he was pulling an invisible rope—not even close. He looked like he'd taken a wrong turn somewhere and shown up a virgin to the hooker convention.

The other mimes were quite adept, producing flowers out of nowhere, pretending to walk tightropes, but this guy...let's just say while he was muscular and fit, and looked good in the tight outfit, I hope he wasn't going to quit his day job.

The crowd began to snicker a little at just how atrocious he was, making me feel uncomfortable for him. "That poor man," I said to Forrest, slowing our dancing to a halt. "Let me go see if I can talk him out of any more performing and into some food. I'll catch you in a bit."

Pressing a quick kiss to his cheek, I slipped off the dance floor and went to see if I could convince the most awkward mime ever he should just grab some food and hang out.

But that was just before the crowd swelled as some of the waiters arrived with fresh plates of the big hit of the night—the shrimp wrapped in bacon and stuffed with jalapeño cream cheese.

When I managed to find my way past them and the crowd waiting for the food, the awkward mime had disappeared.

But Bart hadn't. He strolled up to me, tall and maturely handsome, his shock of thick white hair even whiter against his tan. "Stevie! Have I told you how good it is to finally meet you in the flesh?"

I smiled up at him, remembering my words to Win

that I was going to try to leave my baggage behind me. It wasn't Bart's fault my mother wasn't Donna Reed. "It's good to finally meet you, too. Where's my mother?"

"Oh, she's floating around, working her magic on all her old friends, if you know what I mean," he said on a wink.

My mother didn't have any old friends here in Ebenezer. And when he used the word "magic," I grew a little nervous. Did he mean *magic*-magic? Or magical charms? Either could apply when it came to Dita.

Hooking my arm through his, I caught a whiff of his spicy cologne. He even smelled expensive. "So tell me a little about you, Bart. Where do you come from? What do you do for a living? What's it like to live in Rome?"

The warm smile never left his green eyes. "It's actually Greece, and I dabble in the market from time to time. Speaking of the market. I'd love to advise you." He leaned in and whispered the next words. "Dita told me all about your recent coup and it sounds like you need an investment planner. I'm your man. If you're looking, of course."

"I'll keep that in mind—"

Bart's phone rang, interrupting any more conversation. He held up his phone, the shiny Rolex on his wrist flashing in the dark. "You'll excuse me, won't you?"

I smiled and patted his arm. "Of course. We'll have a nice long chat later, after the party."

Bart nodded and moved back off into the crowd of people, stepping around Sandwich, who was looking very smart in his tux, even if his bow tie was a little off. I nudged him with my shoulder. "Find any sardines in the sea of escargot and goat cheese?"

He barked a laugh, his shortly cropped dark hair glistening beneath the lights. "No sardines ever again for me." Dropping his hands into his pockets, he smiled wide, his easygoing expression much different than the one I'd witnessed just two months ago at the scene of a murder. "So, this place, Stevie? It's pretty amazing."

I curtsied and winked. "No big deal. Just a couple of marathons on the DIY channel, YouTube videos, and some two by fours and paint. Easy-peasy."

Sandwich smiled, flashing his white teeth. "You wear it well, Stevie. This house somehow suits you, and you look great tonight, by the way. Not that you don't always look great, but tonight, you look extra great. Thanks for inviting me. Good eats."

"Miss Cartwright?" someone drawled from behind me. Someone who was the bane of my existence.

Ah. My favorite police officer was here. I turned to find Officer Nelson, also known as Dana (I was still snickering over that), and occasionally known by me as Officer By The Book, looked quite dapper all dressed up. "If it isn't Mr. Sunshine and Chuckles. Are you having a nice time, Officer Nelson?"

His lips lifted at the corners, otherwise known as the rare beast called a smile. "I am. This shrimp is pretty dang good." He held up his hors d'oeuvre plate to show me, his always-serious eyes dancing with a flicker of delight.

"Good. I'm glad to see you're enjoying yourself. So, anyone save your life lately?" I teased, batting my eyelashes in reference to my last tango with a killer.

Sandwich snorted. "Told ya, she grudges and she never forgets."

I didn't know Officer Nelson's story. He was already a part of the Ebenezer Falls Police Department when I moved back. I didn't know where he came from or where he'd been before here. The only thing I can tell you is, he's one tough nut to crack. Like walnut-tough to crack. Wheedling information out of him about a crime and any hints or clues is about as easy as getting a hand mirror away from my mother.

Speaking of my mother, I promised Win I'd find her and warn her about Hugh. Where was Hugh, anyway? It was like he'd disappeared.

I grinned at Sandwich. "You don't rack up points if you forget, Sandwich," I teased.

Officer Nelson held up a shrimp and saluted me. "I, for one, *never* forget, Miss Cartwright."

As I chuckled along with them, Chester waved to me, pushing his stout body through the crowd.

"There's my girl!" Chester, Forrest's grandfather, surrounded me in a warm embrace, wrapping his arm around my waist and chucking me under the chin. "Pretty as a picture, you are. Saw your mother with that guy Bart. Still looks just like she did the day she left Ebenezer. It's uncanny. Handsome couple, the two of them, huh?"

"Not nearly as handsome as you, buddy. Who'd you

buy all that good looking from?" I joked, straightening his white and red polka dot bow tie and letting my hands rest on his chest.

He looked up at me, his eyes crinkling at the corners, his balding white head shiny. "Aw, you stop, young lady. I'm just the gardener."

"Bah. I'd have never made it without you, Chester. You're the flower whisperer, as far as I'm concerned." When his face turned appropriately red, I asked, "Did you get something to eat? I made sure they had pickled herring and crackers just for you."

"I'm fine, toots. You go enjoy your company. But save an old man a dance, would ya? Forrest ain't the only one who's got twinkle toes."

I barked a laugh and pressed a kiss to his round cheek. "I love you, Chester. You're one of a kind."

Letting go of him, I turned and scanned the crowd, hoping to locate my mother and Bart, or even Hugh at this point, but to no avail. They were somewhere swallowed up in the crowd of partiers.

So I strolled through the people who'd gone off and formed their own groups, waving, smiling, thanking everyone for coming, reintroducing myself, passing the time and avoiding the inevitable questions about my sudden wealth and my day job as Madam Zoltar 2.0.

There was some kind of commotion over by the big champagne glass of water, but I couldn't quite catch what was going on before someone grabbed my arm.

"Stevie Cartwright!"

I was caught off guard for a moment until I looked

a bit closer to the man calling my name and recognized him. "Elias Little?"

"Yeah!" he said on a grin. Sticking out his hand, he grabbed mine and pumped it. "Good to see you after all these years!"

I'm pretty sure Elias knew little to nothing about me—at least not from high school. We'd traveled in very different circles then, but he hadn't changed much. Still wearing those horn-rimmed glasses, still sporting a crew cut and kind brown eyes.

"You look great, Elias. It's good to see you, too."

He leaned in as though he were going to share a secret (also, he still smelled like band practice—resin and a hint of sweaty, secondhand band uniform, to be precise). "So, wanna give a guy a scoop?"

"Scoop?"

"Yeah. All this." He spread his arm, covered in a brown tweed jacket, and waved it at the house. "Didn't just happen, did it? I mean, you had to get the money from somewhere, right? So I was hoping to do a feature on you in the *Herald*. You know, hometown girl makes good while she reads your mind or something? There's gotta be a story there, Stevie—there always is."

I snickered. "I don't read minds, Elias. I speak to the dead on behalf of the living."

He gave me the skeptical look everyone gives me, the dimples on either side of his mouth fading. "Riiight. A medium. Either way, I'd love to feature you in my column. Whaddya say?"

Just as I was about to politely decline, I heard a

scream—a scream that chilled me to the bone, slicing right through me.

Oddly, it was a familiar scream.

One I swear I'd heard before.

In that moment, I wondered if the Bats had disobeyed orders to stay put in my room.

But then I saw my mother—on the top step of the porch stairs—her face riddled with horror and disbelief, the light shawl she wore falling about her slender shoulders as she clutched it to her breast.

My stomach sank right to the bottom of my sparkly shoes when she cried out, "Bart! It's Bart! He's dead!"

CHAPTER 4

I ran for the front steps, my ridiculously high heels sinking into the brand-new sod. Grabbing the wrought iron and wood banister, I pulled myself upward just in time to keep her from falling on the porch floor in a graceful heap.

I tapped her face with my fingertips, brushing them across her flushed cheeks. "Mom? Mom!"

She crumpled against me, heaving a long sigh as Sandwich and Officer Nelson plowed up the steps and forced me to move out of the way.

"Put a call into the paramedics, Paddington!" Officer Nelson ordered, scooping my mother up to lay her flat on the porch and check her breathing.

As everyone began gathering around, their curious eyes on us, what my mother had yelled before collapsing finally registered and had me pushing my way past one of our local doctors, who'd come to help.

I stepped into the entryway, my heart throbbing in

my chest. There was plenty of activity still going on in the kitchen as the French chef shouted orders to his staff and loud music played amidst the chaos, so wherever Bart was, it wasn't in there.

Closing my eyes, I swallowed hard and opened them again. Turning to my right, I looked into the dining room, ablaze with a rustic candle chandelier and a table full of housewarming gifts we'd asked everyone to forgo, but had somehow managed to amass anyway. I saw nothing.

I took a deep breath and decided to venture to the parlor. There was a loud thump before I entered, making me wary, but I went in cautiously anyway, and that's when I saw him.

Bart, in a heap on the floor, the sheet from the cirque acrobat wrapped around his neck.

Instantly my eyes went to the pulley above him— the one the engineer had said wouldn't fall down in an earthquake, after I'd mentioned my misgivings—but nothing looked out of place or askew.

And what would Bart be doing climbing an acrobat's sheet, anyway? He looked like he took great care of himself, and I wasn't sure if that was due to the fact that he was a warlock, or because he worked out. But he sure didn't look like the kind of guy who'd want to float around in the air on one of those silky sheets.

Now I doubted myself. *Was* he a warlock? (I can't tell who's human and who isn't, since I lost my powers.) I couldn't remember if my mother had said one way or the other...?

No, wait. Now I remembered. Yes. Yes, he was definitely a warlock.

Rooted to the floor, I could only gape at my poor stepfather, his body twisted at an odd angle as though someone had hoisted him up toward the ceiling and let him crash to the floor. By the looks of it, he'd broken his left leg from the impact, given the way it was twisted awkwardly behind him.

There'd been a struggle, of that I was sure. The gorgeous crystal vases housing calla lilies and hydrangeas were smashed on the new hardwood floor of deep walnut. The lamp on top of the chest of drawers was tipped over and one drawer was crooked.

"Dove?"

I sighed in relief when I heard Win in my ear. "Yes?" I managed on a squeak, wrapping my arms around my waist.

"Come away. Don't linger."

"As if. You know me better. I can't just walk away. I never walk away."

"I *do* know you, but this is quite personal."

"More personal than my favorite tacos in the whole world?" I asked, referring to how we'd solved the mystery of my favorite taco man's death.

"He was your stepfather, Stevie."

"But…I didn't even know him. I knew Tito better than I did this man my mother married."

My first thought about that statement was how crazy it sounded. Bart had been married to my mother for quite some time now, and I didn't know a single thing about him.

"Regardless, it's still jarring. Come away now, Dove. The police are on their way and your mother will need you when she awakens."

I nodded, numb from the scene sprawled out before me. "Do me a favor, Win?"

"Anything."

"See if you can locate Hugh. I haven't seen him all night, since I left him in the parlor. You don't think..."

"Don't jump to conclusions, we don't know anything at this point," Win said.

"You know what we *do* know?"

"I'm afraid to ask, but I'm going to face that fear. Is it the tingle?"

Nodding, I winced. I didn't have to say another word for Win to understand. Whenever foul play was involved, I always got a tingle up my spine.

It didn't necessarily have to equate to murder, though the last two times I'd been right on the money. Sometimes it could be an event as simple as someone shoplifting or lying. It was once a much stronger tingle, when I was still a witch, but it never failed me, and I was getting it now about Bart.

"I'll attempt to locate The Huge Granite posthaste then."

Carlito and Liza were the next to get to me, pulling me from the entry of the parlor and toward the kitchen.

Sirens sounded and lights flashed outside the big

picture window as members of the Ebenezer Falls Police Department rushed in, along with the two detectives I jokingly called Simone and Sipowicz, their serious faces in place.

"You all right, Stevie?" Liza, asked, her wide eyes filled with concern.

Carlito handed me a water bottle, his handsome face grim. "I'm sorry you had to see that, Miss Cartwright."

As Carlito and Liza brought me back into focus, I heard my mother calling for me in that sweetly pleading tone.

"Where's my baby girl?"

Inhaling, I smiled at Carlito's and Liza's sympathetic gazes. This certainly wasn't the first dead body I'd seen. I could do this. "I'm fine. Promise. I'd better go see if she's okay." I patted Liza on the arm, only vaguely noticing how beautiful she looked tonight in her emerald-green slip dress.

"I'm here, Mom," I called, stepping back out onto the porch, where she sat while the doctor hovered over her frail form.

Pretty as a picture, she sat on the bench swing that Win, Belfry, Whiskey and I sat on every night while chatting about the day's events, her hair mussed beautifully around her flushed cheeks.

Pushing my way through the throng of people, I sat down beside her. "What happened, Mom?"

Her full lower lip, the one she used for the trademark

Cartwright pout I just couldn't perfect, trembled. "I don't know. I went to see where Bart was. I...I couldn't find him anywhere and then..." She began to openly sob, tears streaming down her face and falling to her gold lamé lap.

I did what I've always done when my mother's upset. I wrapped an arm around her shoulder and squeezed her trembling form close. She always looked so helpless, so frail when she wept, that all my defenses fell away. "I'm so sorry, Mom. I don't know what to say. Tell me what I can do to help."

"Miss Cartwright?"

Both our heads shot upward (I didn't know if my mother had changed her name this last marriage or not), and I encountered one half of my favorite pair of detectives. Simone and Sipowicz—or Simone, to be precise, better known to Ebenezer Fall-ers as Ward Montgomery. He was good cop to his partner's bad cop. If anyone was going to question my mother, better him than his partner the yeller.

I'd had an encounter with these two, where one smiled at me while the other pounded his fists against the desk like he was Fred Flintstone.

Under the porch lights, Detective Montgomery's hard face didn't give anything away, but I knew he'd want a statement. "We need to ask you some questions," he said gruffly.

Mom's slender shoulders shook harder as she clung to me.

"Can we do that a little later? You can see how upset

she is," I said, trying for those Thumper eyes my mother was so good at.

But he never blinked. "I'm afraid we can't. I'll be as gentle as possible, but we really need her impressions of tonight."

Well, at least my record for failing miserably at flirting was still intact.

"So if you'd please let me take your mother's statement, *Sipowicz* will get yours over there," he said with a hint of sarcasm as he pointed to the other detective, who was leaning against the doorframe, just shy of rubbing his hands together in devilish glee.

Enter bad cop. Detective Sean Moore. He was the one who was supposed to put the screws to you while his other half held your hair back and let you vomit your tale of insidious doings.

Rolling my eyes, I rose and smoothed my hands over my dress. "It was just a joke," I retorted before heading toward my second-least favorite cop.

He motioned me inside the house and pointed to the dining room, pulling out one of the high-backed chairs for me. "You know, *Stevie,* I noticed something tonight."

Lifting my chin, I gazed into his eyes, hard as ice chips. "Did you? What's that, Detective Sean Moore?"

"Murder follows you around. This is the second body you've been in contact with."

Ya think? "*Phew.* A for astute."

He poised his pen over his notepad. "Where were you all night, Miss Cartwright?"

"Sunning in Aruba. I just got in on the redeye. Wanna see my tan lines?"

"Funny. Answer the question. *Please.*" If Officer Nelson was a walnut, this guy was a brick.

So I lifted my shoulders and shrugged, gripping my temples with two fingers to ease the oncoming ache. "Where do you think I was? This is my party. I was all over the place with my guests."

"Did you see Mr. Hathaway go inside?"

I cocked my head and bit the inside of my cheek. "Is that his last name?"

Detective Moore raised an eyebrow. "You didn't know his last name?"

"I didn't." Sweet Pete on the beach. I didn't know my stepfather's last name.

"How could you not know your own stepfather's last name?"

Because I've had so many? "I guess it just slipped my mind. Tonight was the first time I've actually met Bart. My mother...she's been traveling with him since they eloped and they only just got back to Seattle this evening."

He scribbled on his small spiral notepad, his lips thin. "You know if there was any trouble between them?"

"As far as I know, they were very happy with each other." I think. I didn't know...

"Did they argue tonight?"

Suddenly I was defensive on my mother's behalf. She was capable of many things, but murder wasn't one of them, and if that's the avenue he was taking, I was going to throw up a big roadblock.

I held up a hand. "Okay, hold the phone here, Sipowicz. I have to ask myself, are you seriously considering my mom had something to do with this? Look at her. She weighs a hundred pounds soaking wet. How do you think she could have hauled Bart up on that pulley with her skinny little stick arms? They'd have cracked like toothpicks. And did you happen to see the size of Bart? He's two hundred pounds easily. You're barking up the wrong tree here, Detective Sipowicz. Maybe Bart committed suicide. Have you thought about that angle? Put that in your pipe and smoke it."

"How do you know he was pulled upward by the pulley?"

Oh, right. There was that. "I just assumed that's how he was killed," I said—then cringed.

Gosh, I never knew when to shut up. No one had mentioned the word "murder" in association with Bart.

Detective Montgomery stopped scribbling. "Who said he was killed?"

"Oh, no one said he was killed, all right? It just seems kind of fishy that he's got a sheet wrapped around his neck and he's a crumpled mess on the floor."

"I thought you said maybe it was suicide?"

I rolled my eyes. "Stop trying to catch me in a lie that doesn't exist. I was theorizing, is all." Out loud. With my big mouth.

Moore leaned back against the wall and smiled like a Cheshire Cat. "I hear you do that a lot."

"Well, to be fair, I *have* solved two murders, haven't I?"

"Testy, testy tonight, aren't you?"

You bet I was. There was a dead man in my parlor and I didn't even know his last name. I couldn't very well continue to blame my mother for not being involved in my life if I didn't even try to get involved in hers. *Do unto others, Stevie Cartwright.*

She'd been married to Bart for over a year now and I'd made no effort to contact her, other than perfunctory congratulations when she texted to tell me they'd tied the knot.

But I decided I was better off staying on the defensive. "Sure I'm testy. Wouldn't *you* be testy if someone died at your housewarming party? You know, I wish you guys were as diligent about those jerky kids who keep ding-dong-ditching me because I stole their favorite drinking spot."

I'd been ding-dong-ditched five times since I'd moved in, and when I'd mentioned it to Sandwich, he'd given me that boys-will-be-boys speech.

He appeared to digest my words before his face relaxed just a bit, his posture going from rigid to loose. "I'm just doing my job. My job is to ask you questions. You do want me to do my job, don't you? So we can figure out what happened to your stepfather?"

He was right, and I was still holding a grudge about my interrogation after Madam Zoltar's death, when he'd also just been doing his job. "Fair enough. Keep asking."

"Did you see Bart with anyone else tonight? Notice anything unusual?"

I didn't know Bart well enough to know what was unusual. "I saw him here and there tonight. He was mingling with the other guests, talking, eating and doing what people do at parties. We chatted for a bit and then he had to take a phone call."

"A phone call? Do you know from who?"

As I crossed my legs, I forced myself to remember this was for the greater good. "I have no idea. He just said he had to take it. He was a rather successful businessman, maybe it was some hot stock tip."

Detective Moore just grunted and scribbled on his pad. "Anything else you can add? Any suspicious activity? Anything out of the ordinary with anyone else at the party?"

"Nothing that I can think of."

Flipping the small notepad closed, he glared down at me in bad cop mode. "That's all for now then. We'll be in touch."

Just as I rose to go check on my mother, one of the troupe members who'd been a part of the champagne glass act rushed in from outside and took a towel from another male acrobat.

Her slight frame trembled as she dried herself and smiled at the man who'd handed her the towel. Unlike K, in a very American accent, she asked, "Where's CC?"

Huh. A two-letter name? Definitely a rage-against-the-machine move on CC's part.

"Out talking to that cop with the poker face," he said, hitching his thumb over his shoulder.

Her blue eyes, enormous in her tiny heart-shaped face, widened. "Is she telling him what happened with the dead guy earlier?"

I slowed my exit from the dining room and turned my back to the couple, trying to melt into the wall so I could eavesdrop.

"You mean that she slapped him for being a pig?"

My eyes widened. Bart? A pig?

"He was disgusting, making comments about her breasts. He deserved to have his face slapped!"

"Well, now the guy's dead. That doesn't look so good for CC."

"Don't be ridiculous, Al. She didn't kill him. She slapped him for being inappropriate," the tiny woman said with disgust in her tone, her teeth chattering with every word.

"Well, the cops asked her where she was at the time, and she was on a break. A break *alone*. That looks suspicious."

"Interesting," Win remarked in my ear.

"Look who decided to show up to the party," I whispered, pressing my fingers to my Bluetooth in case I was caught talking to what looked like myself.

"I've been here almost the whole time, Cheeky One. Except, of course, when I went on the hunt for Hugh, whom I was unable to locate unless he was in the loo—a

61

place I'm unwilling to check. You were holding your own just fine with Detective Dog With A Bone, so I thought I'd hover and see what I could see with your mother."

"And did you find anything?"

"I found that even sobbing, she's still quite beautiful."

Grating a sigh, I closed my eyes. "Not helping, Win."

"Not much else to report. She claims she was in the ladies' room, freshening up before she continued her search for Bart. As she made her way back out to the front lawn, she saw him in the parlor."

No matter what my mother did, I would never wish her coming upon anyone, let alone her husband, sprawled on the floor with a sheet wrapped around his neck, dead. But that she was alone when she'd found him wouldn't look good to the law.

So I crossed my fingers and asked, "Was anyone with her? Did anyone see her go to the ladies' room?"

"Unfortunately, no. However, she's stuck to her guns and repeated the same story four separate times for Detective Montgomery, word for word."

"Is he still with her?"

"Oh, indeed. He's comforting her as we speak."

"Then I'd better get back out there before they end up engaged." I hated saying that about my mother, but it was the straight-up truth. She'd only had one husband who'd died—a mortal, for all intents and purposes—and not one day after his funeral, she was drumming up replacements.

I often wondered if it was because she was afraid to be alone. Yet, I couldn't reconcile that with her behavior *after* she said "I do." Once she'd nabbed a man and locked him down in wedded bliss, she didn't want anything to do with him.

She was too busy socializing and having her hair done to spend quality time with her new husband. So maybe it was just the thrill of the chase, and when she captured her conquest, the fizzle ran out.

I slipped out of the dining room and through the entryway, skirting the new crowd who'd entered as the police milled in and about, asking questions of each of the guests.

Stepping out onto the porch, I saw my mother sitting with Detective Montgomery. He had that enthralled look on his face all men had when they were caught up in Dita's spell, no matter how powerful they were.

Great googly-moogly. I had to act fast. "Mom?" I held out my hand to her and smiled. "Come with me and I'll get you some of that tea you like so much."

Detective Montgomery patted her hand and gave her his card when she shot him a questioning glance. "It's fine, Miss Cartwright. I've got all I need for now. We'll be in touch."

My mother rose, fragile as a wilting flower, took two steps and collapsed against me, letting me help her inside. Forrest came up from the rear and flanked her from the other side, taking most of the weight off me as we led her to the kitchen, which had now begun to clear out.

I sat her down on one of the chairs by the enormous windows overlooking the Puget and set off to make her some tea, but I didn't have to bother. Carmella, my contractor Enzo's wife, was already on it.

She held up the cup, her normally messy bun atop her head looking quite sleek tonight. She wore the pretty gold and blue sparkly caftan I'd given her for her birthday just last week. "I got this, kiddo."

"How did you know what she liked?"

"Oh, your mother and I had a nice chat earlier. I learned plenty," she said on a wink. I wasn't sure if it was meant to warn me she knew what a diva my mother could be, or if mom just dominated their conversation with all things Dita enough that Carmella now knew her bra size.

Taking the steaming cup from her, I smiled warmly and planted a kiss on her cheek. "Have I told you you're the best lately and that I positively adore you?"

She tweaked my cheeks with chubby fingers and grinned. "Just the other day when I brought you some stuffed manicotti, I think. You were talking all sorts of gobbledygook. Lifelong commitments, moving in together. Now go be with your mother. I'll make sure everything else is handled with Petula and crew, *capisce*?" she asked in her New York accent.

I blew out a breath in relief. "Marry me, Carmella. Leave Enzo and let's just do it," I teased.

Her chuckle, warm and hearty, rang in my ears as she made her way out of the kitchen.

"You look beautiful tonight, Carmella! Tell Enzo I said so!" I yelled after her, smiling as I brought the tea to my mother.

Forrest looked to me, his eyes full of genuine concern, because that's just who Forrest was. A good guy. "Should I leave?"

My mother's hand snaked out and grabbed his wrist. "No man as handsome as you should ever ask that question." Then she chuckled, tinkling and airy as she smoothed her hand over her hair and batted her eyelashes.

Uh-huh. I give you the *real* Dita.

I grabbed Forrest's hand, too, and motioned him to sit next to me. "It's fine. Stay, please." I could use the support.

Then I looked into my mother's eyes—eyes so like mine. "So what happened, Mom? Was Bart in a bad space?"

She shrugged her shoulders and lifted her eyes, letting tears fill them. "He was fine, Stevie. Everything was fine. I don't understand…"

"Understand what? Do you think he would harm himself? Do you think he'd…" I couldn't say it out loud.

My mother shook her head. "I don't know. As far as I knew, he was very happy."

That statement worried me. As far as she knew? The trouble was, she never looked deeply enough or past her own needs and emotions to know if anyone else was suffering, ever.

So I patted her hand and encouraged her to drink her tea by pushing it toward her. "Have some tea, Mom. It'll warm you."

But my mother flapped a hand and wrinkled her pert nose. "Forget the tea. I just told that woman I liked it because don't *all* mothers my age drink tea? The best way to make friends is to be just like them. Find me some whiskey, Stephania, honey. That'll warm me up just fine while I hunt for Bart's insurance policy."

Yep.

Heeere's Dita.

CHAPTER 5

As the last staff member cleared the kitchen, I let Forrest take my hand and lead me to the front door and back out onto the porch.

The lights still glowed everywhere, leaving a dreamy ambiance that, had a death not occurred here tonight, would leave me feeling warm and fuzzy.

Bart's body had been removed and taken to the morgue while my mother sobbed, something I wasn't sure was real or for show. All the guests in their fancy clothes had gone, too. The questioning was over for the time being. There was nothing left to do but be alone with my mother. And I hated that I dreaded it.

"You gonna be okay?" Forrest asked, pulling me close.

I let my cheek rest on his chest and nodded. "I'll be fine."

He pressed his chin to the top of my head. "Good to

know. So lunch this week if you can break away? Bring your mother if you'd like."

"You don't really want me to do that, but you're a standup guy for asking anyway."

His deep chuckle rumbled in my ears. "She's quite a card, your mother."

"Um, yeah. She something all right." Leaning back in his arms, I smiled up at him, his warm eyes comforting me. "Thanks for sticking around during this mess."

"I wouldn't have missed tonight for the world. I'm sorry it ended so badly."

"Me too. So lunch later this week it is. I'd better get back inside before my mother breaks the Internet trying to figure out Bart's passwords."

"I was a little surprised she was already thinking ahead. Very levelheaded of her."

It took everything I had not to snort out loud. "Someday, I'll tell you all about my mother and her level head."

"I can't wait," he teased, pressing a quick kiss to my lips. "Night, Stevie."

"Night, Forrest," I murmured back, wiggling my fingers as he let go of me before disappearing down the steps and across the lawn.

Kicking off my shoes, I stooped to pick them up and decided to wait just another moment to go back inside and help my mother.

"Stevie? I have intel," Win said, his tone ominous.

I sighed as I looked up at the stars. "Intel?"

"A spirit here—no face, just a voice—says not to believe everything you see."

My head hung between my shoulders as a sardonic laugh spewed from my lips. "Oh, that's hugely helpful. Bet it has to do with my mother. I think Dita just proved what she shows the world isn't real. If that spirit's contacting you because of her, it should be telling that to all the people she encountered tonight, including Carmella, who bought her Mary Poppins routine lock, stock and tea."

"Hold on—more coming..."

Did I want to know what was coming? Would it be something horrible about my mother? Some piece of information I was better off not knowing?

"The spirit says—a male spirit, in case you wondered—your mother isn't what she seems... How curious, don't you think?"

Rolling my eyes, I headed back inside. "Tell your spirit he's like twenty years too late. I've always known she gives good face. She's only been my mother for almost thirty-three years. If he really wants to help, tell him to find Bart. Some answers would be nice."

"I've been waiting here on Plane Limbo since you found him, but no sign yet. Either he immediately crossed or he's drifting."

"Well, if you see High Planes Drifter, tell him we have some questions, would you?"

"I am nothing if not your minion, Dove," Win joked.

"Did you ever find Hugh?"

How could a man claim to be my father then take

off without another word? I wanted to talk to my mother about it, but it was a pretty precarious time to bring up something she never wanted to talk about to begin with.

"I haven't seen him since his confession. I looked everywhere, too. I'd like to chalk this up to someone attempting a scam with you, but my gut says something else."

"Perfect. Then I'll have to ask my mother about him. Not looking forward to that conversation."

"But you must protect yourself, Stevie, and your mother."

"Stephania? Who are you talking to? I thought everyone had gone home?" my mother called from the kitchen.

I can't believe I'm saying this, but it's a relief to finally tell another living soul I have a ghost. "It's my ghost, Mom. His name is Win. Or Crispin Alistair Winterbottom, if you're into long names that sound like they belong to a British butler."

"Oh, *Stephania,* will you never learn?" Win asked on a chuckle.

She cocked her head, looking up from the laptop as I took the seat across the table. "Your ghost? I thought you could no longer hear the dead? You said you lost your powers, during our last phone call."

"I did. And we didn't have a phone call, Mom. I left you a message and you sent me a text back saying Bart said you shouldn't get involved because of council reprisal."

"Must you make mountains out of molehills, Stevie?"

No. I mustn't. This wasn't healthy. No rehashing, especially now that her husband was dead. We had more important things to discuss—like anything that would be helpful in finding Bart's killer.

Dropping my shoes in the corner by the mudroom just off the kitchen, I shrugged my shoulders. "I don't know how I can hear Win. I just can. He showed up one day, and we've been together ever since."

I wasn't terribly interested in telling my mother everything that had gone down in the past couple of months since I'd lost my powers. She never really listened anyway unless it had to do with her. If I kept that in mind, if I could just accept her as is, this visit could turn out okay.

She stopped pecking at the laptop and gazed at me. "I was relieved when you said you'd lost the ability to talk to spirits. I never liked you talking to the dead."

"I distinctly remember you telling me it was creepy." Yes, that's right, folks, my own mother, a witch herself, thought I was creepy because I had the ability to speak to the afterlife.

She took a delicate sip of her whiskey, her pinky finger extended. "It was, and still is."

Gritting my teeth, I nodded. "You're probably right, but Win's the reason I have all this."

"Do tell her it's a pleasure to meet her and give her my condolences, would you, Dove?" Win requested.

"Win says he's pleased to meet you and he's sorry about Bart."

Mom's perfectly plucked eyebrow rose. "Are you talking to him right now?"

Tracing the pattern of the wood tabletop with my finger, I nodded. "I am. It's why I have the Bluetooth. So everyone won't think I'm talking to myself."

"Well, tell him to go away!" she snapped. "We have personal business to discuss!"

"Mom? Did you just hear what I said?"

"Yes, dear. You said you have a ghost."

"A ghost who gave me all *this*! The house, more money than I know what to do with in two lifetimes, a stress-free financial future, a car, his *friendship*, Mom. I'm not booting my ghost out because you think he's creepy. Win knows everything there is to know about me. We have no secrets." Well, not on my part, anyway.

"See *Stephania* stand up for her creepy ghost. I'm all aglow here on Plane Limbo," Win teased.

And then everything I'd just said obviously sank into Dita's brain. She stirred in her chair. "Wait, are you telling me that this ghost gave this house to you?"

Ah. Now I had Dita's attention. Not that it should matter. In a couple of days, she was going to be rich, if what she said about Bart and his life insurance policy held true. Not to mention, he had a villa in Greece. People who had villas in Greece had many bank accounts, and probably lots of olives in those bank accounts.

I smiled, leaning my head on my hand. "He did. It

didn't always look like this. That's why we had a house-warming party. But if not for him, Bel and I would be out on the street. I had nothing when I was booted out of Paris by Baba Yaga—"

"You have money?" she asked, now sitting up straight, effectively cutting off all talk of me and my tale of woe.

"I do. Plenty of it."

"Why would a *ghost* leave you his money? Was he once a lover?"

I think my cheeks turned twelve shades of crimson as I looked at my mother. "No, Mom. It's a long story, but it has to do with a murder and a woman named—"

"Well, how much money?" Mom closed the laptop, her interest clearly piqued.

Whoa, slow the roll now. Why did she care? I could see if she was between marriages, but she surely had boatloads of cash. "Why does it matter?"

"Because I might be in a—"

"Dita?" a voice full of wonder said from behind us.

"Make room for daddy," Win muttered.

～

"*H*ugh?" my mother whispered, her lower lip trembling, a perfection of lip gloss and fragile glass. "Is that you?"

So he really was Hugh Granite? My jaw unhinged.

Hugh smiled that perfect smile and strolled toward

her, his hands outstretched in a welcoming gesture. "You're as beautiful as always, Flower."

And he called her *Flower*.

"Is that *really* you?" Dita asked in her own tone of wonder, taking his hands and letting him pull her to her feet.

If this were a movie, things would be all slow motion and heart-tugging music would be playing right now and I'd be dripping the salt of my tears on my popcorn. I actually had to blink to believe I was really seeing this reunion.

Wowwowwow, were they perfect together, too. More perfect than even Mom and Bart. They were all things beautiful and lean, graceful and supple.

I rose from my seat because I was drawn to their magnetic pull, their combined charisma that heady, but I tripped on the leg of the chair and stumbled, falling into them instead.

As I crashed into Hugh, his strong arm went around my waist. "Are you okay?"

Looking up at him, falling into his gorgeously concerned eyes, I now didn't just stumble, I apparently stuttered, too. "I'm…yes…um…"

"Stevie? How could you be remiss in telling me Hugh was here?"

My mother's question, her eyes wide with curiosity as she demanded an answer, angered me.

My jaw unhinged for the second time today. "Oh, I don't know, Mom. Maybe because you were here with your new husband? Or maybe the same way you didn't tell me he was my *father*?"

"Bloody hell, Stevie. There are gentler ways. Have we still not perfected our subtleties? In order to garner the results you wish, you must read your antagonist, not rile her. Stand down, Dove."

Dita gasped, gripping Hugh's arms, but he took a step away, disentangling himself from her and putting an arm around my shoulder, his gaze locking with mine. "All these years, *you* didn't know either?"

Was this really happening? Right here in my sparkly kitchen? Numbly, I shook my head. "I had no idea who you were—or that you didn't know I existed."

His eyes went from smiling to angry, narrowing in on my mother. "How could you deny my beautiful daughter knowing she had *me* for a father, Dita?"

Okay. That wasn't exactly the noblest response a child hoped for, but it would suffice. Plus, my dad thought I was beautiful. That was kind of preen-worthy, coming from a movie star in Japan.

But now my mother narrowed *her* eyes, raising her hands in the air.

Oh, goddess. I knew what lifting her red-tipped nails meant. A spell was coming, and I had no defense against her magic. There was a sudden cool wind in the kitchen, swishing my mother's hair around her face as her eyes went brilliantly hot.

Sweet Pete in a thong, bad spell alert!

So I jumped in front of Hugh and shook my finger

at her in stern warning. "Mother! Don't you dare use your magic!"

But she was seething, her eyes flashing dark, her signature wind whipping the takeout menus around on the fridge.

"I should turn you into a urinal!" she shouted at Hugh on a dramatic sob before sweeping past us and out of the room with a huff.

But my father just chuckled, his eyes twinkling as he looked at his shortly clipped nails and buffed them on his suit coat. "Still the same old Dita, I see."

Obviously he was accustomed to my mother's melodrama, but he had some splainin' to do. In that second, something dawned on me. Was Hugh paranormal?

"Where have you been all this time, Hugh?" Then I held up my hand. "I mean tonight. Not all my life. Let's start there."

He blinked as though I'd gone mad. "In the upstairs bathroom, running lines, of course."

Was this all really happening? I worried my lower lip with my teeth. "Lines?"

"Certainly. You don't get to be an international star if you don't know your lines, Daughter." Then he paused, dramatically, lifting his chin when he spotted his reflection in the windows before taking my hand. "You said we'd chat later. It was obvious you were very busy with your beautiful party, and being a star, I didn't want to distract from your shining moment, as so often happens when I'm in a room. It's only natural people recognize me from my many movies and appearances and create a fuss. So I took my leave and went upstairs to memorize my lines for my next movie and let you have your spotlight. I think you'll find I can be very gracious, indeed."

I'm pretty sure Hugh had no idea how incredibly arrogant he sounded. In fact, I know he didn't, simply because he looked at me with such tenderness. He really believed he'd given me some rare gift and he didn't think it was at all arrogant.

And who was I to tell him otherwise? Yet, it was the way he presented this gift that intrigued me and touched my heart. Without an ounce of reservation. He was what he was, and he didn't hide it. Egotistical or not, I had to admire that.

So I patted him on the back and waved him to a chair. "You're a real sport, Hugh. But do you have any idea what happened down here while you were holed up in the bathroom?"

"A party, of course. I was so engrossed in learning my lines and correcting some monumental error on the part of the writers, who have obviously made a mistake, casting me as anything other than a strapping man of wealth and great intelligence."

"So you were in the bathroom for *five* hours? The party started at seven, came to a screeching, murderous halt at nine, and it's almost twelve now. Didn't you hear all the chaos?"

He winked and puffed his chest out as he sat, pulling a pair of earbuds out of his jacket pocket. "I had these in. Music soothes me when I rehearse. Also, I'm nothing if not studious. I like to prepare all my angles and make notes for the cameramen so they feature me at my absolute best."

I sat down next to him. "Someone was murdered during the time you were perfecting angles, Hugh."

He gasped. His look of surprise, whether acted or real, was on point. *"Who?"*

"Mom's husband Bart."

Hugh made a sad face. "Poor Dita. No wonder she's so out of sorts."

I nodded. Sure. That was definitely the reason. Obviously he, too, was blinded by my mother and her wicked charms. "So can I ask you a couple of questions?"

"Of course, Daughter."

I had to wonder why he kept giving me a familial label. Maybe he was using it out loud so he could adjust to it, as much as I was using it internally in order to do the same.

"Mom never told you about me?"

He sighed, long and wistful. "Unfortunately, she did not. Alas, our love affair was fleeting—like sands through the hourglass, it came and went. We were never meant to be, you see. Ill-fated from the start."

"Star-crossed lovers," I whispered. If I'd ever had fantasies about my parents and how they met and fell in love, this one was high on my list.

"No," he said with a shake of his head. "It had nothing to do with stars. We met at a rodeo convention in Galveston, Texas. She was a rodeo girl and I was traveling with a production of *Oklahoma!*

"Hah!" Win barked in my ear. "Bloody fabulous!"

Hugh cocked his slick head, frowning. "Who is that?"

My brow furrowed. "Huh?"

"Who's the fellow with the British accent?"

My eyebrows rose in surprise. "You can hear him?"

Hugh chuckled a laugh. "You're delightful! Of course I can, Stevie. I didn't say so earlier because he was offering sound advice and I didn't want to frighten you further, but I'm one of the few warlocks in the world who can communicate with the dead."

No. Way. I'd never met anyone else who communicated with the afterlife. I knew others existed, but we're rare. With the exception of Baba Yaga, who could communicate with Satan himself, I suppose, this was a first for me.

I must have inherited my powers from Hugh.

"Me too!" I yelped in excitement, until I realized that wasn't really the case anymore. "I mean, I used to communicate with the dead. Not so much anymore since I lost my powers, though."

He gasped again, the intake of breath making me jump as he gripped my hands in his larger ones. *"You lost your powers?"*

"Well, I didn't really lose them. They were slapped out of me. It's a long story. I'll tell you someday when you have extra time on your hands."

Now his face was grave, exaggeratedly so, but still,

grave with concern. I think it was concern, anyway. "Who would do such a thing to my daughter?"

"Again, looong story. But a good one, too. Anyway, introductions are in order, I guess. Win, meet Hugh. Hugh, Crispin Alistair Winterbottom. Or Win, as we call him."

"A pleasure, sir," Win said, his warm aura surrounding me the way it always did when he wanted to let me know he was being supportive.

My father (my father!) lifted his square, dimpled chin and nodded regally. "The same. We have much to talk about."

"Indeed, sir. I'm happy to answer any and all questions. Shall I take my leave so that you might have privacy with your daughter?"

I loved the way Win said *privacy*. It always cracked me up when he used a short "I". It was so upper-crust British.

"I have nothing to hide," Hugh offered amicably. "You're more than welcome to stay. I'm more interested in hearing how my daughter lost her powers."

"Like I said, we'd need a lot of time to ride that pony." I wasn't ready to rehash just yet. "So, mom..."

He winked, his strong jaw lifting. "Yes. Your mother. She's quite a handful, isn't she?"

"You're not angry with her?" I asked in disbelief. "I mean, she didn't tell you I existed and probably never would have."

Was I angry with her? Should I pile that on top of all the other things I was angry with her about?

"No, Daughter. Certainly I was at first. But that passed. Anger is a wasted emotion if there is still treasure to find. Finding out about you was a treasure. I won't allow anger to interfere with what I hope will be a budding relationship with you. Dita…is Dita. I might have only spent one night with her, but she's easy enough to figure."

Then I looked at him pensively. "So one last question. Does this mean you're going to disassociate yourself with me as well, because I'm not part of the coven anymore? There aren't many left who are willing to associate with me."

I prepared myself for the inevitable answer. He *was* a lot like my mother. She didn't like messes of any kind. I imagined that trait was something she looked for in a man, too—even if it was only for one night. When the goin' got tough, Dita got goin'. I wanted to be ready for the rejection.

Though, I couldn't really blame him. I was a sticky proposition, especially if you were only just meeting me for the first time. Were *I* Hugh, I'd cut ties and behave as though this had never happened.

"Don't be absurd," he responded as though the suggestion was unseemly, his eyes intense and glittering. "You're my *daughter*. Now that I know you exist, I'll never leave you. Well, not unless a big lead movie role presents itself. But then you can come to the set to visit me. I'll show you all of the Hugh Granite techniques I've perfected over the years and you can see your father in action. It will be wonderful!"

Tears stung my eyes. Okay, so sure, he was vain and full of himself, but he was willing to do something my mother hadn't been—stick around. "How did you find out about me?"

"Ah," he said forlornly, his lips forming a sad pout. "A spirit came to me. One I lost just recently."

My curiosity piqued, I asked, "Who?"

"Your great aunt Imelda. Unfortunate broom-cauldron accident," he murmured, making a sad face that bordered on comical. "She's part of an afterlife coven called Seventy and Saucy. This is where she met your mother's aunt Prudence. The moment she realized you were the daughter no one ever told me about, she contacted me. What a shock to find out about you!"

Running my fingers over my eyes, I pinched my temple. "I bet. How long have you known?"

"I only just found out two weeks ago. The moment I was able to leave the set of my last movie, I snapped myself here. I would have left sooner, but contracts and agents, you know. However, now we meet, Daughter." Hugh's smile went warm and gentle again as he patted my hand. "So tell me, how is it, if your powers are gone, you can still hear this man? *Who* is this man, pray tell?"

We had a lot to catch up on. "Another long story I promise to share when you have the time. So do you have a place to stay? Are you staying here in town or do you have to hurry back to being an international star of stage, screen and film?"

"For you, I have all the time in the world. I'm between movies, and I'm staying at a charming inn, which is quite close to your beautiful home and has many cats."

I fought a yawn. The day was catching up with me, but I didn't want to lose this connection yet. I wanted to bask in the knowledge that my father, the man I'd wondered about all my life, was here—right in front of me.

"So you're a warlock who can talk to dead people."

Hugh grinned and winked. "I am. But we can talk all about this and more tomorrow. Maybe for lunch? Wouldn't that be wonderful? Now, it's time for all beautiful daughters to be in bed so they can remain as beautiful when they wake. Walk me to the front door?" He rose, tall and perfect, and held out the crook of his arm to me while everything around him fell away.

I took it, still in a warm bubble of acceptance—until we passed the parlor, that is. That was when I shuddered.

Bart's body had been taken to the morgue, the sheet once hanging from the ceiling removed as evidence, the pulley and all the mechanical workings dusted for prints. But from the corner of my eye, I saw something shiny flash under the chest of drawers with the long, skinny legs and made a mental note to check it after Hugh left.

As we stopped at the front door, he drew me into a warm hug, resting his chin on top of my head. "Will you be all right staying here tonight? Such a tragedy, and to have to deal with your mother's sorrow, too? I can't even imagine the stress. I'd be happy to stay with you, if you'd like, Daughter."

But I shook my head. How could I ask him to spend time with the woman who'd never told him he was a father? Surely he'd want answers, and while he deserved them, in all fairness, her husband had just died.

"I'll be fine. But maybe we *could* have lunch tomorrow? If I can get away?"

Hugh leaned back in our embrace and ran his fingertip down my nose. "As you wish. For now, I shall take my leave." Squeezing my arms one last time, he raised his own in the air, snapped his fingers, and was gone in a wisp of emerald green smoke.

Just like that.

I stood there for a minute, still basking in the presence of Hugh, unsure what to do next.

"You've had quite a night, Dove. The Bats arrived in all their maddening fluffiness, your father finding you after all these years, and of course, there's Bart. Hugh was right. You need rest."

I turned around and headed back to investigate the shiny object I saw under the chest of drawers. "But not before I take one last look in the parlor."

"Stevie? Is that a good idea? Maybe this one is too personal and we should let the authorities do their job rather than immerse ourselves in Bart's death."

I sank to my knees as near the chest as I could get, careful not to disturb the yellow police tape blocking everything off, and leaned forward on my hands until my cheek almost touched the floor.

"You see what I see, International Man of Intrigue?"

Win's sigh rasped in my ear. "I do."

"Still wanna leave it alone?" Win loved a good mystery as much as I did.

"Do not touch anything, Stephania Cartwright. Especially after you promised Sardine you'd stay out of this room until they could clear it," he warned, just as I straightened and reached for the fireplace poker.

"It's Sandwich, and c'mon, Win," I grunted as I stretched as far as my arm would allow from behind the barrier of the police tape. "You know me better than that. This isn't my first murder." I wiggled the poker beneath the chest until I hit pay dirt.

"We don't even know if it's a murder."

"We do too." Sweeping the poker under the chest, I continued to swipe at the shiny object until it came into view. "Woot!" I cheered, dropping the poker and sitting back up to get a good look at whatever it was.

"A money clip…" Win muttered.

There was that tingle again. "With the initials BH. For Bart Hathaway?"

"And a piece of paper, not money, mind you, attached to it. Can you read it without touching it?"

"It's a phone number." As I read it off to Win to commit to memory, I shoved the money clip back under the chest of drawers to the exact position I'd found it in.

Then I ran to find my phone, yelling to Win to repeat the number.

As he rattled it off, I grabbed my phone from the countertop and punched it in, turning it on speaker.

As the other end answered, a recording began to play. "You have reached the Washington State Penitentiary. Our hours are…"

CHAPTER 6

I popped an eye open. "Uncle Ding?"

"Yes, Gorgeous?"

"Get out of the top of my nightgown this instant!"

"Aw, c'mon, Uncle Ding! What'd I tell you about leaving Stevie alone? You're giving bats a bad name. Don't be a dirty old bat!" Belfry chirped.

Ding pushed his way from the top of my pajamas, poking his head out to gaze at me. "I was just tryin' to get warm. It's cold here in this cotton-pickin' state!"

Belfry crawled up along my arm as Ding exited off my shoulder. "That's what a blanket's for, Uncle Ding. Now stay out of Stevie's boobs and go have some breakfast."

I watched with grainy eyes as Ding took flight, swooping into the bathroom where I'd left the Bats some fruit last night before crawling into bed beside Whiskey, snuggling up against him and literally passing out.

"How you feelin', Boss?

"Like I saw my mother for the first time in over a year again, then I met my father, and then someone was murdered at my party."

"*Your what?* Dita has a baby daddy?" Bel cried.

I stroked the top of Bel's tiny head. "Of course she does. I didn't just hatch." I think at one point in my life I must've thought I had, because my mother had been so tight-lipped about the subject. I'd thought all sorts of thing, but I'd never thought Hugh Granite.

"Well, who knows with your mother? I wouldn't put it past her to have conjured you up."

I snickered. "Stop. You don't think for one second she'd do something like that on purpose, do you? If that's the case, I'm laying bets I was a spell gone horribly wrong." Then I chuckled, because I could actually joke about my origins and feel no pangs of stinging regret.

"Morning, Dove! Up and at 'em. Your mother's in rare form this fine day and I believe your help will be needed." Win's warning slipped into my ear in his husky-silky tone.

Last night rushed back to me in a flood of my mother's expensive perfume and my father's crazy but sweetly overblown ego.

"Now what?" I groaned, scratching Whiskey's ears when he set his big head on my thigh for our typical morning snugglefest.

"She's been on the phone for what seems like hours,

calling all sorts of insurance companies and bank officials, only to come up dry."

Stretching, I asked, "Dry? For what?"

"Money, Stevie. If what I'm hearing is correct, there is *no* money."

I bolted upright, almost knocking Bel from the bed. "No money?"

Bel hopped into my lap. "You heard Winterbutt right. Bart had no money."

Scrubbing my hand over my bleary eyes, I tried to shake the sleepies off. "But he has a villa in Greece, for goddess sake! Who has a villa in Greece if they have no money?"

"It was a lease," Bel said in a deadpan tone. "Old Bart was leasing it and when they left, he owed five months of back rent. Won't be long now before they come confiscate that Mercedes he'd been hiding in some storage garage somewhere, either."

This wasn't happening. I plucked up Bel and shoved the covers off, swinging my feet over the edge of the bed. "There must be some mistake…"

"The only mistake is Dita's, thinking Bart was wealthy," Win said. "She was just about to chew someone else out as I came to wake you."

My stomach rolled in turmoil. What about all the yacht parties and jet-setting she'd claimed they did before she'd stopped communicating with me? "Okay, okay. Let me grab a shower so I can figure this out. There must be some error. I *hope* there's some error."

Just as I was making my way to the bathroom, Dita flew in the door, her face paler than normal, her lavender nightgown covered by the smallest scrap of a matching bathrobe. "Stephania! Thank goddess you're awake!"

Brushing my hair from my face, I shot her a look of sympathy. "What's going on, Mom? How do you feel this morning?"

Her small frame trembled, but not in sorrow—in rage. She held up her cell phone and shook it at me. "It's that Bart! Oooh, I could kill him!"

"Already taken care of," I sniped.

The guy wasn't even cold yet and she was too busy hunting down his money to even care how he'd ended up dead? She wasn't upset he'd died; she was upset he hadn't made finding his money easy enough for her.

"Don't you take that moral highroad with me on today of all days, young lady! I will not stand for your self-righteousness!" she cried at me, pacing the length of my bedroom floor, her nightgown floating about her dainty kitten-heel-clad feet.

Dang. I'd done it again. I kept breaking my pact with myself to accept Dita for who she was and love her anyway.

"Mom!" I yelled. When she got like this, there was no calming her. She'd work herself into a state of hysteria if I didn't rope her in. I motioned to the chair by my fireplace. "Give me the phone and sit down, *please.*"

With a huffy exhale of breath, she plunked down in

the chair and held out the phone. "Maybe you can talk some sense into these people."

"First, I'm sorry. That was uncalled for. And no. That's not what I'm going to do. I'm going to take a shower and make you a nice breakfast and we'll figure out what's going on. And try to remember, you're in mourning. You know, for that guy who put a ring on it? The police are going to be watching you very carefully. You don't need the kind of heat they'll bring if you keep harassing bank officials. It looks bad. It looks like you were only in it for the money."

She looked at me in outraged astonishment. "I was!"

"Bloody fantastic!" Win quipped.

But I cringed, annoyed that Win thought this was funny. It wasn't funny to take advantage of someone—to use them for their money.

"Mother! You can't say things like that! Do you have any idea how bad this looks for you as it stands? If Bart really doesn't have any money, the police might come to the conclusion you were angry enough to kill him for lying to you. Pipe down, for Pete's sake."

Dita blanched, her skin going even whiter, if that were at all possible. "*Me?* If I wanted him dead, I'd just snap my fingers, for goddess sake. Why would I bother to string him up like some Christmas lights?"

Had Bart still been hanging by the sheet when my mother found him?

"Was Bart..." I swallowed hard. "Was he hanging when you found him, Mom?"

She closed her eyes and shuddered. "I don't remember, Stephania. He was just there. I told the police everything. Please don't make me repeat that horror."

Then something else occurred to me. Something I wouldn't necessarily be able to tell anymore because I was no longer a witch. Bart was a warlock. Had he tried to use his magic to stop his killer? It was a natural, almost kneejerk defense.

"Did you smell magic when you found him?"

My mother's gaze found mine as though she just realized something crucial. "Yes!" Then her eyes clouded over. "But I can't remember if it smelled like Bart's," she sobbed.

I stiffened, fear coursing through my veins. "You didn't say anything like that to the police, did you? Call me crazy, but worse has been revealed in a time of anguish."

"Of course not, Stephania! I'm not an idiot."

"Okay, then did you see anything else that might help us? Anything unusual other than the scent of magic?"

"No! Now stop grilling me as though I'm the guilty party here! I don't know who'd want to kill Bart. I told the police that, too. In fact, I don't know much about his past at all."

"Because you never investigated his past, Mom." She'd just seen dollar signs. "This is going to look bad to the police, Mom. You could end up a serious suspect."

"Well, I don't care! It's just as I said. If I wanted Bart dead, I'd have taken care of it with my magic."

Closing my eyes, I prayed for patience. "Mom? You cannot use that as a valid alibi for how you couldn't possibly have killed Bart. We live with humans here in Ebenezer Falls. They won't get your justifications, and you cannot kill anyone, *ever*, anyway. Not according to Baba and the coven word. Understand? And maybe you should talk to my father so he can help you work on your sad face, so if the police question you again you'll at least look like you're sorry Bart's dead."

"Stevie, we've talked about this. You'll only add fuel to the fire," Win chastised.

Crossing her arms over her chest, Mom gave me the death glare. "Don't even speak his name in my presence, Stephania. I won't have it today."

I know, I know. I swore I was going to accept Dita for who she was and love her anyway. But not when it came to something as important as this. Nuh-uh.

"Mom? All you have to do is answer one teeny-tiny question and we don't have to talk about Hugh ever again. No talking it out. No repercussions. No blame. No drama. Just one question. Deal?"

Sucking in her cheeks, she gave me a curt nod of her sleep-tousled head. "One question and that's it. Then we have business to take care of."

I swallowed hard. Now that I was about to ask the most important of questions, I couldn't believe how nervous I was or how much I really wanted what I was about to ask to be true.

Rubbing my hands together, their clammy surfaces

cold, I looked her in the eye. "Is Hugh Granite really my father?"

Dita took a deep breath. The early-morning gray of the oncoming rain through the wide expanse of windows made her look tiny for only a moment before she sat up straight, her spine rigid. "*Yes*. Hugh Granite is your father."

I let out a breath I didn't even know I was holding and left her with these words: "Thank you for answering. I'm going to take a shower, and when I'm done, we'll have some breakfast and figure out what happened with Bart."

Tears stung my eyes as I made my way into the bathroom.

I had a movie-star father.

In Japan.

And I liked him.

And that was pretty cool.

~

"Why are you wearing that ridiculous outfit, Stephania?" my mother asked as I looked at yet another account Bart owed money on.

Belfry rolled to his back on the towel I'd set him on and looked up at my mother. "You deaf, lady? Didn't we just relive the whole Madam Zoltar 2.0 story?"

But I pressed my finger to his chin to quiet him. "Because I work, Mom. I have an appointment today as Madam Zoltar. Remember what I told you over the eggs Carmella was kind enough to make—and you complained about?"

Carmella had come to check on my mother and me this morning to find we hadn't eaten yet. And no one didn't eat when Carmella had an apron and a gourmet kitchen at her beck and call.

"Well, they were runny."

"So is your mou—"

I pressed another finger to Bel's snout to shush him. "And they were *free.* Like I told you earlier, I'm dressed like this because this was how Madam Zoltar dressed when she was giving readings and communicating with the dead."

She rolled her eyes, bored with me already. "But didn't you just tell me you could no longer communicate with the afterlife?"

"Yes, but then I *also* told you about Win, my conduit. He helps me talk to the spirits. So in honor of Madam Zoltar, I took over her business and I have appointments for readings today that were made a good deal in advance of your surprise visit. You didn't RSVP until the last second. I thought you weren't coming. Anyway, that's why I wear the caftan and the turban."

"You'll never get a man dressed like that, Stephania," she scoffed, flicking at the linen napkin on the table of our kitchen nook.

"Well, that's good, because I don't want a man who bases his attraction to me on how I dress. I want a man who bases his attraction to me on my mind."

"Brainz, we want braaainz!" Belfry chirped on an infectious giggle.

I would have laughed under normal circumstance, but not after the hour I'd just spent going over Bart and Dita's finances. Pressing my fingers to my temples to ease the ache in them, I closed my laptop with resignation.

It was true. Bart had no money. He'd been scamming Mom all along, using credit cards he'd run up to the max to stay afloat, robbing Peter to pay Paul, and it was all catching up to him today.

"So it's true then?" Mom asked, her tone filled with worry.

"It sure looks that way. His credit cards are all maxed out. In fact, the first-class flight to Seattle took him right over the top. The Mercedes was a lease that's going to be repossessed any minute, a lease he also paid for with a cash advance from his credit card. The villa in Greece, the yacht in Aruba, the condo in Miami, the wine-of-the-month club, a couple of other unmentionables I can't even believe you tolerated—all leased. All paid for with credit cards. Didn't you have credit cards as his wife, too, Mom? Didn't you *ever* look at the bills and see the mess he was in?"

Now she looked hesitant—and that made me nervous.

"Mom? If we're going to do this, and I'm going to help you, you're going to have to lay everything on the table for me. All of it. I want the truth. Don't let me get caught with my pants down and make me look like a fool, and don't you dare get defensive either. Now spit it out."

Fluffing her silk scarf (a new one; not like the kind I hunted down at secondhand stores, mind you), she twisted the multicolored fabric in nervousness. "I did have credit cards, but they weren't all in his name. Some were in mine."

"And where are they now?" I held slim hope they were shredded in the trash, but I knew better.

"Pick me, I know! I know!" Bel squeaked.

I gave my familiar a stern look that said enough really was enough. "Mom?"

"In my purse," she hedged, biting her lower lip.

"Burning a hole in it, I suppose?"

Shrugging, she ran her finger over the rim of her teacup. "I have some debt…"

"Mom, where did you meet Bart?"

"At a convention."

Sweet Pete in a mini-skirt. I had a bad feeling I was in up to my eyeballs because she was being purposefully evasive, but that didn't stop me from diving head first into the pool. "For?"

"Millionaires," she said on a guilty whisper.

Well, of course she had. Where else would someone like my mother go to hunt down her next husband? "So he told you he was a millionaire?"

Mom looked at me as if I was insane to question such a thing. "How else could he be registered at the convention?"

"I smell rotten things in Denmark, Stevie. I do

97

believe we have a legitimate con artist on our hands, Dove."

"Seeing as I'm pretty sure you weren't working the convention—though, I've heard back in the day you were super adept at them, Rodeo Girl—Bart was probably registered the same way *you* were registered. By making things up and presenting false documents."

I watched as her mind worked, watched as she considered creating some tall tale in her head to cover her scam, so I gave her the "don't even" glare.

Finally, Dita looked me right in the eye, her beautiful gaze narrowed. "He thought I was an heiress with a trust fund, all right?"

Win began to laugh in my ear, so loud and so hard, he wheezed. "Priceless! They scammed each other! Oh, bloody good show!"

"So he thought you had money, too?" The magnitude of not just the pretense of riches, but the mental work it required to keep up such a ruse fell on me, full impact. "Oh, Mom. Haven't you learned after all this time? Stuff like this catches up with you. I thought after husband number three hundred and eight, you'd get it. And you've married *other* men and didn't have to pretend you were rich to get them to say I do."

My mother let out an annoyed sigh, smoothing her silky hair back over her shoulder. "Don't exaggerate, Stephania. I've only had five husbands, *counting Bart*. But he told me he would only marry a woman of his ilk, and when I peeked at his net worth, well, you know the rest of the story."

Oh, what tangled webs we weave... I cleared my throat. "So you pretended to be 'of his ilk' before you even knew if he had ilk himself? How'd you manage that?"

Dita didn't look guilty when she told me. Not even a little. "Masters, my last husband, left me some money, and of course I have credit cards..."

"*Some* money? Wasn't Masters a legit multimillionaire?"

"He was, but he left most everything to his greedy children and his various charities. Some diabetes foundation or another, the hunting club, etcetera."

Now for the biggest question of all—the one which would determine how much debt she was really in. "How much did he leave you, Mom?"

"Enough to—"

"*How. Much?*" I wasn't letting this go. If we were going to try to fix this, we were going all the way.

"Two hundred thousand dollars."

Win groaned with me.

Licking my lips, I said through clenched teeth, "And where is that money now, Mom?"

Looking out the window at the boats, she drummed her fingers on the table. "Well, I had to prove to Bart I was an heiress, didn't I? So I bought a car and some small trinkets. They were investments..."

"While I lived like a pauper in a fleabag motel and ate dollar tacos to make my money last? Nice, Mom."

Dita turned her eyes to me, all doughy and soft. "I didn't know, Stephania."

I fought the urge to be petty, but it slipped out anyway. "Because you didn't *want* to know. Bart told you he didn't want you to know."

Mom swallowed, licking her lips. "That's fair."

"So, in other words, all the money you had is gone, yes?"

"Yes," she said in a weak voice.

"How long did you think you could keep making him believe you were an heiress with a big fat trust fund?"

"Do you want the truth?"

"Nah. I want you to lie to me. Of course I want the truth, Mom!"

Her shoulders lifted under her powder-blue cashmere sweater. "Until someone better, maybe richer came along. I had my eye on a shipping magnate."

I popped up from the table, my work boots clomping on the gorgeous hardwood floor to keep from throttling her. "Okay, I need a breather and it's almost nine. That means I have to go because I don't want to be late for my nine-thirty at the shop. Let me mull some of this over and we'll reconnect later this afternoon when I'm done with work."

"And what do you expect I'll do all day? Hang around with those disgusting mutants upstairs?"

Count the credit card companies you owe? Plan a funeral for your husband?

"Count, Stevie. Do the three-count. In this instance, maybe five or even ten. Whatever it takes to keep your cool. Remember, as we discussed. Be clear and concise with your requirements for this relationship, but don't give in to fits of sarcasm. And no passive-aggressive stabs at her clear inability to focus on anything but herself, or her lack of sensitivity after abandoning you in your darkest hour," Win encouraged. "The time to hash her faults as a mother out are for after this is handled. And I wholly encourage you to do such. Don't let her take advantage, but wait until the dust of Bart's death settles."

He'd been coaching me for the past couple of days, ever since he knew my mother was coming to visit, offering skills on how to deal with emotional terrorists. I'm still not sure if it's the same as the kind of terrorists *he's* dealt with, but so far, it was kind of panning out.

So I counted to ten in my head, got my boundary ducks in a row, and said, "Mourn your husband properly, keep your mouth closed and don't talk to anyone. Also, please don't call the Bats disgusting. They're an extension of Belfry, who's one of the best friends I have in the world. That means they're always welcome here forever. Just because you don't want a familiar, doesn't mean I don't. They've been given strict instructions to stay out of your way, but I won't have you insulting them. They're my guests."

Then I scooped up Belfry and tucked him in my purse, calling for Whiskey, who loved to ride in the car no matter where we went. "Whiskey! C'mon, buddy! Vroom-vroom!"

Those two key words had him bounding down the

stairs and, from the sound of it, stumbling over his big feet on the last step before he skidded into the hallway entry. He righted himself and scurried to stand by my side as I latched his leash on his collar.

Kneeling down, I pressed a kiss to the top of his head. "Who's the best boy ever?"

And that was when I noticed what he had in his mouth. A business card with bite marks on it.

Groaning, I tapped his wet nose. "Hand it over, dude, or no vroom-vroom for you."

Bel peeked his head out of my purse, his tiny claws, clinging to the edge. "Whiskey! Dude, what have I told you about eating everything off the ground? Swear, someday you're gonna get the clap just because you can't resist snarfing stuff up. Spit it out!" he ordered.

Whiskey let his tongue unfurl, plopping the card into my hand. I held it up under the light coming in from the front door. It was a card from Parties by Petula, pastel pink and festively decorated with a three-tier cake with sparkling white bows.

As I flipped it over, I read a name scrawled in pencil on the back.

Bart.

CHAPTER 7

I looked at the business card from Petula again as I waited at the store for my eleven o'clock to arrive. A man who wanted to attempt contact with his brother who'd died last month.

The day had gone even grayer and drizzlier, but the store cheered me up. I loved what we'd done with Madam Zoltar's. It soothed me today, with the healing crystals I so adored surrounding me, and what was left of my glued-together snow globe collection (trashed after a run-in with an angry spirit) on a shelf.

We'd added antique rocking chairs outside for those who chose to pop in and chat (spirits and people alike), and as word got out, we were beginning to grow our clientele.

"I assume we can speak freely now that we're out of your mother's presence?" Win asked.

I nodded, pulling my turban off to run my fingers through my hair. "Thank goddess, yes."

"You sound exhausted and the day's only just begun, Stevie. Didn't sleep well last night?"

Yawning, I rolled my shoulders to ease the tension. "My mother takes the stuffing right out of me. All this keeping my feelings to myself is work, Win. I used to let off steam with sarcasm and my razor-sharp wit. If I can't use those, she uses up all my life points," I complained on a laugh.

Win barked a laugh of his own. "She is a great deal of work and far worse than I imagined."

"Admit it, you thought I was exaggerating, didn't you?"

"I'll own that statement. Yes. I thought you exaggerated. I was wrong. But I'm proud of how you're handling the shambles her life is right now. I realize there's a great deal of fodder to be had, but you have on your restraint pants and you're wearing them well. So let's refresh, yes? Beginning with Masters."

"Her ex-husband?"

"Poor sap," Belfry chimed in.

"Yes. Well, it seems he may be the spirit from last night who warned us Dita wasn't what she seemed. He revealed himself to me just this morning as your mother frantically entered incorrect passwords for Bart's credit card accounts. Who uses muffinloveshis-bunny as a password?"

I snorted. "Did he have any other gems from the afterlife?"

"Just the one, but I fear he's simply striking out as a form of payback. While we obviously can't dismiss his

104

statement, we surely should be on the lookout for retaliation."

Leaning back in my Madam Zoltar chair, I sipped my cup of freshly made coffee. "Fair enough. I'll make sure to keep my ducking skills brushed up. So let's move on to the bigger mystery. Why the heck did Bart have the number for the Washington State Penn, and do we call the police and mention they missed a piece of possible evidence? Do we show that potential piece of evidence to Momster and see if it really was Bart's?"

Win scoffed. "Well, the first is obvious. His BFF's probably in doing twenty for some scam or another. Grifters like Bart don't make close friends often, but they do make contacts. Maybe he was trying to reach out to one of them?"

I thought about that. Sure, if Bart had been doing this all his life, maybe he did have connections to others like him. "Maybe. But it's not like we can call up the pokey and ask if a Bart has called recently."

"Point. But if we could get our hands on his phone records…"

"Right. Because Officer Dana Do-The-Right-Thing Nelson's going to just hand them over to me?"

"Then consider that a dead end for now. Also, yes and no. You do tell the police about the money clip and phone number, because if Sardine Pickles finds a connection to the Penn and Bart's death, you're going to begin working that charm you've been brushing up on to find out what he knows. And I vote no on telling your mother. She has the eye of the tiger, and it has nothing to do with whether Bart was killed or not."

I felt such shame over my mother confessing her motives. "I have to give her credit for her honesty. She made no bones about why she'd married Bart."

"True enough. You know, there's something I've been wondering. If your circle of witches is so small, why haven't you ever heard of Bart and his unsavory reputation? He is a warlock, is he not? And why doesn't he—or for that matter, your mother—just conjure up some money and a villa in Greece? One spell is all it would take."

Everyone thought that. Everyone thought we could have whatever we wanted with a flick of our wands. But not true. Not if you liked living as a free witch.

"It's pretty easy to slip under the radar in the witch world. Some choose to live with humans and others choose places like my old hometown, Paris, simply because we didn't have to hide our magic there. We're as scattered as humans are, so, while close-knit, we don't all barbecue together. Second, we're not allowed to use our magic for personal gain. Not that it doesn't occur, and not that my mother hasn't done it, and obviously Bart did, too. But something as big as a villa in Greece with no work history would make Baba Yaga and her council of goons sit up and take big notice."

"Have you ever used your magic for personal gain?"

I chuckled and batted my eyelashes. "I don't magic and tell. So moving right along—the business card from Petula with Bart's name on the back?"

"Now for that, we get out the old detective's kit and investigate thoroughly. You definitely should ask Petula if she knew Bart, or maybe if someone working for her knew him."

Resting my chin in my hand, I wound a piece of hair around my finger. "You know, I've been thinking. Maybe considering all the debt Bart was in, he *did* take his own life. I'd hate that just as much as murder, but he owed everyone and their grandmother money, Win. It isn't unlikely."

"But does the word suicide make your spine tingle the way murder does, Dove?"

"No." No, it definitely did not.

"Then we proceed as such."

"Fair enough. I'll call Petula and see if she can give me a couple seconds of her time later this afternoon. Next up, my mother's debt." Ugh. The mountain of it made me want to curl up in a corner.

"That can be handled, Stevie. You know it can," Win said with his usual generosity when it came to any hardship in my life.

"*No*. No it can't. No way am I letting you dig her out of this mess."

"It's *your* money, Stevie."

I shook my head, resting my palms flat on the table. "No. That's not how I've ever considered it. If we call it anything, we call it *our* money. Period. Technically, you're still around to see where it's spent. It's like bringing the Invisible Man to the bank, and then making him watch you piss away his hard-earned money on the horses or something, knowing he can't do a thing about it."

"I don't see it the same way, I guess. But if you'd like to call it our money, then let's consider how *we* can help Dita with it."

"It won't be by paying off her credit cards. I just can't, Win. Let's be honest here. She has a pretty cold heart. And I don't mean just with me, with everyone. Bart's not even dead twenty-four hours and she's looking to find insurance policies and cash. That's not forgetting Masters, who was a really good guy, by the way, and how she called his kids greedy. My mom's selfish, and you shouldn't have to pay for it. We'll figure something else out. Credit counseling, bankruptcy, I dunno…"

"How about we revisit this particular subject later?"

In other words, Win didn't want to fight. But neither did I. "Done deal. Onto the magic portion of this investigation. My mother said she smelled magic when she found Bart, but she wasn't sure it was Bart's magic."

"Please explain this smell of magic, would you?"

"Witches intuitively sense when magic is used. We can smell it, feel it. It's a vibe of sorts, and the scent is unique to each witch. After a time, once you get to know someone, you can identify a person's magic by the scent."

"Then we consider magical foul play. Which means you must tread carefully. Without your powers, no amount of spy training will save you. I won't watch that happen, Dove."

Win was incredibly overprotective of me, but this time he was right. I was no match for magic anymore.

"Oh, something I failed to mention last night. One of the Cirque acrobats was talking to another male acrobat about a woman named CC, who slapped Bart."

"Hmmm," Win purred. "Interesting. Why did she slap Bart?"

"Apparently, he made a very inappropriate comment about—"

"Her boobs," Belfry piped in.

I sighed. "How did you know about that, Bel? I just overhead the conversation. I didn't see it happen."

"Sonar, baby. I got it and it's honed to a sharp point. I hear all sorts of stuff I'm not supposed to hear—when I'm awake, anyway. When the sirens began wailing and the cops were crawling all over the house, they woke me up."

I smiled at him, tucking him into his towel. "If only that sonar had picked up something around the time when Bart was killed. Anyway, yes. According to these two acrobats, this CC was offended by something Bart said and she slapped him."

"So you remember who the acrobat was, Mini-Spy?"

"I didn't get her name but I know what she looks like, and they're all staying at the inn, sharing the few rooms available until the police clear them to leave town and go back to Vegas. Easy enough to check on them." I added that to my list of people to talk to about last night.

"Then one last thing, Dove. The commotion I mentioned last night with Hardy Clemmons."

"Oh yeah. You said you didn't see what it was about, right?"

"Correct, but he's worth talking to anyway."

"Then I'll add him to the list of people we should wow with my subtle yet charming interrogation skills. So are we done briefing for the moment? Anything else you can think of at this point?" I asked, scrolling my cell for my Ebenezer Falls phone app for the *Herald*.

"Your father. *The* Hugh Granite. I hate to say it, but can we rule him out? He *was* unaccounted for the better part of the evening."

I thought about that for a moment. It was only fair to consider him. He was the only outsider in Ebenezer Falls, and suspiciously enough, he'd appeared on my doorstep the night his old flame's husband was killed.

But after talking with him, that didn't sit well with me. "Okay, if we go on my gut, which I'm trying not to pepper with my giddy girl feelings about finding my father, then I'd have to say he just doesn't seem capable. He could have come back for my mother a hundred times over the years and he didn't. His motivation, if anything, would certainly be jealousy, right? A crime of passion? Seems a stretch to think Bart was the one to send him spiraling into a murderous rage. Mom's been married five times over the years since they were yeehawing it up in Texas."

"All valid points. Now on the flips side, talk to me, Dove. Tell me how you feel about him and his presence after a night of rest and letting this information sink in."

I smiled. I couldn't help it. "He's pretty vain, huh?"

Win's chuckle warmed my ear. "But in the most charming of ways, wouldn't you say? I've never seen anything quite like it. He refers to himself in the third person as though he's an entity—nay, a force. Yet he's utterly, unabashedly unaware he's doing so in the most delightful way."

I agreed a thousand percent. "Did you see the way the two of them looked at each other?"

Win hummed in my ear. "As though right out of a movie."

"I'd sure like someone to look at *me* that way someday."

"Maybe someone already does."

I waved a dismissive hand, giving Whiskey belly rubs with the side of my foot. He loved a good scratch. "You mean Forrest? Naw. He's not there yet, if he ever will be. But then, neither am I. You know what one of my first thoughts was when my mother and father saw each other for the first time again after all these years?"

"What's that?"

I hesitated only for a moment before I said, "You and Miranda. You two looked at each other in the picture that way, too."

I was referring to the only piece of evidence I had that Win really existed once. A picture I'd found in the back of the closet of our house, in which he was smiling down at a gorgeous redhead with complete adoration in his eyes.

Win was everything I'd secretly thought he'd be and more. Dangerously dark, all angles and chiseled lines, his face rugged and raven's wing hair almost exactly as I'd imagined.

When I first saw the picture, it left me breathless… and then it dredged up feelings I didn't even know I was having until I had them. Feelings I wasn't comfortable with at this point in my life. Feelings that there was nothing I could do about anyway.

I waited in silence while Win processed what I'd just admitted. It was like pulling teeth when it came to the subject since I'd found the picture. I only knew one thing—he thought Miranda, the woman he'd loved, had killed him.

When he finally spoke, his voice was stoic and husky. "I admit, I was once very much in love with her."

"Right. And then she murdered you." I waited again, keeping my poker face in place.

"That she did," he responded in a sharp tone.

"And then?" I coaxed him with a hopeful glance.

"And then I don't know, Stevie. I have no answers as to why she betrayed me so deeply. But she did," he replied, his voice tight with tension, like an arrow ready to spring from its bow.

"But she's dead, too, right?"

"That *is* the rumor at MI6."

"Have you investigated that rumor, Spy Guy?"

"How would you suggest I do such?"

He was getting snippy again, a clear sign I was pushing too hard. But it was time for some honesty. We'd beat around this bush a hundred times over the last month or so. Him giving me bits and pieces of his former life and the mystery surrounding it; me backing off and letting him breathe until I wanted to scream.

I don't know why it was so important to me to know what went down with him and Miranda. Maybe it's because I know it's important to Win. Otherwise, he'd just tell me what happened and it would be done.

So I cracked my knuckles and decided to jump into the deep end. "Listen, Win, I'm going to lay something on the table here. You know everything about me and I've been as open as possible about all the things in my life, good and bad. But the time has come for *you* to be as open with me...or this will never work. I'm going to end up feeling resentful if our relationship is so one-sided. It's obvious your death and the events leading up to it bother you. It's unresolved and it will eventually affect how you feel about everything we do together. I'm not asking you to put your heart on your sleeve. Just state the facts and maybe I can help you find out what happened with Miranda. And that's all I'm asking. So you think it over and let me know."

"Is this an ultimatum?"

I made a face. And men always say *women* don't listen to the facts, that we cloud them with our emotions. Poppycock with a capital P.

"Does it sound like one, Win? I don't remember

saying you had to tell all or I was hitting the road. What I said was, things between us are very one-sided and I'm open all the time, but you not so much. *That's* what I said. Then I offered to help you find out what happened the day you died and what happened to Miranda. Women don't have to be from Mars and men don't have to be from Venus if we listen to what the other says and really hear the words."

"It's men who are from Mars, and women from Venus."

"Yeah? Well, Venus was just made a planet again. We women didn't even have our own planet for a little while there, so I borrowed Mars."

"No. That was Pluto."

"You're deflecting. You're avoiding. You're driving me out of my mind! We're a good team together, Win. We are. You *know* we are. Let me help you figure it out. Wouldn't you feel better knowing if she really betrayed you? What if she didn't and you've been persecuting her all this time for no good reason? What if your memories of your love affair don't have to be tainted with doubt?"

His sigh was long and low. "Maybe I'm just not ready to find out the details? That's the best I can offer you right now, Stevie. If you want my squishy girl feelings on this, here they are. I was deeply in love with Miranda. My alleged homicide—and I only use that word because you're correct, I don't know with one hundred percent accuracy she was the one to actually pull the trigger—all points back to her being a double agent, and taking sensitive information I'd given her then feeding it to a sworn enemy. Thus making my demise a forgone conclusion, either way. Right now, it's all speculation on my part, but I'm not clear as to whether I'd rather leave it alone because it would cut me deeper or because I was played for a fool. Does that work for you? Or did I leave out an emotion you haven't demanded I display?"

I simply smiled. He was still testy, but less defensive. But I still wasn't prepared to lend him my theory on the possibility of Miranda still being alive. I'd thought a lot about the potential for faking her death, and it was pretty high. She had been or was, after all, a spy. I kept that card close to my chest for the time being.

"See how easy that was?" I puffed my chest out and pretended to be Win. Lowering my voice and using a British accent, I repeated what I'd heard. "I loved Miranda. She hurt me. I don't have all the facts. I'm not sure I'm ready to hear the facts. Those are my squishy girl feelings on the subject, Dove."

Belfry whistled his approval. "Niiice, Boss. You forgot a 'bloody hell,' but good show!"

Win laughed, leaving me relieved. "I'm quite used to keeping things close to my chest. That's what spies do, Stevie. We don't get involved."

"Oh yeah? Well, guess what, Winterbottom? You're involved with *me*." I thumbed my chest. "Whether you like it or not, I got you, babe. I'm your earthly eyes and ears. So stop being so quick to wheedle information out of me and offer up some of your own. My book's written. You know it all. But we're only on chapter one of your opus. So, speaking of chapters, let's turn the page. Did Miranda buy the house before you? Why does everyone in town talk about a woman living at our house, but either dying or disappearing?"

"Yes. She bought it before me and I bought it from her estate. I bought it because…well, because it reminded me of her. We'd had plans to…renovate it."

Again, my heart twisted. He'd bought a house because the love of his life died. But that also meant Win bought it before he found out she'd allegedly betrayed him. Setting aside his reasons for buying the house, now we were getting somewhere.

"It was easy enough to find out, if you'd contacted the real estate agent who sold it, Stevie. It's a matter of public record."

I shook my head and wagged my finger. "Um, no. You don't get to call me a slacker amateur sleuth. It's all I can do every day not to start digging things up on the Internet about you."

"I've been scrubbed, you won't find much."

"But that's not why I don't do it. I don't scour the web because you asked me not to, so I don't."

"Which was how I knew I could trust you."

My heart skipped a beat, a solid beat. This was even more unfamiliar than all the other emotions Win evoked in me. "All good things. Now trust me some more and tell me why she bought the house? Was the intent for the two of you to retire from spying and live out your spy lives in Ebenezer Falls?" I waited, my pulse racing like a Kentucky Derby mare.

But the jingle of the chimes on the front door thwarted all further conversation as I assumed my eleven o'clock had just arrived. "This ain't over, Spy Guy," I muttered.

"I'd be disappointed if you kept your claws sheathed," Win quipped.

"Daughter!"

Oh, hey, look. My *dad's* here.

I fought an enormous grin as he sauntered toward the back of the store. He wore a casual sports jacket in a crisp navy blue with a pale blue lightweight sweater beneath it. His hair was shiny and black under the store's lights, slicked back away from his forehead, and his eyes were blue pools of warm greeting.

I jumped up, startling Whiskey, who immediately hauled himself off the floor, his big body knocking into a chair before he came to rest at my side, sniffing the air.

"Hi…" Dad? I wasn't sure I was ready for that title yet. "Um…Hugh. What brings you to Madam Zoltar's?"

He smiled broadly, holding out his hands to me— hands I took without reservation. "Every father wants to see where his daughter works. I thought maybe we could have that lunch? Somewhere private, of course. Perhaps my room at the inn? The mob of people seeking my autograph somewhere public would only interrupt our getting to know one another."

I fought a giggle along with Win, who sputtered a

cough. "I have an eleven o' clock appointment, but it shouldn't take long. We could meet back at the inn around noon, maybe one?"

And I could do some snooping.

Hugh cupped my chin. "Perfect. Shall we say one o'clock? I'll take care of everything."

I grinned, standing on tiptoe to press a shy kiss to his cheek. "We shall."

Hugh gave me a quick hug before turning to take his leave, but he stopped mid-stride and cocked his head.

Which made me cock *my* head in confusion.

Which is what I'm guessing was the inspiration for Win to bellow, "Intel alert!"

But wait. Then *I* heard something, too.

"Don't believe a word he says, y'all! He's the one! He's the one!" yelped a disembodied female voice, dripping with Southern charm.

CHAPTER 8

My eyes flew open wide in shock. "Was that... Did I...?"

"You heard her?" Win blustered, his shock just as clear as mine.

"Who are you?" Hugh demanded, his normally smiling face going hard.

"He ain't who he says he is, bless his wee heart. Not who he says he is. Not who he says he is! Not who he says he is!" the voice repeated, picking up steam in an almost eerie echo-like taunt.

"*Who* isn't who he says he is?" Win demanded, his shout abrasive to my eardrums.

"Yeah?" I asked into the room, my eyes flying to Hugh. "Who are you talking about?"

"He did it! He did it! Y'all are gonna find—" And then the voice cut out completely on me. But obviously not for Win and Hugh.

"Identify yourself!" Win demanded in an almost

simultaneous request with Hugh, whose face was getting harder by the second.

"Whoever you are, we need to know *who* you're talking about," Hugh said from stiff lips, his words curt.

And then she was back, but only momentarily. "*Hiiim!*" she screamed so loud, another one of my patched-together snow globes shattered and crashed to the ground. Gosh dang it. What was it about my snow globes being used as a point of reference for attack?

Whiskey began to bark wildly, running toward the shelf housing my globes as Belfry flew up in the air, landing on my shoulder to burrow into my hair with a shiver. "What's the deal, Boss? Who's at it now?"

I grabbed Whiskey to soothe him, stroking his big head as Win said again, "You're not making any sense!"

Hugh held up one of his perfectly manicured hands and narrowed his eyes. "Identify yourself or I'll end this conversation right now! I can't help if you don't tell me what you're talking about!"

And then there was silence and the remains of my snow globe in pieces on the floor in a small puddle of water.

I broke the quiet when I asked, "Did anyone recognize the voice?"

"No. Never heard it before, Dove."

The storm clouds on Hugh's face suddenly parted and his warm charm returned in their place. "Neither have I."

And then the spirit's words sank in. Not the fact that I'd actually heard them, that crazy could be addressed later. No. It was the words themselves. The spirit said "he" wasn't who he said he was.

Hadn't we gotten the same message just last night from who we assumed was Masters about my mother?

And what other "him" was in the room aside from Hugh?

My eyes went to his face, now sunny and cheerful. "When pressed to identify who she meant, the spirit said 'him.' There's only one *him* in the room," I murmured, my legs wobbly.

But Hugh looked astonished, his eyes going wide. "Daughter, surely you don't think she meant *me?*"

I backed away a little, grabbing the broom in the corner. I hated that I did, but I didn't really know Hugh. I'd been so exhausted last night, I hadn't had time to look him up on the web. That chore was on my list of things to do later this afternoon.

But just because he had a website didn't mean he wasn't capable of murder.

"Stevie!" he yelled, his voice harsh and rife with disappointment. "I would never say I was something I'm not. I am The Hugh Granite!"

"But are you two Hugh Granites? Movie stars kill people, too…"

He reached for my hands, his eyes imploring me, but I was afraid now, so I took another step back, putting the broom between us.

"The spirit said nothing about killing anyone, Stephania! And spirits often become confused."

Oh, you bet I knew that. I could spend all day telling

you stories about the confusion spirits can experience, or even create because sometimes they're not in their right minds. They're as confused as those they're trying to contact. But this had been very specific.

I swallowed the nervous lump in my throat, licking my dry lips as Win spoke in my ear. "He's correct, Dove. She said nothing about murder. Let's think this through. Remember how we talked about controlling our impulses, Stevie."

Was I hearing Mr. Ultra-Cautious right? Think it through? We knew nada about Hugh, except what he'd told us. Were we just going to take him at his word because he was my father? Maybe we'd discounted his involvement in Bart's death too soon?

"*Please think this through*," Hugh echoed, his eyes filled with hurt.

So I held up my hand, letting the broom handle rest in the other. "I'll do that. But I'd like to do it alone, if you don't mind," I said from stiff lips.

"I guess our lunch is off then?"

Gosh. Even as I added him to my list of murder suspects, he was still adorable. I hated seeing the hurt on his face, the way his wide shoulders slumped in defeat.

Lifting my chin even as my legs trembled, I nodded. "For the time being. I'd like you to go now, please."

Now he lifted his jaw, square and defiant. "I shall, but this isn't over. I won't give up on us, Daughter. You'll see you were wrong and I'll wait until you do." He all but clicked his heels and pivoted, heading toward the door where, just before he opened it, he squared his shoulders and smoothed back his hair.

And then he was gone, with just the chimes to announce his departure.

I finally let out a heavy breath, my fear dissipating, leaving me sad.

"How are you, Dove?" Win finally asked.

"Horrified. Mortified. Disgusted for even suggesting such a thing."

"But better horrified than dead, m'love. You must take precautions on the off chance your instincts, and mine as well, are wrong."

"It can't be him, Win." *Please don't let it be him.* "But who else could the spirit have meant?"

"She was quite evasive. I don't know what it is about the spirits, but 'twould seem many get stuck on repeat. We can't take everything they say as reliable."

I nodded sadly, my heart heavy. "Did she say anything else?"

"Nothing either Hugh or I could understand, certainly."

"Okay then. For now, Hugh stays on the list," I offered with more resolve than I had. "What else could she have meant? He was the only *him* here."

"It could mean many things, Dove. Let's let that go for a moment and focus on something absolutely amazing. You heard the spirit as clearly as both Hugh and I! Surely that's cause for a twerk?"

A small rush of excitement skipped through my veins before it fizzled. "I don't have a twerk in me right

123

now. I mean, this has happened before, right? A brief glimpse into my old life then nothing for weeks and weeks."

I was referring to the last major bind I'd been in when another madman was chasing me down and I'd shot sparks from my fingers, just like I'd once did when I was a witch, casting spells. But I'd quickly fizzled, and then nothing until today.

"That's true, but that's not to say you won't experience this at more frequent intervals now. Never give up, Dove," he soothed, his warm aura surrounding me as though he were using his arms to envelope me in a hug.

"Yeah," Bel agreed, tugging my hair as he nuzzled my cheek. "Don't give up, Boss. This might only be the beginning of you getting your powers back."

Biting the inside of my cheek, I didn't say anything more. I was too torn up about Hugh. Grabbing my turban, I put on my Madam Zoltar garb just as the chimes rang on the door, signaling my next client's arrival.

Setting aside my anguish, and the image of my father so hurt, flashing through my mind's eye, I set about doing what I was here to do.

I put a warm smile on my face, held my hand out and welcomed him, and made him comfortable.

But my heart was damn heavy while I did so.

◞

*A*fter I called Sandwich to let him know about what I'd seen under the chest of drawers in the parlor—keeping the information very vague, of course—I decided, before I headed to the inn to question some of the Cirque acrobats, I'd stop in and see Chester and Forrest for a cup of coffee and an egg salad sandwich. I needed some comfort food to ease the ache in my chest.

I tied Whiskey's leash to the post under the awning Forrest had put up for customers with pets and kissed his muzzle. "I'll be right back. Promise to bring you a treat."

As I entered, Chester grinned at me from his favorite ice-cream-colored table and waved me over. "There she is. Come give ol' Chester a hug. One's in order after last night, Sunshine."

I leaned down and dropped a kiss on his rosy cheek, letting him give me a good hard squeeze, inhaling the comforting scent of his Old Spice cologne before I dropped into a wrought iron chair next to him.

He was like a lighthouse beacon on a dark and stormy night. I still wasn't ready to tell him or Forrest about my father's sudden appearance, but Chester knew of Dita's shenanigans. Even if he didn't say it out loud, I knew he sympathized.

Chester chucked me under the chin. "You okay, Kitten?"

"Well, I've been back in Ebenezer Falls for what,

three months, and everywhere I go, someone ends up dead. Ya think it's me?"

He chuckled, putting his hand on his round belly. "I think it's coincidence, kiddo, and a whole lotta crappy luck. But it ain't you. You're too pretty to always be on death's stoop."

Forrest, tall and handsome in his white apron with the logo of the coffee shop on it, made his way to where we sat, a cup of coffee and an egg salad sandwich on wheat toast on a plate. "I figured you might need lunch and caffeine." Then he rooted around in his apron pocket and pulled out a foil bag of blueberry Pop-Tarts, handing them to me with flourish. "To drown your sorrows in after your sandwich," he teased, his eyes sparkling.

"You're the best."

Forrest nodded and grinned. "Yep. I kinda am."

I patted his hand as I dug into my sandwich, unable to think of anything to say that wouldn't be awkward. They both knew my mother from my younger days. I wouldn't be at all surprised to find they considered her a suspect and they were just too embarrassed to tell me.

"So any news?" Chester asked over his round glasses. "Any word on what they're calling this latest round with the Grim Reaper?"

"You mean have they labeled it murder yet? Not that I'm aware of."

My mom had been blowing my phone up all day, but it isn't about anything to do with the police or the investigation. It was about how the Bat twins, Com and Wom, were too noisy and she couldn't nap. Or how I'd failed to provide her with Perrier, or a mountain of other complaints I mostly ignored.

I set my sandwich down, my appetite almost nonexistent, and tried to gather my thoughts as I looked around the room. That's when I saw Hardy Clemmons over in the opposite corner of the shop by the counter, sipping a coffee and eating a Danish.

Hardy was our mailman and newish to town. At least, he was newer to me. He'd been kind enough to make the treacherous climb to our mailbox before we'd had the driveway installed, precariously perched at the end of our lawn just before a steep drop off the cliff. Hardy was in his late fifties, nice enough looking, with a full head of hair and a ruddy outdoors appeal.

Rumor had it he was once involved with the richest woman in Washington, but she broke his heart when she cheated on him and left him for someone else.

Now was as good a time as any to ask him what had happened last night at the party. I was up and out of my chair and crossing the shop's floor to Hardy's table before Forrest could remind me I hadn't finished my sandwich.

"Hi, Hardy. How are you?"

He paused in taking a bite from his Danish and eyed me over the top of the thick white icing. "I'm okay, but what about you? Crazy night last night, huh?"

I nodded, my expression grim. "May I sit?" I

motioned to the chair across from him and he nodded his consent.

I dropped down into the chair, tucking my purse against my chest. "Can I ask you a couple of questions, Hardy?"

His bushy salt-and-pepper eyebrows rose. "Is it about the package left on your front lawn? I don't know how many bloomin' times I have to tell that moron I have for a fill-in he's supposed to ring the doorbell and leave it in a covered area, for Pete's sake. It's not a darn newspaper. I'm sorry that happened, but it'll never happen again. Promise ya that."

"No, it's nothing like that. The package was fine, Hardy. Simple mistake is all. I wanted to ask you about last night at the party." I fought a wince, hoping whatever had happened wasn't too serious.

He set his Danish on the plate and sat back in his chair, his eyes growing suspicious as he wiped his fingers on the napkin and tucked his hands under his armpits. "If it's about that argument, the police already asked me plenty, thank you very much. Those of us they didn't get to last night had to go down to the station for questioning. They lined us up like a herd of cattle and took statements from all of us. I already explained."

An argument? That must have been the commotion Win mentioned. "I'm sorry there was trouble, Hardy, and I don't want to bring up bad feelings, but what was the argument about? I hope it wasn't over the shrimp wraps. They were pretty popular," I teased, flashing him a warm smile of sympathy.

He only half-smiled before his weathered face went sour. "No. Though they *were* darn good. The argument was with your mother's husband—the philanderer! He had the nerve, after all this time, to stroll up to me like he never cheated with my girl back in the day!"

Oh, Bart. You were a dirty, dirty boy. "I know it's a sensitive subject, but could you maybe just tell me a little about what happened? If you're not comfortable then by all means, tell me to beat feet. I can take a hint."

Hardy popped his lips and gazed at me. "Oh, I'll tell ya all right. That man jumped into bed with my fiancée, Clara Rawlings, just three days before we were going to get married. That's what he did. Then he has the nerve to offer his hand and smile that stupid smile of his like he didn't ruin my life—in front of everyone at the party? No, sir. Not on my watch," he scoffed, throwing his napkin on the table in disgust.

"Clara Rawlings? Isn't she Lou Rawlings's daughter?" I asked in disbelief. The Rawlingses were some of the richest people in the state of Washington. They were always in the news for some charity or another.

And then it hit me.

Once a grafter, always a grifter. Bart had likely played Clara the same way he had my mother.

Hardy bobbed his head, reaching for his mailbag. "That's the one. Used her all up then dumped her. She eventually came back to me, tail between her legs, cryin' and carryin' on about how he'd only wanted her for her money. But no way was I takin' her back after that. Once a cheat, always a cheat. Serves 'em both right."

"So Bart once lived here in Ebenezer Falls?" How could that be? From the chatter at the party, no one appeared to recognize Bart.

But Hardy shook his head, preparing to rise. "Nope. He met her at some yacht club party in Seattle I couldn't go to because I was out earnin' an honest living on my mail route. I lived in Seattle before I moved here a few years back. I know it was almost twenty years ago, but danged if it didn't sting, him wantin' to make amends, all smiles and fancy suits."

Talk about a coincidence. The world grew smaller still.

I gave him another smile in sympathy. "I'm so sorry, Hardy. If I'd known…"

He patted my shoulder. "How could you have known? It isn't your fault, Stevie. I was just as surprised as he was. I guess he thought he'd slather on some of that charm he's so famous for, and all would be forgiven. I told him if he didn't get the heck outta my sight, I'd tell your mother what a cad he was. I didn't like him, but I sure didn't kill him, and I got an alibi that says so."

I rose then and squeezed his hand. He was such a nice man. "I know this will sound strange, but I think my mother was duped by Bart, too, and I'd like to investigate. Do you remember the name of the yacht club, Hardy? I'm sorry if that brings up painful memories. If it's too much, I'll back off."

"Can't ever forget it. Sure wish I could. The Anchor Yacht Club. That's the name. It was the annual party they had every year. Clara begged me to go. Sure wish I'd taken off work now, but I was determined to prove to her father I could take care of her without his money."

I saw it written all over his face, the pain he'd suffered at the hands of betrayal, and my impulse was to hug him. Instead I smiled and thanked him. "Appreciate it, Hardy."

He winked then; obviously all was forgiven. "You tell your mom I hope she feels better, and just between you and me, she's better off he's dead."

He gave my shoulder one last pat and headed out the door.

"A viable suspect no doubt," Win uttered. "He had an ax to grind."

Closing my eyes, I pressed my fingers to my Bluetooth. "But he claims to have an alibi."

"How do we know that alibi panned out? We don't. Which means we'll have to find out."

Nodding, I rolled my head on my neck and prepared to head over to the inn to find this CC before I considered rattling Officer Nelson's cage. I don't know that I was up to playing cat and mouse with him right now.

Not after the incident with my father.

"Stevie?" Forrest called from the other end of the now-empty shop.

My head swung in his direction as he pointed to the TV mounted just behind me in the corner.

And what to my wandering eyes did appear?

My mother on the boob tube in her tiny rain gear.

CHAPTER 9

So forget every single word I said about accepting my mother for who she is, loving her without reservation; I was no longer immortal, and that meant I didn't have a lifetime of anger to waste, blah, blah bah.

Psychobabble be darned. It was officially *on*.

Because I was going to open up the biggest can of whoop you-know-what I could find the minute I got my hands on her.

As her beautiful face flashed on the TV, her big eyes watery and red-rimmed, and she carried on about finding Bart's killer with a reward (a *reward*, folks!), it was all I could do not to hop in my car, race home and run her over.

"A reward? How does one cough up a reward when one is in, as you Americans say, the hole?"

I pressed my hand against the Bluetooth and

clenched my teeth. "You try and swindle your daughter out of it, that's how. Win, I swear, I'm going to—"

"Hold that thought, Dove. You've been accused of murder once. Lightning can strike twice. Do not say such words in a public place."

I was enraged as I sucked in gulps of air and forced myself to say goodbye to Forrest and Chester. "As you two can see, I have some things to take care of, but thank you for lunch, Forrest." I gave him a quick peck on the cheek and a hug to Chester before I somehow managed to leave without throwing something.

I untied Whiskey's leash with my shaking hands. Stomping along the sidewalk, I ignored the rain battering my face, thrusting the key fob at my car like I was preparing to joust with it. Sliding inside as my ever-faithful Whiskey jumped in beside me, I gripped the steering wheel and clenched my teeth even harder. Even my cute Fiat in red and white—the one thing I'd probably fight Win to my death over, should he ever threaten to take away everything he'd given me—didn't bring me any peace.

Not today.

"I'm going to kill her, Win. *Kill her.* I'm going to grab her skinny bird arms and break them one at a time. Then I'm going to drag her by her lustrously shiny hair and wipe the floor with it!" I shouted, starting my car and pulling out to head home. The drive was a total blur of pine trees and the Sound.

"Dove, 'kill' is a strong word. How about just a good talking to?"

"Uh-huh," Bel agreed. "Let's just give her one of those come-to-goddess talks. Killing is so messy. Haven't you learned that by now?"

But there was no stopping my tirade at this point. She'd been back here all of a day and everything was totally upside down.

"Didn't I tell her to stay put in the house and keep her pretty lips shut? I think I did. But what does she do? She calls a press conference! All this does is draw attention to herself, which we don't need. What's next? Will she go on live TV and summon a spell? Use her magic wand? This is unacceptable! The rule of the coven is clear: if you want to commune with humans, lay low. This is hardly low, Win!" I said on a shout, hitting the heel of my hand against the stirring wheel.

"But Hugh doesn't lay low. He's an international movie star. I don't get the rules of your people, Stevie," Win said.

"But he's not out on live TV talking about murder and he didn't scam his husband! He's not bringing the kind of attention my mother is. She needs as little focus on her as possible. What do you suppose the police will do with this scam she pulled on Bart? They'll instantly suspect she killed him because he really didn't have any money! Dita did this for a reason. To keep the focus on *her* and maybe to collect some sympathy cash in the process. I'm sure there's more ulterior motivation, but that's who Dita is, and for all the acceptance I'm supposed to be doling out, this is unforgivable."

I screeched to a halt just I pulled up into the driveway I so adored, right next to the cute Mercedes convertible Mom probably didn't even own, and popped open the door, racing up the steps and into the house—where mass chaos ensued.

"Dirty Deeds" by AC/DC played so loudly, the entire house shook.

Com and Uncle Ding were flying in circles around the chandelier in the entryway, tinkling the crystals with their tiny fluttering wings.

Wom was bathing in a tub of Cool Whip on the kitchen counter. Blops of the creamy confection were all over the floor and countertop, and even one of the curtains.

Vases were tipped over, drawers were open with kitchen towels, silverware, potholders all spilling out.

In the middle of all this, my mother was on a chair with a broom, screeching at them to stop, while Mom Bat snoozed in a corner under the leaf of one of the leftover arrangements from the party, completely unaware, with Bat Dad nowhere in sight.

"Stop this instant, you filthy animals!" my mom yelped, swishing the broom in the air with hapless swipes, her slender calves straining to keep from falling out of her deep-purple heels.

Whiskey rushed in, barking and pulling at my mother's flowing skirt.

As I took in the scene, the utter madcappery seeping into my usually serene life, my eyes narrowed.

"All of you—knock it the heck off!" I bellowed

above the music, the satisfying echo of my own voice reverberating in my ears.

All motion stopped as one Bat boy hovered and Uncle Ding swooped to land on the banister of the staircase, his tiny eyes blinking in surprise. My mother snapped her fingers to turn the music off then froze in place, teetering slightly on the chair she perched upon.

"You two?" I hissed, pointing at Com and Uncle Ding. "Get your butts down here now and knock it off. If you can't be respectful of your surroundings, you're going to end up in a dark closet for the remainder of your stay!"

"Awww," Wom complained from the kitchen. "Why you gotta be so mean, Stevie? We're bored!"

"I'm telling you, Wom, get out of that container or I'll put the lid on it and seal it up tight. *Cool Whip* is not for playing!"

That's not what Uncle Ding says," he leered on a giggle.

"Get over here *now*!" I pointed to my secondhand pink Coach purse, where Belfry peeked out of the top edge.

Wom swooped over and tipped his whipped-cream-covered body over the edge of my handbag, but Com was more reluctant.

"I don't have to do what you tell me, Stevie. You're not the boss of me!"

I originally raised my hand to scold him with a well-pointed finger, but what I ended up doing left us all gasping.

I zapped him.

Yep. By all that's holy, my finger swizzled a weak but steady current of electricity, making him drop like a fly hitting a bug zapper. Lucky for him, I caught him in my hand and plopped him in my purse.

"Stevie! This is bloody enormous!" Win said, his tone congratulatory.

I looked at my finger and shook my head. "I don't get it…?"

Why all these stalls and starts? Was it some kind of residual magic? Was someone taunting me?

No. I couldn't go there. I'd never sleep at night if I thought the person who'd stolen my powers, the almighty warlock Adam Westfield, was stalking me from the great beyond.

"What does it matter, Dove? You used magic!"

I grinned from ear to ear. I had. It was only another blip, but it was certainly less of a stretch of time between uses.

"You singed my butt, Stevie!" Com complained from inside the dark confines of my purse.

I looked down into the interior and wrinkled my nose at him. "You'll get more than a butt singeing if you don't knock it off. This is Win's home. You absolutely cannot behave like you're some wild animal on a rampage. Save that for outside, buddy!"

Com blew me a raspberry but nestled quietly against his brother.

Then I looked up at the target of all my discontent. I

held out my hand to Dita, my temper almost in check. "Mother, get down from that chair now."

She placed her fine-boned fingers in mine and stepped down, swishing her scarf over her shoulder before dropping the broom. "I was just trying to get them to behave," she said, obviously affronted.

I cornered her next, right up against the entryway hall, and narrowed my eyes. "Did I tell you to stay inside and keep your mouth closed? I did. I distinctly remember telling you to talk to no one and not to leave the house. So what do you do? You get on the local news and offer a reward for Bart's killer? Where are you getting this reward, and what about being on the local news is 'laying low'?"

My mother gave me the best charm-your-britches-off smile she had in her arsenal and shrugged her shoulders. "I was trying to drum up some sympathy. You never know what that can bring. And you're not poor. We *do* want to catch Bart's killer, don't we?"

"Not with Win's money, we don't! Mom, you can't just offer something that isn't yours. Bart hasn't even been dead twenty-four hours and already you're offering up *someone else's money* for information leading to the arrest of the killer."

"Please stop calling it my money, Stevie. I gave it to you," Win interrupted, clearly aggravated.

"Your money, my money, whoever's. That's not the point, Win!"

My mother cringed as though Attila the Hun had arrived. "Is *he* here?"

"Yes, Mom, he's always here. He's my friend, and he stays. End of. Back to the topic at hand. What possessed you to call up the local news? How is that keeping you out of the spotlight? Now every crackpot who ever saw Bart, and plenty who didn't, are going to be calling the police station with their crackpot tips! Don't you think about the repercussions before you do things like this?"

Straightening her spine, she put her fingers to my shoulder and pushed me back. "Of course I do, Stephania. There's already a Kickstarter fund for Bart's funeral in progress."

My eyebrow rose. I knew exactly what this was about, and it had nothing to do with giving Bart a proper burial. "You do realize you have to use that money for an actual funeral? Not a shopping trip in Milan, don't you?"

Mom sucked her cheeks inward and gave me a haughty look. "Oh."

"Yeah. Oh," I said, deadpan.

Mom then tried the cute act, putting her hands behind her back and smiling sweetly. "So you're angry then?"

"If you call breaking her skinny bird arms 'angry,'" Win quipped.

"Oh no. Don't play cute and coy with me. I'm not one of your boyfriends, Mom. I'm the person who's trying to keep you from making a spectacle of yourself, because from the sounds of it, there are a lot of people who had a reason to want to whack Bart."

I decided against telling her about the number for the penitentiary for the moment. She knew so little about Bart already, I was almost certain she wouldn't know anything about that phone number he had.

Mom made a reproachful face, as though she'd been taking acting lessons from my father. "What a horrible thing to say, Stephania!"

"More horrible than a Kickstarter fund for a funeral you never planned to have for him?"

She gave me the silent glare, stepping around me and moving toward the kitchen. As she went to the fridge, I chased after her, setting my purse on the counter.

"Hey, ease up there, Boss!" Bel squeaked in protest.

"You cannot run away from me, Mom. No more running away. Now you get on my computer and you cancel that Kickstarter. When the coroner's ready to release Bart's body, we'll pay for the funeral."

"Fine," she huffed, taking the Perrier I'd had delivered for her and slamming it on the counter.

"Now, we have some things to talk about. Sit at the table. *Please*."

Mom opened her peachy glossed lips to protest, but I stood firm. "Not a word. Sit."

Strolling to the chair at the kitchen table, she dropped down in it and crossed her legs, her face petulant and defiant.

I grabbed a regular old water, though what I really needed was a martini with *two* olives. "So, mind explaining to me why I keep hearing about Bart and his penchant for taking things that aren't his? And I'm not talking about just money."

She twirled her hair around her index finger and bristled in her seat. "I don't know what you mean."

"I mean that not one, but two people now have had run-ins with Bart, and they've both involved Bart taking something that wasn't his or saying something he shouldn't have. First it was one of the acrobats at the party. The one in the champagne glass. Apparently, Bart said something inappropriate about her body parts. Then it was Hardy Clemmons, who had a bit of an altercation with him at the party over something that happened years ago."

She sighed and flicked the flowers in the vase on the table, as though I were once again boring her. "Well, don't make me guess, Stephania. What happened?"

"Hardy says he stole his fiancée. You'll probably know her. She was a Rawlings. Clara, to be exact. And rich. Very rich. It happened twenty years ago, but clearly the leopard's spots never changed."

I watched my mother with close attention to her eyes. I could always tell when she was lying by watching the color of her eyes change. But nothing happened.

"I know the name, of course. I grew up here in Washington. But I know nothing of Clara and Bart."

She was definitely telling the truth. She might know Bart had been a bit of a perv, but she didn't know about that particular incident when he was especially shady.

"Well, do you know anything about his behavior with the acrobat at our party?"

Suddenly, her shoulders sagged, and I wasn't sure if she was doing some more acting or she really felt defeated. "I didn't know about that, no. But Bart wasn't above shenanigans."

"Shenanigans how?" If she said open marriage had been on the table, I was out.

"He was very flirtatious, just the way I am, Stephania. I might be conniving. That's the word you used once, right? But I'm not blind."

Okay, yes. I admit I called her conniving *once*. It was after my fifth-grade vocabulary test, where I'd learned what it meant. The definition fit her to a T, so when she made me angry, I flung the word at her like an arrow because she'd hurt my feelings.

How was it that she could remember an argument from when I was all of ten, but she couldn't remember my birthday? Good gravy.

"So let me get this straight. The grifter hooked up with the grifter but the grifters didn't know they were grifting each other?" Perfect. The sanctity of marriage was beyond my mother's comprehension. Marriage was just a rung on the ladder to her. A way to climb the totem pole until she reached the top.

"That sounds so callous," she murmured.

My gaze was one of disbelief. "That's because it *is*, Mom. What you do, tricking people into believing you love them, is callous. If you knew Bart was a dirty bird, why did you marry him in the first place?"

143

I shouldn't have asked the question unless I wanted the real answer.

"Because he had money, of course! Listen to me, Stephania, and listen well. I'm going to be on this earth for a very long time. A *very* long time. I don't want to be on it alone and poor."

"Well, here's a crazy concept. Get a J-O-B! Those are the pesky things that earn you money for the long haul here on Earth. Imagine the satisfaction you'll discover when you don't have to bat your eyelashes to pay your light bill."

"Listen to you preach when you have all this!" Mom swept her hand around the room as though I'd made "all this" magically appear.

My chair legs scraped the floor as I rose to wrap my hands around her long, swan-like neck, but Win and Bel stopped me.

"Nooo!" they both yelped in unison.

"Stevie, she doesn't have the depth to understand what you've been through. I implore you to keep your hands to yourself," Win urged.

"So no jumper cables?" I asked from a clenched jaw with equally clenched fists.

"We have rules, Stevie!" Win reminded.

"But that was pertaining to you. We had no rules about *me* using the jumper cables," I muttered in a whisper-yell.

"Boss! Back off. As your familiar, I'm warning you. I'll pluck your eyebrows razor thin if you touch her. You'll look ridiculous. Promise! Winterbutt's right. She doesn't know any better, and seeing as you're not taking the time to teach her to *be* better, you'll have to suffer her piss-poor behavior. We've talked about this, Stevie."

What Bel said was true. Because I avoided confronting my mother about how crummy she treated me—and everyone else, for that matter—I enabled the poor behavior.

Win began the mantra. "And we're counting, Stevie. One-two-three, and breathe. And again, one-two-three. Solving this by mutilating her fingers isn't the way, Dove. The way is to confront her with direct and precise terms—which you've chosen to avoid. This is what happens when you allow a situation to go unhandled."

My mother gave me that innocent blink as though I were some wild animal just let out of its cage, so I closed my eyes, blocking her out.

Counting in my head, I slowed my breathing and sat back down, gathering myself before I said, "Mom, before I had all this—and I'll remind you that when I came into all this, I was on my last leg after being kicked out of Paris—I *worked*. Remember? As a 9-1-1 operator. I paid my own bills and I took care of myself. I didn't do that by marrying hordes of rich men."

Dita was one of the reasons I was so fiercely independent, because she'd always been so dependent on men to provide for her—and our lives had always been up in the air because of it.

"Then more's the pity. If we brushed your hair and

spruced you up, you'd be able to find a rich husband."
She reached for a strand of my hair, a helpful smile on
her face.

But I batted her away and looked heavenward while
internally, I seethed. "How about the cigar cutter? Just
one little finger."

"Stevie!" both Win and Bel yelped.

I rolled my head on my neck to loosen up the strain
between my shoulder blades and tried to find my
sorely lacking patience. I gentled my tone and futilely
went back in. "Mom? That was a low blow."

Mom sighed. "I'm just trying to help, Stephania. I
want you to find happiness."

"Um, yeah. I don't need that kind of help or that
kind of happiness. It's insulting. So here's the deal: I
don't want to find a rich husband. Even if I didn't have
all this because of Win, I wouldn't want to find a rich
husband to pay my bills. I'm in charge of my own ship,
and that's the way I like it. You know what else that
affords me? I'll tell you what that affords me. A life free
of worrying about finding the next millionaire. A life
free of a man who was more than a little shady. A life
free of a man who is now likely dead because of that
shady behavior. See what I mean?"

She waved a dismissive hand at me, but her eyes
flashed something new—something I'd never seen
from Dita—or maybe I'd just never looked for it.

Sorrow.

It was there and it was real, but it only lasted for a
mere second before she put her vapid coat back on.

"Fine. I can't sit and listen to this nonsense anymore because I have a mani/pedi scheduled at three. Now, if you're done badgering me with your speeches of empowerment, may I go?"

"No!" we all bellowed, including Wom, and Com.

"Mother, this isn't a party! There's a murder investigation going on surrounding your *husband*. You're not to be out sprucing up for your next coup! Now, from here on out, you stay put. You don't go out. You don't call the press. You don't talk on the phone to anyone but me. You don't *talk*. Period. If I have to say it again, I'll wash my hands of the whole thing. Clear?"

She pursed her lips as she looked at her current manicure. "Crystal, you tyrant. But if anyone comments on how poorly I look, I'm directing them to you."

"You do that. Now, has anyone aside from the press called you today? Have you heard anything from the police?"

"How should I know? I haven't checked my phone. I'm going upstairs to nap. You've exhausted me. My phone's over there on the counter if you want to look at it and check."

With that, Dita made another dramatic exit, sweeping out of the room in a cloud of floral perfume and swishy, ultra-feminine clothing.

Win yawned in my ear, his warm aura surrounding me.

"Do you need a nap, too?" I asked as I crossed the kitchen to grab Mom's phone.

"Bloody hell, yes. She's infuriating. How did you survive a childhood with her without losing your mind?"

"What doesn't kill us makes us stronger," I quipped, scrolling my mother's phone. I held it up. "The police have only called ten times since this morning. Argh! This woman!"

Mom Bat flew into the kitchen, her chubby body wobbling in the air before she landed on the counter in front of me. "Stevie, dear?"

"Deloris," I said on a warm smile, stroking her head. "I'm so sorry. I've been so caught up in everything, I haven't had the chance to say a proper hello to you, but I promise, we'll sit and chew the fat after things quiet down a bit. Maybe tonight out on the porch? If it clears up, the stars out here are amazing."

She wiggled her stout body and rubbed her head against my hand. "That's lovely, dear. We can do that later. Right now you have more pressing problems."

"You mean my mother? Hah! Tell me about it."

"No, dear. I mean your mother's car."

I snorted. "You mean the Mercedes? She said Bart took that out of storage when they landed here in Seattle. But I'm pretty sure that's not really *hers*-hers." Nothing was really hers-hers. Everything had been bought with credit.

Deloris looked up at me with her big brown eyes filled with concern. "The repo man seems to think so, too, dear. They're hauling it away as we speak."

I dropped Mom's phone and ran to the door,

cracking it open with Whiskey hot on my heels. Sure enough, two big, burly men were putting a boot on her swanky powder-blue Mercedes.

But I laughed. Probably for the first time today. I couldn't help the relief I felt.

One less thing to worry about Dita getting into more trouble with?

Check!

CHAPTER 10

"*R*andom question?"

"Hit me."

"Why doesn't the lovely Dita have a familiar like you?"

I snorted at Win. "Because if you were Dita, would you want a guide to steer you away from all the bad things you do? Like marrying men for their nonexistent money?"

Win's hearty laugh rang in my ear. "Point for you. So you don't have to have familiars? It's not mandatory?"

"Nah. It's highly recommended, but not a requirement. Unless you screw up. Then you have no choice. You end up assigned to one. Familiars are only guides to our consciences. But Mom's never been able to keep one around for very long, either. They all end up running and screaming like they're on fire after just a week with her. So there's that."

"See my shock and surprise," Win said dryly.

I laughed as I put off the inevitable. Then I sobered and fessed up. "I don't know if I can do this, Win."

"You don't have to if you don't want to, Stevie. I reminded you of that before we got in the car. It's not your job to find out who killed Bart."

"Yeah, but if I don't, my mom can't leave town."

I heard Win's teeth chatter. "Did you hear that? That was my full body shudder. She's more than a handful, and I'm sorry I ever doubted your reasons for avoiding her. Forgive me, Dove."

I looked out my windshield at the quaint Sunshine Inn with its rows of English countryside flowerbeds in purple and pink. The cottage feel to the whole place, made warm and cozy by the owner, Coraline, was perfect. I loved her gardens. I loved that she served tea with blueberry scones and clotted cream to her customers. I loved everything about the atmosphere she'd created.

Yet, inside was a man I feared might have something to do with Bart's death. I don't know why or even how that might be possible, but I couldn't tick Hugh off the list after that spirit all but pointed her southern finger at him.

"But that means I have to go inside the Sunshine and risk the chance I'll run into my father."

"You don't really believe Hugh had anything to do with this, do you? Where's that tingle you're always talking about—that gut instinct of a sleuth?"

"Then what did the spirit mean, Win? Have you been able to find out?"

"Sadly, I haven't, Dove. You know how this rolls. They're all quite scatterbrained. I've yet to meet a spirit who has a message to send who isn't. Aside from me, that is."

I tilted my head in thought. "Yeah. Why is that? Why are you so clear-headed?"

What Win said was quite true. The spirits often were very scattered. Not always, but a great deal of the time. Which is why, when they attempt to get a message to the other side, it's almost always choppy and fragmented.

I don't know if some things get lost in translation through the veil, but mostly it never translates in a conversational manner the way it does with Win. We talk all the time as though he's in the room with me. Only, he isn't.

"Because I'm me and I have a good handle on where I am. I hear through the Plane Limbo grapevine that if you're unsure about whether to cross, or your death was particularly tragic, everything you do comes across as confused. I'm not at all confused, Dove. I know where I want to be and how I want to get there."

I nodded. This subject, the one where Win claimed he was going to get back to the earthly plane by some miracle, was a sore one. For me, that is. I was almost certain there was no way back. In all my years as a witch, I'd never heard of a way back. But to poke a hole in Win's bubble just wasn't in me—or wouldn't be in me until it absolutely had to be. When he needed a good dose of reality.

Win cleared his throat. Probably because he took my silence on the subject to mean I wouldn't engage. "Now, back to your father. Are you sure you want to keep him on the suspect list?"

"Loosely, at least. Again I say, what did that spirit mean? Who else could be the infamous 'him'?"

"Fair enough. I'll heed your hesitation. Now, what did the police say when you called to tell them you thought there might be more evidence?"

Leaning my head on the door, I looked up at the sky, which had begun to clear. "I told them I thought I saw something under the chest of drawers they might have missed when I was looking for Whiskey's ball. A small fib, in the scheme of things, I guess. Sandwich said to stay out of the parlor and wait for someone from forensics to clear the room because if we disobey —and I think what he meant was, if I disobey his order —we'll have to move out and stay in a hotel. I just got settled at our house. I don't want to haul everyone out of there."

Win clucked his tongue. "Bart's money clip led nowhere anyway, and certainly no one at Washington State Penitentiary is going to answer questions from you, a mere civilian. It's better off in the police's hands. So we leave it alone until we ask your mother what Bart would be doing with such a thing. Not that I expect she'll have an answer. It seems she was quite happy to let him roam freely, accosting women and running up credit card debt. Now, next task. Have they ruled Bart's death a homicide yet?"

I shook my head. "Sandwich said as soon as he knew, I'd know, because we're next of kin—sort of. I don't see how it can be anything else but homicide, but I guess there are plenty of causes of death we know nothing about that could be responsible for the poor man left dead in the middle of our parlor."

"And finally, have you looked your father up online yet?"

I gripped my phone with the sparkly pink cover. I'd started to and then I'd erased the search before I pressed enter. "No. Not yet. I guess I just don't want to…"

"Get more deeply involved in his life if he's the one who killed Bart," Win finished for me.

My stomach lurched. "Yeah. That. I'm still a little raw, I guess."

"Then let's go home, Stevie. Take a load off for today. Hole up in the Batcave and rest. You deserve that after this chaos."

But I squared my shoulders and turned my car off. "I can't. It's not in me to just give up."

"It's not giving up to take a break," Win chided.

"Do killers take breaks? No. They kill more people. Maybe he's just waiting for his next victim and if we don't stop him, he'll kill again. Do spies give up? Did *you* ever give up?"

"Well, I will admit, there was this one time in Bulgaria. We'd been on this mission, trying to locate a nuclear weapon being sold to some pack of despicable arms dealers. I'd been in deep for over four months when the sale was finally about to take place. Just as we were finalizing details for the trade-off, a mole, still unidentified, gave me up. Which naturally scared off the buyers. Just made it out of there by the hair of my chinny-chin-chin. If giving up were ever to happen, that would have been the day I decided to do so."

"But the question is, did you give up and let the pack of scoundrels have the nuclear bomb, thus obliterating the entire world?" I asked, digging in my purse for my sunglasses.

"The world wasn't their goal, m'love. Chicago was. Nonetheless, no. I didn't give up. I went back in undercover in disguise and managed to catch the buyers."

I could sit and listen to Win's spy stories all day. They were fascinating. "Exactly my point, Spy Guy."

"You're not dealing with arms dealers, Stevie. The world really isn't going to blow up if you take just one day off."

"You said it wasn't the world. It was Chicago."

"Don't mince words. The point is, nothing is blowing up today."

"Says you. Like my mother doesn't even resemble a nuclear bomb just a little?"

Win's response was to chuckle. "Point for my spy-in-training."

"I'm going in. Stay on standby."

"Copy that. Good luck on your mission, Mini-Spy."

I giggled as I got out of the car, grateful I'd changed

into some jeans and a light sweater with an accompanying shrug. The rain might be breaking, but the air was becoming chilly.

Thankfully, I didn't have to go far to locate the acrobats and there was no sign of Hugh. They were all out back on the terrace of the inn and its beautiful surroundings, lifting each other high, twirling with ribbons, bottles of water everywhere. I spotted the one who'd mentioned her friend's run-in with Bart immediately.

She was the tiniest woman of the bunch, her hair smoothed back tight from her face in an immoveable bun, her leotard in black, her legs strong as she bounced on a small trampoline.

My head bobbed with her up-and-down motion, fascinated by the ease with which she flipped and tumbled on such a tiny surface without worrying she'd fall on the brick terrace and crack her tiny skull open.

I tucked my purse under my arm and shielded my eyes from the sun that had finally burst through the clouds, calling up to her. "Hello there! Do you remember me? I had the party the other night."

Instantly, she slowed her bounce until she came to a complete stop, and looked down at me. "I remember," she said, her tone dry.

"May I speak with you?"

"About?" she asked with clear hesitance. She was touchy. I understood that better than anyone. I bet Simone and Sipowicz had grilled her. You didn't want to talk to *anyone* after an event like that.

"About the other night at my party and your friend CC."

The acrobat scanned the crowd before she hopped off the trampoline and came to stand in front of me. I felt like Gigantor compared to her as she gave me a wary glance. "What about her?"

I stuck my big man-hand out to her Tinkerbell-sized one and said, "I'm Stevie Cartwright. You are?"

She took it, but it was like she was putting her Jessica Lange fingers in my King Kong paw. "L."

"As in one letter L? Or E-L-L-E?"

Her big blue eyes assessed me before she responded, "Just the letter L."

"No comments from the peanut gallery," Win warned.

I fought a grin and held up my hands. "I come in peace, swear it. My mother's distraught over her husband's death, as you can imagine. I heard you and one of the other acrobats talking about how Bart had—"

"Behaved like a pig?"

I smiled uneasily. "Yes, that. Surely you understand I want to protect my mother. I was hoping I could ask CC a couple of quick questions about what happened? Can you point her out for me?"

"I can, but I'm warning you. She spent four hours at that police station today, being questioned by two men who are a total parody of television cops. She's pretty battered. I'm not going to let you beat her up all over again to ask the same things they did."

I knew that feeling well. "I promise, no beatings. I'm just looking out for my mom. You can understand that, right?"

L warmed only a little when she said, "She's over by the rose garden. The little blonde with the green leg warmers."

I spotted her instantly amid the hundreds of pale pink and salmon blooms. "Thanks, er, L."

Pushing through the acrobats milling about, I approached CC with caution, but it was unnecessary. She popped up from her chair like her feet were spring-loaded and jumped right into my face.

"If you are here to…" She looked to the man to her left, a thin but intensely muscled very young guy in a white pair of Capri sweats rolled at the knees, no shirt and a man bun. "What ees ze word I look for, T? Ze one wis ze aneemal?" she asked him.

"Badger, *mon cheri*. You do not wish to be badgered." He crossed his arms over his chest and gave me an "I dare you" look.

"Oh, no," I said on a nervous laugh. "I'm not here to badger you. I would never. I'm just here because of my mother. Listen, like I explained to H… I mean, L. I'm just looking out for my mom. You can imagine how distraught she is. Especially seeing as she had no idea Bart was so…so…" *What's the word I'm looking for, T?*

"Such an aneemal?" CC spat, her seductive almond-shaped eyes narrowing.

"Okay, sure, that works. If we have to label, *aneemal*

158

seems like it's a good fit. What did Bart say to you, CC, that upset you so?"

T must be her boyfriend, because he instantly stood beside her in protective mode, wrapping an arm around her waist. "He made ze rude remarks about her breasts! He ees despicable!"

Yeah. It would seem so. But one person's rude remarks were sometimes another person's no big deal. So I wanted to clarify.

"He called my breasts ze fried eggs!" CC shouted up at me. "He said he liked fried eggs!"

Ooo. Yeah. That was bad. What else could I do but apologize on Bart's behalf? "I'm sorry, CC. So sorry that happened. It was rude and crass and had I known, I would have had him removed from the party."

"You deed not have to. He was removed by ze killer. And now that I do not have ze—ze—"

"Alibi." T filled in the blank for her, his gaunt face tight as he seethed the word at me, followed up by a dramatic stance.

Her finger shot upward. "Yes! Ze alibi. Ze police call me ze suspect. But I deed not keel zis man! I would never!"

"Well, *I* believe she deed not keel zis man. What about you, Mini-Spy?" Win said in my ear, his French accent near perfection.

I was certainly leaning that way. "So the police consider you a suspect?"

CC rubbed her arms, her eyes flashing dark. "Oui! Because I cannot account for my whereabouts. I was on a break and no one saw me for sirty minutes total. Ooo, I hate zis state! I want to go back where eet ees warm and no one accuses me of ze murder!"

Another voice from a cluster of the acrobats chimed in. "We did zis for Win! Long live Win!"

My ears perked up immediately, zeroing in on the person the feisty voice belonged to. Yet another gazelle-like woman, this one with fiery red hair and the longest legs possible on someone who wasn't even five-one.

So she didn't know he was dead? Hmmm.

"Stevie, take that Sherlock Holmes hat off right now."

Aw, heck no. This was a real live tiny person who knew Win. Not a chance, buddy.

"You knew Win?" I asked, moving around T and CC to look down at the gorgeous creature.

She lifted her chin and purred. "I deed. He was, how do you say, *amazeballs*."

I nodded. "Yeah. That's the adjective I use all the time to describe him," I said with laughing sarcasm. "So he came to your shows in Vegas?"

"*Oui*. He was most generous to us all. We came to your party as ze favor to heem, and now we are all stuck here!" she yelled, rising to a rigid sitting position, as though being here was a fate worse than death. "It ees reediculous!"

"Stevie. Let this go. We have other, far more important things to deal with."

Nuh-uh. Now *I* had ze eye of ze tiger. "How was he generous?"

Her face softened a little as apparently a memory flooded her. "I deed not speak ze language very well when I come to zis country. He saved me from zis man with many hands when I work as ze cocktail waitress, even though I am ze trained ballerina. Zis man's hands, zey were all over me, and Win rescued me. He found me zis job with ze troupe. I am forever in his debt."

Aha. "That Win. Always a hero, huh?"

"Yes!" she cheered. "He ees always my hero."

I had to wonder how Miranda felt about that. "So was he your boyfriend?"

"Stevie Cartwright, stop forcing the woman to kiss and tell and get on with it!" Win demanded.

But the woman shook her head, thrusting her shoulder forward as she smiled a secret smile. "No-no. Eet was not like that. Though, he was deelicious to my eyes and I would have liked it to be so."

"That's Win. Yummy-yummy," I agreed, rubbing my stomach.

"Stop. You're making me blush," Win joked.

But the small woman just frowned at me, signaling I'd overstayed my welcome. I thanked her before turning back to find CC and T still behind me.

Blowing out a breath, I gave CC an earnest look. "Is there anything else you can tell me about that night? Anything unusual happen that you witnessed?"

CC shook her head, the tight bun at the back of her

head unmoving. "No. I already told ze police everything I know. I told them about what zat peeg said to me, and I told zem about zee other man who argued with heem."

"The other man? You mean Hardy? About so high." I held up my arm to indicate Hardy's height. "Nice head of hair, ruddy complexion? He's our postman here in Ebenezer Falls."

She shook her head vehemently. "No. Zat was not heem. I saw zis man deliver ze mail today. Zer was someone else much shorter zan zee postman. Someone ze peeg had ze angry words weeth. I could not see zis man he was arguing weeth very well, but I remember he was very pale and short. He was in ze shadows and zey were yelling." She rolled her neck and emphasized the word yelling.

Another man? "Are you sure it wasn't Hardy?" I prodded.

CC used a graceful finger to point at her eyes with flourish. "I have zee eyes. Eet was a different man!"

"Ding-ding-ding! New suspect alert!" Win cheered.

CHAPTER 11

*I*nstead of pressing CC for more information, I offered her more apologies for Bart's bad behavior. "CC, won't you let me make this up to you? I'd be happy to. I'm sorry Bart was so rude to you. I'm quite embarrassed." A gift card maybe. A lifetime's worth of kale and water?

But CC flapped a tiny hand at me like a butterfly wing. "*Merci*. That ees not necessary. It ees really not your fault. I do not wish to cause more pain to you or your mama. Now, I must go stretch. Please excuse me." She lifted her chin and sauntered off into the small crowd of acrobats.

I turned to leave, a little deflated. As I walked past all these graceful creatures who moved so fluidly, I felt like Godzilla with my big work boots, crushing all the humans in town as I made my way off the terrace—only to run into Officer Nelson.

I stopped under a big oak on the front lawn of the

inn the moment he saw me and winked. "Aw, look, Officer Dana Nelson, as I live and breathe."

He gave me the typical, "Oh God, is there any getting rid of this pest?" look and we proceeded as per usual. "Miss Cartwright. Snooping, I assume?"

I didn't even try to hide what I was doing. "I am. I mean, after all, it is my stepfather who was murdered. There's a sense of urgency to that, don't you think?"

He peered down at me, his gaze ever intense. "Only for you, Miss Cartwright."

"So listen. Let's get this out of the way, okay? This murder is personal. I realize Madam Zoltar and Tito were really none of my business—"

"As if that would have stopped you?" he said on a raised eyebrow.

"You're right. It wouldn't have stopped me. I've solved two murders in this town now—"

"Let's be fair. You *stumbled onto* two killers—"

"That I'd already figured out were the killers. How I got myself *into* jams with them and how they presented themselves to me is neither here nor there." Right?

"If that's the way you see it," he drawled.

I smiled facetiously. "That's the way I see it. So, seeing as I'm doing the work of an entire police force, virtually alone, let me have this one, would you please?"

"The entire police force, Miss Cartwright? My, we're full of ourselves this afternoon."

"Okay, so maybe not the entire police department, but certainly worthy of at least three good men. So, in light of the fact that I like to snoop and my stepfather is dead, how about I call in my 'you owe me'?"

"You mean the one from when you saved my life?"

"Yep. That's the one. Remember? I do. Like it was yesterday. Reminisce with me, won't you? You, me, the killer I stumbled upon, a tree, a scary gun, you tripping and losing *your* gun, me falling on top of the killer I *stumbled upon* and saving your life because I took a leap of faith…"

He lifted his square jaw and made a show of pretending to recall that night. "Hmmm. It's vague."

I planted a hand on my hip. "I'm happy to provide details. Especially the one where you told me you owed me. So in light of the fact that I saved your life, maybe you could let me slip through the cracks on this one? Turn a blind eye, whatever. Just let me snoop."

Crossing his arms over his broad chest, Officer Nelson of the dark hair and chiseled face—Dana, to his friends—looked at me long and hard. At first, his unwavering gaze had always left me nervous, as though I'd done something bad and he knew about it. But over the course of these last few months, I'd grown used to this tactic, and I served him up some of my own by staring right back.

He broke first, his eyes flashing with the smallest of glimmers. "Okay. But I'm warning you, Stephania Cartwright, you're not exactly invisible."

"Did you just call me fat?" I teased.

"I most certainly did not. What I'm saying is, you don't hide your snooping very well. You're everywhere.

I can only be blind for so long before someone questions why I'm not questioning it. So carry on, and just this once, I'll leave you alone. But that's your one-time-only pass."

"Fair enough. Now, any news on the ruling for Bart's death?"

"None."

"Any new suspects besides the obvious ones like CC and Hardy?"

"Wow. You move quickly. Maybe you *should* join law enforcement?"

"And stand next to you? I'd be proud, but nah. You have too many rules."

"Rules are what keep order."

"And keep me from snooping. They don't mix. So, any new suspects?"

"I can't comment on any new information, but rest assured, you've covered most of it."

"Any calls coming into the police station about Bart's killer after my mother's television debut? Any tips? Good tips?"

He rocked back on the heels of his spit-shined shoes. "Ah, yes. Your mother. We now have people working in shifts because of her generous offer."

"You want to kill her, don't you? It's okay. I get it. She's a lot."

He rolled his tongue along the inside of his cheek. That meant he was thinking over his words in order to use caution. "Kill is a strong word. Take her phone away is more like it."

"That's more than one word."

Officer Nelson sighed. "Miss Cartwright, are we done here? I have work to do."

"Almost. What'cha workin' on?"

"Picking up my date for an early dinner."

I think my eyes bulged. "*You* have a date?"

"I know you find this hard to believe, but I do have a personal life."

"I *do* find it hard to believe. I thought you slept in your uniform and ate nails for breakfast."

"Well, you were wrong. About the uniform, anyway," he offered with a smirk.

I barked a laugh, my head tipping back on my shoulders. "Anything else of importance you want to share with me?"

His lips went thin, the sure sign he was clamming up. "Can't think of a thing."

I could never read Officer Nelson. He was aces at being stoic and keeping his secrets, and nowhere near as easy to trip up as Sandwich, but he always had the good information, making him worth a try.

So I patted him on the arm. "Good talk. Okay, so this is the part where I go snoop until my eyes roll back in my head, and you go away. Nice seeing you, Officer Nelson."

He tipped an imaginary hat as he moved around me and headed up the walkway to the front door of the Sunshine. "And you, Miss Cartwright."

I skipped down the sidewalk, the sun beating down on my head as I walked to my car.

"Well done back there, Dove. I'm impressed at how far you've come when it's time to cash in favors and ask questions. You handled the acrobats well, not to mention our fair Officer Nelson, with nary a bump in the road," Win praised.

I curtsied before I got in the car. "He owed me one. I'm not sure we can chalk that up to my finesse."

"Still, you cashed it in with clear and concise demands. Accept my praise and like it."

My cheeks turned red. "So home now, I guess? I called Petula, who said she could squeeze me in later tonight so I could ask her some questions about the other employees she hired. We really need a list of all the waiters and waitresses, the chef's staff, etcetera. But it's getting close to dinner and we don't have a whole lot else to go on right now. Except for that mystery man CC mentioned."

"Yes, a pale short one. Remember anyone fitting that description?"

As I started the car, I shook my head. "The whole party was such a blur, I can hardly remember any of it until Bart was killed."

Win tsked me with a cluck of his tongue. "I'm sorry, Dove. I so wanted that night to be special for you."

"It's okay. I told you, I'm a Cheese Whiz and crackers kind of girl. We could have broken a bottle of cheap dollar-store peach wine on the porch beam and I'd have been just as happy." That was the truth. The finer things in life were great, but they weren't as important to me as Win and Bel and Whiskey.

"I'm determined to teach you to love caviar and champagne and graduate your palate from kindergarten."

"Newsflash. I'm never, not ever, going to love stinky fish eggs. It's Cadbury or nothing."

"Someday I'll show you myself what you've been missing out on."

I clammed up. That was never going to happen. Not ever. Not even as much as I wished it could happen. Rather than address his comment, I drove, letting the peaceful ride back to the house with the tall pines and boats on the Puget soothe me.

I pulled into the driveway, again silently thanking the pavement gods I didn't have to rappel up the side of my lawn to get to the steps, and pressed the garage door button.

Yep. I even had a garage now. One that led into the laundry/mudroom with shiny silver appliances, shelves galore and a big sink. No more wet grocery shopping for me.

Whiskey greeted me in the mudroom, his tail furiously wagging, his favorite tennis ball in his mouth. I knelt down and scratched his big head, kissing his muzzle. "After dinner, I promise we'll play, okay?"

He licked my face in agreement, trotting off to the kitchen to sit in his favorite spot where the sun shone in from the tall windows by the kitchen table.

And that was when I saw the mess—everywhere.

My mother's clothes were strewn from one end of the kitchen to the other. The beautiful white cabinet doors of the upper row were flung carelessly open, while the complementing steel-blue of the bottom rows were just ajar.

The fire alarm beeped at regular intervals, it's annoying chirp going right through me. There was black soot on the hardwood floors with pieces of charred material in it.

Glasses were piled high in the sink, discarded bottles of my mom's favorite Perrier scattered over the vast landscape of our Italian creamy-white and blue-veined countertops.

Bel was on one of those counters, a tiny bandana on his head, made out of one of my old Carolina Herrera scarves I'd found at a bargain-basement price, as Com pushed at a can of powdered cleanser and yelled, "Timber!" Letting the substance puff out onto the countertop.

Wom sat atop a sponge, twisting his tiny body to cleanse the counter surface. Even Uncle Ding was in on the action. Using a toothbrush held in his mouth, he was disjointedly scrubbing the shiny copper faucet of the vegetable sink.

Bat Dad stood beside them and oversaw the process of whatever it was they were doing. "She'll be back any minute, boys. We've got to clean this up!"

"Too late, boys," Deloris called, her wings flapping wildly as she hovered over the countertops.

"Ma!" Belfry cried. "You were supposed to be our lookout!"

"What is going on?" I yelped.

Bel was the first to react. He launched himself into the air, flying straight for me to position himself in front of my face. "It was just a little accident. We'll clean it up, Boss, Promise. No big deal."

"Yeah," Uncle Ding grunted, spitting out the tooth-brush. "Some accident, leavin' us here to clean up her mess while she goes off to take a long hot bath and a nap. I've never been treated so bad in my life!"

"Belfry? Explain," I ordered.

"I got this, Nephew," Uncle Ding groused. He kicked the toothbrush into the gorgeous copper sink and strutted to the edge of the countertop, his little hands on his very round body. "Your mother's a slob. She spent all day complaining about how bored she was while she changed her clothes like a runway model, then she had a little lunch in every room in the house and decided she wanted to iron her dress for tonight. Well, she forgot the iron was on while she was taking that long hot soak I mentioned, almost setting the house on fire, and now she's napping. Nice, right?"

"Stevie, I caution you. Murder is wrong. Murder is wrong. Murder is wrong. And it's punishable by death in some states," Win warned.

"She left you guys to clean up for her?" I squealed in disbelief.

"Well, she didn't ask. She just left it here," Bel admitted, his face sheepish. "I couldn't stand the idea you were gonna have to come home to this, so I gathered the crew and thought we'd try and handle it on our own."

"Did she not get my call telling her Sandwich was coming over to collect more evidence?"

Com nodded on a tired sigh. "Aw, yeah. She got it, all right. Ignored it. But that guy Enzo—who was workin' on the touch-up paint in the bathroom—let the cop and his team in. They did another sweep of the parlor and took whatever you told them about and left. She never even woke up from...what was it, guys, her second nap of the day?"

"Two, three, they're all a blur," Uncle Ding groused.

"Stephania?" my mother called from the staircase.

Ah, the woman of the hour. "Mother? Please come in here," I seethed, clenching my fists.

"Murder is wrong, murder is wrong, murder is wrong!" everyone chanted in unison.

I snapped my fingers at the peanut gallery. "Can it, all of you! Mother, come in here!"

Dita breezed in looking fresh as a daisy. She had one of my cute maxi dresses on—cinched tightly at her neck because we weren't even close to the same size—a chunky gold bracelet, and she smelled suspiciously like my favorite pear perfume.

As she stopped in the doorway and looked at me as though she didn't see the mess all around her, I reminded myself. *Murder is wrong, Stevie.*

"What do you want, Stephania? I'm very busy."

Murder is wrong, Stevie. "Oh, *reeeally*? Too busy I guess to clean up the mess you made? Mom, have you no respect for someone else's things? Look at this!" I spread my arms wide to encompass the "this" I was talking about.

Mom just shrugged her slender shoulders and tossed her hair over her shoulder. "You have a maid, don't you?"

"No!" I bellowed so loud, Whisky whined. "I don't have a maid, Mother! And even if I did, I wouldn't treat her this way. But *you* don't have a maid either. Know why you don't have a maid? Because you have no money!"

Her bored look of disinterest only served to further infuriate me. "Are you done with your rant now? May I carry on with my evening?"

I might have passed out in disbelief if this wasn't my mother's typical MO. I don't think she ever mopped a floor as I was growing up, or even cleaned a toilet. "No. No you may not. You're going to roll up your sleeves, or in this case, *my* dress, and help us clean this up!"

She didn't look at all concerned. Trashing our beautiful house was of no consequence to someone like Diva Dita Cartwright.

"But I have a—"

The doorbell clanged then, interrupting my internal plan to map out a way to smother her in her sleep.

"That will be for me," she said cheerfully, turning to answer the front door.

"Oh, no you don't!" I yelled, running after her to grab her arm and swing her around.

The expression she gave me was mortified. "Stephania, let go! That's my date Raul, and I don't want to be late. It would be rude."

"Your what with Ra-who?" I squeaked, gripping her arm tighter.

"Rrraul, Dove. Nice name. If you roll the R it's very dark and seductive, yes?" Win offered.

"Win, shut it."

Dita smiled her cat-like smile. I knew it well. Raul was the mouse and she had her kitten heels on. "Raul, Cupcake. He's that shipping magnate I told you about."

"Mother, what did I tell you just this morning? You can't go anywhere with anyone! How can you even consider hunting down a new husband when all the town's eyes are on you right now? Your husband just died *yesterday*, for gravy's sake!"

"I'll wear my sunglasses. They'll simply think I'm out with a dear friend who's come to help me through my grief, Stephania. Now, let me go!" She yanked her arm from my grip and ran to the door, flinging it wide to reveal a very handsome man in a tan suit.

Dark and muscled, lean and sensuous, he lifted Dita's hand and pressed a light kiss to it. His charisma alone, if bottled and packaged, would make millions.

And my mother giggled like a schoolgirl. "This is my daughter, Stephania," she said in her dismissive tone.

Raul didn't even have the time to greet me before she was pulling him out the door and down the steps, the clack of her heels echoing in my ears.

"Murder is wrong, Stevie," Win singsonged.

The cool breeze blew in the door, ruffling the leaves of the arrangements on the dining room table. Defeated, I went to close it, avoiding looking at the parlor. There was no helping her if she didn't want the help. If she landed in human jail for her behavior, Baba would come and snatch her up so fast, her head would spin.

And it'd serve her right. I hope if she does end up in the clink, she has to eat creamed corn every single meal of her prison sentence.

Just as I was about to shut the door on any hope my mother would ever behave like an adult, Hardy's face appeared. "Stevie?"

"Oh, Hardy, I'm sorry. I didn't see you. What can I do for you?"

He smiled and handed me a package wrapped in brown paper and addressed to me. "Figured I'd drop this on the way home. Missed it when I made my deliveries earlier today. Guess I'm still kinda shook up after yesterday."

I leaned against the door and smiled tiredly, taking the lightweight package from him. "That was very sweet. Thank you, Hardy. You have a good night, okay?"

He held up a slender finger as I began to close the door. "One more thing. You kept calling that varmint Bart. I thought it was strange, maybe a nickname for him or somethin', but the papers called him that, too."

There was that tingle in my spine. I frowned. "We called him Bart because that's his name, Hardy."

Hardy's face went hard with a scowl, the sun shining on it and accentuating his high cheekbones. "Not when *I* knew him, it wasn't."

"What was his name?"

"I'll never forget it as long as I live. It was Andrew Forbes."

CHAPTER 12

*A*fter I set the package on the dining room table, I raced to the kitchen to grab my laptop. "Andrew Forbes, eh?"

"You heard the man, and according to him, he told the police Bart wasn't Bart but Andrew. Which means, they'll be looking into it just like we're going to. It's just a matter of who finds what first. So, I need to see if I can look up pictures of the Anchor Yacht Club parties. Maybe we can see if he's mentioned in there."

"My guess is Bart stole identities. Bad Bart," Win commented.

I stopped halfway to my laptop and looked at the Bats and Bel, trying so diligently to clean up Dita's mess. "Guys? Take a break. This wasn't your mess to clean. I'll take care of it, but thank you for looking out for me."

"Wahooo!" Wom screeched, kicking up a cloud of the cleanser as he soared to the ceiling.

But Bat Dad flapped his wings in a curt reprimand. "Wom Bat, you get down here right now, young man! Stevie was kind enough to allow us to stay in her home, the least we can do is help out when she's in need."

Wom dropped to the kitchen's center island like a bomb, dragging his body back to where he'd been scrubbing. "Fine. Let's go on vacation somewhere else next year, huh? How do you feel about Bali?"

I chuckled, tucking my finger under Bat Dad's chin. "I appreciate it, Melvin, but you guys go." I swished my hands at them to shoo them off to better things. "Scoot. You must be due for a nap by now."

Bel flapped his wings and hovered in front of my face, his eyes searching mine. "Boss? I'm gonna be honest. Your mother sucks dirty toes. She's horrible, and I can't stand to watch any more of this kind of behavior from her. Either you handle it, or *I* will. I don't care if it's overstepping my boundaries as your familiar or not. Someone needs to put her in her place. She's mean to you, and I don't like it."

"I know I need to speak to her, Bel—"

"No. You need to set *boundaries* with her, Stevie. Boundaries. Like the kind that make it perfectly clear you're not her punching bag or her cash cow. Enough's enough."

He was right. Everyone was right. It was just summoning up the courage and making the promise to myself that I'd stick to my guns and no longer allow it.

"You're right, and I promise when this is over, I'll talk to her."

"Fair enough. C'mon, guys. Let's let Stevie do her thing. Whiskey!" Bel whistled. "C'mon, buddy, let's play ball!"

As the Bats, Bel, and Whiskey left the room, I sank into one of the kitchen chairs and sighed in relief. The peace settling over the house wasn't just audible, it was spiritual. I felt my mom's tense, hyper presence leave my space and took a deep breath.

"It's been a very long day, yes, Dove?"

I tucked my chin into my hand and kicked off my work boots. "Yes, Spy Guy. Very long."

"What shall we do about your mother? Bel's right, Stevie," Win said, his tone soft. "I don't know that I had the entire picture, or if I really thought any parent could be as despicable as Dita is. Even after you warned me, described her to me. But I have it now. I, unlike Bel, am not afraid to overstep anything when it comes to her poor treatment of you. She might not be able to hear me, but there are other ways to be heard. This must end."

Flipping open my laptop, I shrugged my shoulders. "What *can* I do? It's clear whatever I say means nothing to her. Which is probably why I avoid confronting her to begin with. It's a very bad idea for her to be out with Rrraul right now, but you see how well she listens to me. She's impossible."

"Was she really always like this?"

As dysfunctional as the day was long. "As far back as I can remember. There were no cookies and milk when I got home from school. Actually, come to think of it, when she was between husbands and low on cash, the house kind of looked like the kitchen does right now."

"My heart is heavy for you. You were so under-nurtured. I don't understand how *you* became so nurturing."

My cheeks went hot. Must have gotten that from my father's side of the family. "I wasn't totally under-nurtured. Dita had witch friends from her coven who dropped by from time to time. I could always call them if I needed anything. Mostly, anyway. She was never one to coddle or dote. Everything is always about Dita. Every once in a while she'd do something nice for me. Buy me a cake at the supermarket for my birthday or whatever. I often wondered why she had me in the first place. It's obvious I wasn't planned."

Win enveloped me in his warmth. "She had you so you could help others like Madam Z and Liza and Carlito, and most especially, *me*."

I wondered what it would be like to have a real hug from Win, but I brushed that thought aside as I focused on this new information about Bart or Andrew or whoever.

As I looked at my computer screen, I rolled my eyes. "If you were ever wondering how Dita found so many millionaires, I think this is our answer." Pointing to the screen, I almost laughed at the site she'd visited.

Millionaires.com: Where money *can* buy happiness.

"Bloody hell, that woman is relentless," Win growled.

Rubbing my hands together, I asked, "So where do

we go to find out if Bart is stealing identities? How do we find out?"

"Well, as it so happens, I know a person who knows a person. Now, if I can just *recall* the person who knows a person, we'll figure out a way to contact him."

"Okay, you think about your person, I'll go to the Anchor Yacht Club's website and see if we can find any pictures."

"Then let the games begin," Win said, but with that hint of glee in his tone, a tone that only poked its head out when we were hot on the trail of solving a mystery.

～

Munching on a leftover platter of chicken shish kebab from the party, I stretched. We'd been at this hunt for other identities for Bart for almost two hours and we'd finally hit the motherlode.

Bart—also known as Andrew Forbes, Baker Thompson, Joel Lamar and who knew who else—had certainly been around and back again.

He'd been scamming women for many, many years, living off their money then leaving them high and dry once he'd filled his pockets. How he'd managed to escape Baba Yaga and the council was a mystery unto itself.

The only trouble with Bart's scheme was that my mother had been better at the scam than *he'd* been. He'd likely hooked up with her thinking he could get a little cash out of her to tide him over until he found his next Mommy Got Rocks. Little had he known…

I'd laugh if it all weren't so horrible and, above all, deceptive and cruel.

Win had remembered his person, who, after I'd called and given him the secret spy password, got me access to a national database where I was able to do some serious tracking with the little information my mother had. I began with the name Bart Hathaway—or Bartholomew Hathaway, as I came to find was his full name—and that led me to hundreds of people around the country with that name.

But this particular Bartholomew Hathaway—my mother's Bart, with matching social security ID? Well, he'd been dead since the age of ten. That particular lead opened the door to all of the other aliases Bart used. I wasn't even sure what his real name was. If I were still in touch with my coven members, I'd call in a favor and ask them what his birth name had been.

"There!" Win shouted. "That picture there. Do you see the gentleman with Bart/Andrew/Baker/Joel?"

The pictures from the Anchor Yacht Club had also opened up tons of doors to other pictures of Bart from all over the country, at fancy charity, racing and auction events, to name a few.

"You mean the guy who's almost a head shorter than Bart? The one with the blond hair?" I looked at the picture again to locate him. "Handsome guy, huh?"

"Yes! He's been in several pictures with our man Bart. They might attempt to disguise themselves by changing their hair colors and the styles, but there are a million other things about them that are distinguishable. See the way he has his right hand protectively on his tie? He does that often, and in several of the pictures. Possibly the two are cohorts in crime?"

The movie *Dirty Rotten Scoundrels* came to mind as my eyes zeroed in on the gentleman Win was talking about. One Aiden Gailbraith—that was the name used in the pic at the Anchor Club, anyway. But in the picture at some charity event to save the whales, his name was Ian Solmes.

I gasped. "I think we have a connection!" Sure enough, this man, frequently posing in pictures with Bart, was in a bunch of pictures with—of course—women. Very rich women.

"Isn't being this rich a small circle? Like, didn't any of these women ever talk to each other if they frequent the same events? Maybe in the bathroom at some swanky party? You know, 'hey, I met the hottest guy today, his name is blah, blah, blah. Wanna see a pic?' If we don't look out for each other, who else will?"

"Well, as you can see, they took pains to disguise themselves to a degree. Mustaches, facial hair and so on. But even if some of the women knew, you'd be surprised how little the rich wish to share being fooled, Stevie."

Sighing, my lips thinned. "So much for female solidarity. Jeez."

"Type this Aiden bloke's name into the database and

see what you can find. Maybe we can locate him," Win urged.

"But to what end? How's he going to tell us who killed Bart?"

"Any lead is a lead, Dove. Surely I've taught you that by now? Maybe he knows someone who'd want to kill our favorite scam artist? Certainly Bart's racked up kill points with these debutants? Were I dating him, and he scammed *me*, I'd want to kill him. Or at the very least maim him for a good long while, wouldn't you?"

Win was right. Sometimes I didn't always see the trees for the forest. "Agreed. Though, I can't say I recall any rich women at the party with torches and grenades," I joked.

Win chuckled deep in my ear. "Can't say I recall anything like that either, Dove."

As I tinkered with the database, I hit the jackpot. "Winner-winner-chicken-dinner!" I hunkered down and looked over the information for Bart's friend and his aliases.

"Aiden Gailbraith, also known as Ian Solmes and Hart Lincoln, is now serving time *where*, Dove?" Win asked, his tone giddy with mischief.

My mouth opened and my jaw unhinged. It did that a lot lately. "Washington State Penitentiary, for fraud and tax evasion."

"Bloody well done!"

"Okay, so now what? It's not like we can get in to visit him and ask questions, right?"

"Stevie." Win's warning tone sounded in my ear.

"No. You cannot just drop in and pay him a visit with a casserole."

"Don't be ridiculous. I can't cook. Why would I bring him a casserole?"

"Don't get cheeky with me, Mini-Spy. When one is in prison, one does not receive unannounced visitors."

"But that's in places like Alcatraz, right? He's in minimum security holding, for goddess sake."

"Prison is a form of punishment, Stevie. They don't just let anyone in there or it wouldn't be prison. While he's in minimum security, you still have to be approved to visit an inmate. Approval takes all manner of paperwork."

"So what kind of paperwork do we have to do to get approved? Maybe I should join one of those inmates-for-lovers sites or something?"

"The what?"

"Yeah, you know, women who marry guys they've been pen pals with. Happens all the time. Don't they have a group for that?"

"Stephania Cartwright," Win chastised. "You are absolutely not going to join a group like that! I for—"

He'd stopped speaking for a reason, and if I could see his face, it would be sheepish. We'd already been down the road of forbidding me to do anything.

Okay, so he'd been right the last time he'd told me not to do something, but that was then and this was now.

Narrowing my eyes, I shook my finger in the air.

"Do not use the word 'forbid' with me, International Man of Intrigue. No one forbids me to do anything."

"Well, someone should take you to have your noodle examined, at the very least. That's an absurd notion. To attempt to visit a prisoner by pretending you want to be his pen pal is, as you say, bananapants. It will never work."

Looking at the time on my laptop, I wrinkled my nose. "Fine. But I'm not giving up the idea totally. I think I could pull it off. But for now, I have to meet Petula at her store. We need a list of the people she hired for the housewarming. You coming?"

"As if I'd miss it?"

I pushed the chair back and called out, "Bel! Whiskey! Going for a ride. You guys wanna come?"

Whiskey trotted down the stairs, his gait slower than normal. When he appeared, Bel was on his back, tucked against his ear. "Dude and I are tuckered from playing ball, Boss. You need us?"

I smiled. The two had really bonded. I loved that. Running my hand over Whiskey's spine, I shook my head. "Nah. We're good, buddy. I'm taking Win. You rest up, and forget about this mess, okay? Leave it for me and I'll get it in the morning."

"And if Momster comes home? Want me to leave her a message?"

Tucking my purse under my arm and slipping back into my work boots, I thought about that for a minute. "Yeah. Tell her we found a rap sheet for Bart as long as the state of Texas, and if she doesn't want one, too, she should quit pretending to be something she's not."

"Um, no," Bel said on a chuckle. "I'll just tell her you said to sleep tight."

Laughing, I stroked his head before I was heading out the front door once more, ignoring the wreck of the parlor and the ugly image stuck in my mind. But the package Hardy had delivered did catch my eye. Though it would have to wait for now.

The ride to Petula's gave me time to think about what to do with my mother. I could be spiteful and report her to Baba. That would, at the very least, thwart further machinations and scamming. But then she'd only hate me more than she already did for giving a voice to the conscience she lacked.

All the talking, all the reprimands and chastising in the world were never going to stop her from doing what she did, because they hadn't so far.

Even if she hadn't nurtured me, even if her treatment of me could be callous and dismissive at times, she was still my mother. We'd had some good times, they weren't all bad, and I felt a crazy need to protect her—to protect our lives together. Whether she deserved it or not.

Just as we were about to pass The Sunshine Inn, I noted police cars and a crowd had gathered outside the charming inn's front.

Instantly I thought of my father, and my stomach sank right to the brakes I slammed on to stop and find out what was happening.

My heart chugged in a staccato beat of fear as I looked for Hugh. I saw Officer Nelson first, and pushed my way through the crowd of acrobats and onlookers to catch his gaze.

"What's happening?"

He didn't even give me that look I'd become so accustomed to. The one that said, "Will she never go away?" He simply directed his gaze to CC, who was handcuffed and being stuffed into one of the patrol cars. Her long legs, still in her workout clothes, dragged unwillingly.

"I am innocent!" she sobbed, tears falling down her face, her once-neat bun at the back of her head now scruffy and tangled.

"Wait!" I cried, scanning the police and civilians until I found the familiar face of Sandwich, who was holding the crowd of angry acrobats at bay.

"What the fluff, Sandwich?" I asked, craning my neck around his body as he stood in front of a barrier of tape.

His face was beet red despite the cooler temperatures, his jaw tight. "I'm a little busy here, Stevie."

I looked to the acrobats piled together in a huddle of angry eyes and graceful limbs, my gaze pinpointing L, panic settling in my gut. "*Why* are they arresting her?"

She gave me a dull look, her wide eyes glassy from crying. "They're arresting her for," she stuttered on her words, gulping, and then she spit it out, "*murder!*"

CHAPTER 13

$\mathcal{N}$ either of us spoke on the way to Petula's cute shop in the center of town until we pulled up and parked by the curb.

"This is wrong. CC did not commit this murder, Stevie."

"I know," I said grimly. "But according to T, her boyfriend, the police claim to have some kind of evidence that points to her. When she refused to cooperate for questioning, they arrested her."

"Then we need to pick up the pace a bit and solve this case."

"You don't think she's strong enough to haul him up and hold him there long enough to strangle him, do you? She's maybe all of ninety pounds. How could she keep a guy as big as Bart up in the air for that long?"

Win's sigh was deep. "Did you not see her in that champagne glass the night of the party? It takes enormous effort to get one's body in and out of the glass, let alone sit on that small rim. They're quite strong. I realize their sizes are deceiving, but in order to pull off the acrobatic stunts they do for their shows, they train hard, Stevie. And they aren't weak. Yet, still, I'm certain it wasn't her."

"So am I. So what piece of evidence do the police have that points to her? I mean, she was hardly wearing anything but a skimpy bikini that night and she was in water during the better part of the party. DNA? Finger-nail clippings? Hair? What?"

"We won't know any of that until the coroner rules. But certainly there are plenty of other things to leave behind as evidence. No crime is without."

My stomach roared again, its unsettled bottom rising and falling. I hated this, but I could hardly go to the police and tell them my gut said CC didn't do it. I needed proof. Hardcore proof.

Wiping my palms on the legs of my jeans, I grabbed my purse. "Okay, so let's go in and talk to Petula and see if she'll give us a list of people who worked the party. It's all we have for now. Unless I call up the prison and see if I can get on their guest list."

"Stevie, I'll remind you. I was right the last time you did something I warned could be dangerous. Remember Jacob the fish man?"

I thought of my poor aching butt after that encounter and my sprained coccyx. "Distinctly."

"Do you remember how long it took for your back-side to heal? Then remember this—I'll be right again if you pull a stunt like that. Do you want to end up in jail, too?"

"Don't be silly. They can't put me in jail for pretending I want to visit a prisoner. Maybe I really *do* want to visit a prisoner. How do they know what I'm feeling?"

"Then I hope you like creamed corn."

Win knew how much I hated creamed corn. "Oh, stop. You threatened me with that the last time you thought I'd end up in prison. It's lost its impact. What harm can it do to ask this guy Aiden, or whatever his real name is—"

"I believe we discovered it was Ralph Peterson."

I slapped my hand against the dashboard. "Okay, Ralph. What harm can it do if I ask him about Bart and their scams? He can't beat me up while a bunch of prison guards are standing around."

"Go ask your questions of Petula and I'll send Bel a list of things we can purchase at the prison commissary to tide you over until you're paroled."

I laughed, feeling a little lighter already as I climbed out of the car and stepped onto the curb, determined to find Bart's killer and keep CC from eating creamed corn for life.

Knocking on the glass door of Petula's shop, I admired her front window with the tiered cakes, and beautiful pink and silver tulle strung from corner to corner. Lights twinkled and there was even a rotating bouquet of flowers on a small table.

Her smiling face came into view as she unlocked

the glass door with a big set of dangling keys. She looked winded and her cheeks were red. She wore her trusty white apron, spattered in whatever she was making. Not only did Petula plan a party, but upon special request, she also sometimes cooked for one.

Some of her confections were the most popular in all of Washington state.

"Stevie!" she greeted me with a hug. "Thanks for meeting me here. I have a party to cater tomorrow for Mayor Jenkins and it's been nonstop trouble from the word go."

I stepped into her store, surrounded by the beautiful things she provided for parties, and smiled. "First, despite the death of my stepfather, I want to thank you. The party was amazing. It was everything I could have ever hoped for and more."

Her round face went sad when she grabbed my hand. "I'm so sorry, honey. How's your mother?"

Oh, she's dandy. Off on a hot date with her next husband. "She's doing better than expected," was all I managed.

Petula patted my hand with a vague smile. "Good, good. Listen, I only have a couple of minutes before my mini-quiches are toast. I hate to rush you, but could we make this quick?"

"Of course. I know you were crazy-busy that night, but did you see anything? Anyone? I mean, anything at all unusual?"

Petula rolled her eyes and slapped her hands against the white apron she wore. "If you only knew how tame your party was compared to some. I've seen it all. You know, once, I catered a," she cupped her hand over her mouth and leaned into my ear, "BDS something-or-other party. Land alive, never seen so much leather in my whole life!" Then she chuckled, her face going redder, if that was at all possible.

"So nothing out of the ordinary at all?"

"You know I'm a behind-the-scenes gal, so I don't get to mingle much with the guests. I did hear there was a bit of an argument between your stepfather and Hardy, though. But mostly, it ran like clockwork." Then she frowned, the lines on her forehead deepening. "Except, there was *one* thing…"

I leaned in closer, my gaze intent. "Except?"

"Well, I do remember your stepfather talking to someone shortly before your mother came outside and…well, you know. Gosh, that just came to me now! They were under a tree and I think they were yelling at each other. The reason it struck me was because there were hands flapping and necks rolling, lots of posturing, but I couldn't hear anything because the music was so loud. It was almost like a silent movie. I'd better tell the police that."

My spine tingled again. I was getting closer, I knew I was. "That might be a good idea. One of the acrobats told me the same thing, and if you back up her story, she might not spend a long time in jail."

Petula gasped, her hand going to her throat. "Jail? She was arrested?"

"Yep. I saw them take her away on the way over. But

she said the same thing you did. That Bart was talking to some man in the shadows."

Her eyes were full of concern now. "Then I'll call up that stick-in-the-mud Officer Nelson right away. Oh, the poor thing! You don't think she killed him, do you? Are they calling it murder yet?"

"They're still waiting on the coroner's reports. Anyway, did you know the other person Bart was arguing with? See the other person? Can you tell me what he looked like?"

But Petula shook her head, her shoulders sagging. "No, Sugar. I'm sorry. He was short, and I'm pretty sure it was a fella. But that Bart, he's so big, he overshadowed him. Though he was really pale, as I recall. I only caught a quick flash of him before I had other things to attend."

"Any reason why someone would have your business card with Bart's name written on the back?"

Now Petula blanched, her face flustered. "I don't know…I mean, I hand out my business cards to anyone who can close their fingers around them. I hope you don't think I…"

"No. Of course I don't think that."

"Oh, thank goodness," she said on an expelled breath. "I wish I could be of more help, Stevie. I'm sorry."

Reaching out, I squeezed Petula's hand. "I totally understand. Do you have the list of employees who worked the party?"

She held up a finger. "Yes! It's right there on the

counter. Take it with you if you want. I promise to call Officer Nelson to back up that poor kid's story. And now," she thumbed over her shoulder to her shiny steel kitchen, "I gotta run. Good seeing you!"

I smiled and nodded, grabbing the list and heading for the door. "Thanks again, Petula! Don't forget to lock up!"

I opened the door and scooted out, disappointed I had no more information now than when I'd gone in.

"Don't be discouraged, Dove."

Unlocking the car, I climbed back in and slumped in the seat. What else was left *but* discouragement? "She didn't really tell us anything we didn't already know. Some mysterious guy was arguing with Bart. That's two people with that story. We need to find out who that guy was."

The light was beginning to fade, the sun setting in all its perfect gold and buttery yellow, so it was too hard to read the list. "Let's go home and go over this list while I wait for my mother to get back from her date."

"Bet she misses curfew," Win said on a snort.

"Bet I tie her to a chair until Bart's murder is solved."

"Murder is wrong, Stevie Cartwright."

"So is dating a man one day after your husband is murdered at your daughter's housewarming party."

"She has chutzpah, I'll say that."

Pulling out of the parking space, I went around the circle in the center of the connecting streets, still enthralled by my little town, with all its colorful shops and quirky signs. I loved Ebenezer Falls almost more than I'd loved Paris, I think.

Don't get me wrong, I really miss my friends and my magic, but there was something about the safety of being somewhere you knew every nook and cranny that you couldn't beat.

And this new life I was carving out was pretty great. I had so many things to be thankful for.

I waved to Forrest as I drove by; he was closing up Strange Brew for the night with Chester right behind him. Seeing him with his grandfather always made me smile. The bond he and Chester shared sometimes made me long for something similar in my life.

That thought reminded me of my mother as I drove out of town and toward the house.

"You're quiet, Dove. Penny for them?"

As the sun set and our house came into view, the lawn aglow with the Malibu lights and the windows beaconing rays of welcome, I said, "I was just thinking about how grateful I am to have everything we have. The house, Bel, Whiskey, the shop, you. It's good. Really good, don't you think?"

Win's aura circled me, sending gentle vibrations of light and warmth. "I think. We're very fortunate—all of us."

If I could reach out and hold his hand right now, I would. Just so he'd know how much he meant to us, how he'd saved Bel and me. So he'd feel the gratitude I felt in something other than the words I spoke. I'd like to think we'd laugh, maybe take a walk, were he here beside me instead of just in my ear.

I pulled into the driveway, still in my small cocoon of happiness—and that was when it happened. Just as I reached for my purse.

At first I thought it was merely a trick of the setting sun, its eggplant and deep-blue haze casting shadows over the passenger seat, until I looked closer.

I almost wasn't able to say anything because I think I stopped breathing.

Blinking, I forced myself to focus, gripping the steering wheel and turning to look again. "Win? Oh, my goddess, *Win?*"

He turned to me, his hard body twisting with the movement, dressed in an immaculate suit of shimmery black, his dark hair falling rakishly in waves over his forehead, the ends down to just the top of his collar.

And he smiled then, smiled wide, complete with deep grooves on either side of his mouth. A smile full of white, perfect teeth, a smile warm and inviting.

He lifted a hand with long fingers and saluted me before reaching to cup my cheek. "Hello, Dove," he said, thick and husky, silky and seductive, just like he had in my ear for three months now. Yet, I felt his hand. I felt an ever-so-light bit of pressure, the warm curve of it against my skin, the length of his fingers as they left my cheek and wrapped under my chin.

And at that moment I knew. I knew he was everything.

My heart throbbed so hard, I didn't know what to

say, what to think. Elation coursed through my veins. He'd done it. Somehow, he'd made his image appear. Was that me regaining some more of my power or Win gaining some of his own?

"Win? Is that you? Oh my God—*Win!*" I reached out to press my hand to his, but it fell right through the thin film of his body.

So I put my hands to my cheeks, tears burning at the corners of my eyes, smiling through my tears. "It's you! *How?*"

But then he began to fade, his image shimmering, distorting, his voice becoming muffled and faraway, the words he spoke making no sense.

"Wait! What's happening? Where are you going? No, Win! Don't go. Come back!"

As sure as his image began to fade, I also felt his aura slipping away, like water down a drain. "Nooo!" I screamed into the car. "Come back!"

But he was gone. Just like that. And in his place there was a cold talon, slithering along my spine, an empty hole of nothingness. Desperation and despair clawed at my gut.

And then there was a voice. A very familiar voice. A voice I'll never, not for whatever was left of my life, forget.

"Poor Stevie," the disembodied voice rumbled, deep and antagonistic. "Did you lose your only friend?"

I wanted to cringe. To hide. To run for cover.

But then I thought of Win. He'd never run. He'd jam that gorgeous face of his right into his tormentor's and dare him to do whatever it was he was going to do because no way would Win back down.

No. No, I would *not* shy away from this. I would not be someone's hostage for the rest of my life—not after everything he'd already taken.

So I sat up straight. I lifted my chin. I puffed out my chest. I let my eyes go wide with the vengeance I'd shoved deep down inside and I asked, "What do you want from me?"

His laughter was repulsive, filled with his hatred for me. "I want you dead, Stevie Cartwright. I want you broken, battered, beaten, begging for mercy, and then I want you dead!"

Even though my pulse raced and my heart crashed so hard against my ribs I thought surely I was having a heart attack, I reared up in my seat as though keeping my head above his quicksand of evil. "Then bring it, Adam! I *dare you* to bring it, you sick bastard! Bring everything you have. Bring it allll!" I bellowed out, tears stinging my eyes, hot and salty as they ran down my cheeks and into my mouth. "But you leave Win alone! Do you hear me? Leave him alone. Take me, *but leave him alone!*"

Thunder cracked, so sharp, so piercing, it rocked the car, fracturing the passenger-side window. Lighting sizzled, spewing from the sky with a bolt of a flash.

"I'd be happy to!" he hollered gleefully.

I yanked at the car door, trying to escape, but the locks clamped down in place on each door with a harsh snap. Yet, in that moment, that moment filled with the scent of evil, the ozone redolent with the smell of hatred mingled with magic, I felt an odd sense of calm.

If something happened to me, I'd find Win. I'd *find* a way to find him.

But in the meantime, I realized, his words—the words he drilled into my head over and over, day after day—were still with me.

I flung the seat back using the lever, swiveling my body around and using my feet to kick at the window.

Rain began to slash the car, hitting it in hard pelts. I kicked harder, until I heard that familiar crack Win said I'd hear just before it was about to break.

So I covered my face for the backlash, in case splinters rained down on me, and then I was sitting up again, clearing the shards from the window, jamming my legs into it, using my hands as leverage on the frame to pull myself up and slide out.

I ran away from the house, too afraid Adam would follow me inside and hurt the Bats or my mother. I ran across the lawn just past the gorgeous gardens as the rain pounded down on me and my work boots sank into the softened soil. The temperature dropped quickly, turning the rain to ice, its stinging daggers hitting my skin.

But then I realized there was nowhere to go. Where could I hide from someone who wanted me dead from the great beyond? So I turned into the ice and wind and screamed, "Take me, Adam! Come and get me! But you leave Win alone!"

"Stephania!"

I whipped around at the sound of my name being called.

"Stephania! Come to me now!" my mother yelled into the howl of the frigid wind from the center of the lawn. She held out her trembling hand as the lightning cracked again, a slim figure in a flash of light, offering aid. "Stephania! Come to me now!"

So I ran, grabbing on to Mom's icy fingers and clinging to them.

Her eyes closed as her hair plastered to her head and she gripped my hand so tight, I had to take back what I'd said earlier about her skinny bird arms.

She let her neck arch back, her head resting on her shoulders. Leaning into the wind, Mom roared, "Evil be gone from this place! Evil no longer show your face!"

Everything stopped at once, the rain, the ice, the wind, leaving us both shivering and soaked.

My mother grabbed me, pulling me to her, bracketing my face with her hands. "Stephania, are you all right?" Her fingers roamed my cheeks, my hair. "Did he hurt you? *Who* was that?" she asked, her eyes frantically searching mine as rainwater dripped down her face.

I fought for breath, my full-body tremble in high gear. I shivered violently, shudders racking my arms and legs. "The warlock who stole my powers. Adam Westfield."

CHAPTER 14

*M*y mother handed me a towel and she dried off with me in the kitchen as Bel, the Bats and Whiskey sat quietly, watching us.

Puddles of water formed at our feet, though my shivering had abated some.

Mom grabbed my chin and forced me to look at her. "Stephania, are you all right?"

I gulped air in, kicking my sodden boots off. "I can't find Win," I muttered, utterly desolate. "I don't know what he did to Win." It took everything I had in me not to scream the words.

"Sit down now. I want you to tell me everything that happened back in Paris. I'll make tea to warm you."

I shook my head in misery, the hole inside me widening, my fear mounting with each breath I stole. "I can't sit, Mom. Win's gone. I can't hear him anymore!"

She gave me a stern mom look, one I almost didn't recognize. "I said sit. *Please*. Maybe I can help figure it out." Pointing to the chair, she motioned for me to sit in it.

My legs were like lead as I crossed the kitchen and did as I was told. "Forget the tea. Make it whiskey."

"Good idea. It will warm you from the inside out. Now who is Adam Westfield, Stephania, and why is he so angry with you from the afterlife?"

You know, I wanted to be angry with her for not knowing who he was. I wanted to rail against her, point my finger at her, admonish her for not once asking about what had happened to me.

But I couldn't. I'll never forget the look of pure terror on her face when she called my name out on the front lawn. I'll never forget that she managed to banish Adam and save me. I'll also never understand it. I can't ever recall a time she'd gone to bat for me like that, but here we were, the savior and the saved.

"He's the warlock who stole my powers, Mom. It's a long story."

She poured the amber liquid into a tumbler and shoved it toward me with purpose. "Then drink and tell me."

Between gulps of the burning whiskey and my sobs, I told her everything. The 9-1-1 phone call from Adam's son, that evil warlock's subsequent death, the night he literally slapped my powers from me with one hard crack to my cheek. The end of my journey in Paris.

Mom sighed raggedly, her shoulders slumping, her

long hair drying in thick clumped sheets of chestnut. "I didn't know, Stephania."

"No. You didn't," I whispered quietly. I couldn't condemn her now. I was too tired, too defeated to condemn her, to rail against her lack of interest in me.

"I should have known, shouldn't I?" I heard the guilt in her tone, saw her eyes filled with apologies, but I couldn't connect these two very different people. The caring, motherly Dita and the callous, flighty man-eater who, one day after her husband's death, was off wooing another rich purse.

What difference did it make now anyway?

"I'd like to think you'd want to know what happens to your daughter, but you don't ever seem to..." I couldn't say the words. I'd said them before and she'd never listened, there was no reason she'd start now.

We sat in the quiet for a moment, me in my misery, my mother in whatever emotions she was avoiding, when she finally said, "I'm a selfish woman, Stephania. I know it. I've always known it. I'm disorganized, I'm calculating. I'm vain. I'm even cruel sometimes. And I was not cut out to be a mother. I can't say I even really tried to be your mother—the kind of mother you needed—the kind of mother *all* children need. That's horrible. I know it is, but it's the truth. Hand to heart. But it never meant—not once—that I didn't love you. That there weren't times when I regretted letting you raise yourself. Because I do. But I'd never let anyone hurt you if I was unselfish enough to be aware someone was actually *trying* to hurt you. I didn't know about Adam because I didn't want to know. I dodged your calls because I had my own problems to deal with, and somehow, I thought they were more important... and I'm sorry."

I swallowed hard, my throat dry and burning from the whiskey. That was the most real she'd ever been with me in my entire life. It was the most remorse I'd ever seen her display where I was concerned.

But I couldn't look her in the eye. Her admission made me uncomfortable and comforted at the same time. At least she could admit she'd been a pretty crappy parent, but I wasn't sure that admission was what I'd been looking for all my life.

Did it make it any more valid than what I already knew just because she said it out loud?

So I looked down at the table. "I know you want me to say it's okay, and for the most part, I guess it is. I turned out all right, Mom. I can stand on my own two feet. I have a good life, but I won't lie and tell you it didn't hurt when I was kicked out of Paris. I had nowhere to go. No one to turn to but Bel. We were alone, and for the first time in my life, I was petrified. I learned a long time ago not to count on you for much. But just that once, when everything was falling apart around me, I wish you would have picked up the phone and heard me. Really *heard* me."

I saw a sparkle of something shiny in her eye. A tear? No. My mother didn't cry unless they were crocodile tears. But sure enough, it slipped down her cheek and to the table, splashing against the white surface.

"I'm not a good person, Stephania, but I'm sorry. I truly am—*for everything*."

I felt a little like the world was turning inside out right now, upside down, whatever. I never thought I'd hear those words. I never thought my mother would hold herself accountable for anything, or own her mistakes. But here she was, sitting in front of me, apologizing and giving me the cold, hard facts.

"Stevie!" a voice roared from the front of the house, filled with panic. "Where are you, Daughter?"

My father appeared out of nowhere in a puff of lingering emerald green smoke, his handsome face chock full with worry as he stormed into my kitchen, catching both my mother and me by surprise.

I jumped up from the chair, prepared to tell him to go, but he didn't miss a beat when he scooped me into his arms and hugged me tight. "Stevie," he whispered, his voice husky with what sounded like fear. "I know you asked me to stay away, but I couldn't after the spirits contacted me tonight." Holding me out from him, he asked, "Are you all right, Daughter?"

That was when I broke, when the fear of losing Win became too much for me to hold inside anymore. "Win's gone," I sobbed, falling into his wide chest.

He patted my back and hugged me tighter. "No, no, dear heart. No. It can't be. Tell me everything that happened. Tell me what I can do to make this better."

I sucked in a breath as tears fell down my face. "What did the spirit say about me? About Win?"

"It was your great aunt Imelda. She told me you

were in grave danger and I had to come instantly. *Who's responsible for this?*" he demanded in his game-show announcer's voice.

Pulling me to a chair, he set me in it, moving his close to mine, and as we three sat there, my mother who was coming to grips with her mistakes, my father who never knew I existed, and me, the bereft offspring of two people so different than myself, we talked—long into the night.

~

"*D*aughter, you're awake!" my father said from the chair in my bedroom with a wide, welcoming smile. "I'm so pleased to see you and your beautiful eyes looking back at me."

I rolled to my side as I tucked the blanket under my chin, those beautiful eyes Hugh spoke of sore and grainy from crying.

Hugh had stayed the night. He'd insisted, so he could watch over me and be sure no harm came to me while I slept.

He rose from the chair and sat beside me on the bed, nudging me with his hip, still looking as perfect as he had the night before. "Did you sleep well? I made you coffee. A special blend your wonderful friend Enzo suggested. I met him just this morning as he prepared to build an arbor in the backyard, with my new friend Whiskey by my side. He is truly delightful and we've promised to dine together soon."

I smiled up at him even though my chest was heavier than an elephant after a good meal. My parents (wow, weird to use that word in relation to me, right?) had forced me to take some special brew they whipped up with their magic then tucked me in.

I have to say, at almost thirty-three, it was a little bizarre. Nice, mind you, but bizarre. But I still let them, relishing a moment when there was nothing but the three of us. I heard their distant whispers as they talked in the hall and Bel hunkered down near my cheek with Whiskey at the crook of my knees, and I slept, knowing they'd look out for me.

"Did you hear anything more about Win?" I asked groggily, my words almost catching in my throat.

This time, when Hugh's eyes went sad, it was genuine. There was no Academy Award winning performance in his gaze. "Don't doubt I'll find him for you. I promise you, no matter what, I'll find him."

"Thank you," I murmured, the words coming out raw.

Hugh took the coffee from the nightstand and held it up with an enticing grin. "Come, Daughter. Sit up and have some. It's delightful and it will help to get the day started. We must find your Win today. That will take energy."

My heart bounced in my chest with hope and dread. "Do you think we can?"

"Between your mother and I, yes. Now come." He held out his hand and pulled my sore body to a sitting position.

I was more hopeful in the cold light of day as Hugh fluffed the pillows and I accepted the steaming cup of coffee he handed me.

But we had something between us I had to get rid of —something we needed to talk out.

I sipped at the coffee, my taste buds thanking me for dousing them in delicious caffeine. "I'm sorry I told you to leave the store, Hugh. I..." What other nice way could you explain you were afraid the man who was your father was a killer?

Cupping my chin, he smiled that camera-ready smile. "Think nothing of it, Daughter. I had some time to think about what you said and I understand now. Why would you trust someone you'd known for less than an hour? Yes, I was hurt. But truly, I had no right to be. You know nothing of my integrity, my character. I've had no time to prove to you I'm worthy of your trust. It was only fair you suspect I might have hurt your mother's husband. I accept this, but I hope after last night I've changed your mind."

"I think you're in the clear. Thank you, Hugh. Last night meant a great deal to me." It really had. Last night left me wondering what it would have been like to come home to Hugh after school. What it would have been like to take him to the father-daughter dance at school.

He held two hands to his heart. "And to me as well. Now up and at 'em, Daughter. You must shower and dress as we make plans to find Win." He clapped his hands and motioned toward the bathroom with his infamous smile.

I slid out of what I fondly called my nook bed and put my feet on the floor, feeling very wobbly. Hugh was there to grab me, steadying me and taking my cup of coffee.

On impulse, I hugged him, letting my head rest against his suit jacket. "Thank you. I don't think I would have made it through last night without you."

"Of course. Now shower," he ordered on a laugh against the top of my head.

As I righted myself and headed in the direction of the bathroom, my eyes widened. There was a huge poster on the wall by the bathroom door of Hugh, smiling of course, his two thumbs up in the air with his name in artsy lettering.

"I thought you might like a pick-me-up each morning when you wake, Daughter," he said.

I giggled as I tapped the poster with my fingers. "Can't think of a better way to wake up than to a full-size poster of you."

Closing the bathroom door, I peeled off the night-gown my mother had stuffed me into last night and marveled at the turn of events. My mother's apology, my father's unwavering support.

And then I thought of Win, and the possibility I'd never hear his voice again. The wonder at seeing him for the first time. How handsome he was. How much I wished he'd been the one to wake me this morning the way he almost always does.

Tears threatened to fall again, but I shook them off with a fierce determination to keep it together as I turned on the taps and adjusted the water.

Wearily, I climbed in, keeping the hope that Hugh's words held true and we'd find Win. As the warm water washed over me, I began to relax.

"Stevie!"

I heard my name hissed and instantly thought Adam was back for round two.

"Stevie! It's me. It's Win," he whispered, hoarse and low.

Grabbing the shower curtain, I wrapped it around myself and poked my head around the side to see if he'd appeared again. "Win?" I whispered, frantic to hear him respond. He sounded far away—muted, duller than normal, and it scared the daylights out of me.

"Dove, it's me. I'm all right."

My knees went weak with relief, so weak, I had to cling to the tub's edge to keep myself upright. As the water from the shower pelted me, I swallowed the enormous lump in my throat. "Where are you, Win? Tell me so I can help!"

"I'm back on Plane Limbo," he said, though he still sounded weak, utterly worn out.

"What happened?" I asked, fighting that dang sob in my voice, the shaky waver of fear.

"It was Adam. He… I don't know if I can verbalize what happened. It was dark, cold, so ugly. It's too…"

"Oh, Win! Oh, goddess, I'm sorry! One minute you were there, the next you were gone. How did you make yourself appear? Why did you do that? Do you think that's why Adam came for you?"

His sigh was tired, his breathing erratic. "I think so, Dove. I just need to rest. Just let me rest, and everything will be fine."

If there were a way, I'd pull him close and hug him, bring him whatever he needed to heal his wounds, make him soup or Pop-Tarts or caviar, or whatever he wanted. But I was helpless to mend what was broken, separated by two worlds.

"Are you okay, Dove? Did he hurt you? I'll kill him if he hurt you."

My fingers clutched the shower curtain. "You can't kill him, he's already dead, Win. Just rest. I'm fine. My mother helped me with her magic and my father's here."

"Good. Very good," he said, his voice beginning to fade.

"Wait. Did you say you were back on Plane Limbo?"

"Yes. Yes, I'm back."

"Can you see me? I'm naked! We had an agreement, Crispin Alistair Winterbottom!"

"I have my eyes closed, goose. Don't be ridiculous. I always treat you with the respect a lady deserves."

And then a thought occurred to me. "Hang on one sec, Win. I'll get my father."

"Wait. I thought I heard wrong. Hugh's here? I thought you said he was on our list of suspects?"

"I'll explain later. Just find somewhere to rest and hold on. And keep your eyes closed!"

Jumping out of the shower, soaking wet and all, I wrapped a towel around me and threw the door to my bedroom open, poking my head out. "Dad! Win's back!" I smiled so hard, my cheeks hurt.

Hugh rose from the chair by the fireplace and grinned. "How wonderful, Daughter! How is he?"

Water slid down my nose and I blew at the drops falling to my lips. "I think he's hurt. Can you help?"

"Oh, of course! Win, where are you? Talk to me, please."

"I'm here, sir, reporting for duty."

But my father shook his head. "No. You must rest now. I'll call upon Stevie's great aunt Imelda to aid you. She'll know what to do."

"Thank you, Sir."

I could tell Win was fighting to keep his voice steady in light of the fact that my father was here, but he was shaky. So shaky.

"Finish your shower, Dove. I'll be fine."

I just nodded, closing the door and leaning against it. Win was back. Thank the goddess, Win was back.

And I'd called Hugh "dad."

If hearts could hug you tight, I think mine was hugging me for giving it the joy this morning's events brought.

CHAPTER 15

"Stevie? You cannot do this. Have you ever been to a place like this, Dove?"

I smiled. I didn't care that Win was disagreeing with me. He was back in my ear, where he belonged. But that wasn't going to stop me from doing what I had to do. And I had to do this so peace could be restored in our home.

Okay, this isn't just about peace. It's also about the fact that I'm nosy as a dog on a coon hunt, but whatever. I had a niggle deep in my gut that said I was on to something, and now that Win was recuperating, I couldn't let it go.

"Nope. I sure haven't, but I'm all about firsts. I'd never climbed out of a window to keep from being caught by a madman, run through a graveyard in my bare feet while a killer chased me with a gun, been tied to a chair with duct-tape with a gun to my head, or eaten squicky fish eggs and Steak Diane either. But they were all firsts. You have to experience firsts in order to discover whether you don't want seconds. Especially the fish eggs. "I mock shuddered. "I never want those again."

I pulled into the parking lot of our destination and found a space, looking at the vast expanse of the building I was about to enter. My mother had used her magic to fix my car window, strangely silent and somber this morning as she did.

I think the events of last night and our talk hit home. I don't know how hard or if the impact will have a lasting effect, but she'd been a very different Dita this morning. We didn't talk for long, but she'd pulled me into a tight hug before going back upstairs, her gait slow.

Win recaptured my focus when he said, "I don't know how you managed to pull this off. Is this what you do whilst I'm fighting foes on Plane Limbo?"

My pulse sped up at Win's words. Adam had come for Win and tried to do the same thing he'd done when he'd taken possession of the Bustamantes' *abuela* in our shop a couple of months ago.

He'd literally attempted to possess Win.

Win had fought him off, but it was Adam's intent that it would be Win's hand responsible for killing me, according to the spirit gossips. Already weak from bringing his image to my plane, Win was caught off guard.

But my Spy Guy? He was as tough as nails, and

somehow he'd fought Adam off, swearing he'd protect me with everything he had in him.

According to the spirit world, via my dad, Win was all the talk of the afterlife this morning. They were all cheering his strength and courage when up against the almighty Adam Westfield.

But I was fretting. As my great aunt Imelda had set about the task of easing Win's suffering through her otherworldly magic, I paced the length of our kitchen in panic. Maybe the only answer was to have Win leave me forever. If nothing else, it would keep him safe from the repercussions of my troubles.

Win wouldn't hear of it, and those were brave words. But he wasn't invincible and he'd never be as powerful as Adam, who'd proven he wanted me dead— and he hadn't shied away from trying last night.

What would happen when my mother found her next husband and my father went back to Japan to begin his next movie and I was alone and powerless?

But I didn't want Win to see me fret. My worry would only burden him when he needed to stay sharp and watch his back. "You're not the only one who can be spy-like, International Man of Mystery. I called while I was in the bathroom yesterday between stops at home and Petula's. I gave them my sob story about how I'm Bart's stepdaughter and he's dead and it was awful and they hooked me up. Easy-peasy. But you know what this means?"

"What does this mean, Dove?"

"It means you really *do* close your eyes and give me privacy when I'm using the ladies' room."

He barked a laugh, much stronger than anything coming from him this morning. "I'm no peeping Tom, Mini-Spy. When I make a promise, my word stands. Now, I'd like the truth."

I stared out the windshield and did my best impression of vague. "The truth?"

"Yes, the truth. You didn't really call the prison and charm your way into a visit. No one knows your masterful flirting techniques better than I. In other words, they are horrid. So how did you *really* get on the list for a visitation with Ralph?"

"I can't believe how underestimated I am."

"Stevie…"

Oh, there was that uppity British warning tone, letting me know I'd been caught and the only thing left to do was admit it out loud. I think Win keeps a scorecard with perverse pleasure about how often I'm yanking his chain.

"Fine. My father used a little bit of magic to help me along, okay? I've admitted it."

"I thought your people couldn't use magic for personal gain?"

"My people can't. But would you call being allowed to visit a criminal in prison personal gain? If so, we need to reevaluate what personal gain means to you, Spy Guy."

Looking to the passenger seat, where I now assumed he sat when we were in the car, after his appearance last night, I said, "Listen. You should be resting right now. Why don't you go do that and let the grasshopper make her sensei proud?"

"Not on your life. I'm not letting you go into a prison without at least my advice in your ear. Do not argue this point with me. If you wish to make chit-chat with a criminal, I'm your wingman."

"I'm not making chit-chat. I'm just going to talk to the guy. He's in for tax evasion, Win. Not murder one."

"I don't care. Prisons are bleak places where more than just tax evaders lay their heads to rest. No more arguments."

"I'm doing the right thing, Win. Now that Bart's death has been labeled a murder, we need anything, even the smallest of information to help us find whoever did this."

This morning, as I'd gathered my wits while Win healed—with my great aunt Imelda and my father at his side, working their mojo—I found two new voice messages on my phone. One from the prison, granting me visitation with Bart's partner in scams, and one from Sandwich, who'd informed me the coroner was ruling Bart's death a homicide—which was why they'd hauled CC in yesterday.

"Tell me again what the coroner's report said?" Win insisted.

I grimaced. "The coroner's report said the pulley was designed to release when the acrobats used their legs to push off from the ground or the ceiling, and it was fully functional and in good working order upon inspection."

"So absolutely not a suicide?"

"Sandwich said the probability of Bart committing suicide was low—very low. Meaning, someone likely suspended him there and strangled him with the sheet."

"But that wasn't what killed him, correct?"

I looked in the rearview mirror and smoothed my hair back. "Correct. His windpipe was crushed from the pressure of the sheet around his neck."

"Which likely means, the person who suspended him there was no weakling. Damn. The poor sod."

What I didn't understand was how no one saw or heard anything. But Sandwich said that was likely due to the music and the fact that most of the staff was using the French doors off the dining room to get to the front lawn. According to much of the staff testimony, the walk was easier when carrying heavy platters and it was less time consuming, keeping the food warmer.

"So they didn't just arrest her for not cooperating? They really do have evidence against her?"

That was the worst of it. The damning evidence against her. "Fibers from her bathing suit were found on Bart's dinner jacket."

While both CC and another acrobat, D (yep. You guessed it. One letter) were the only two in bathing suits, D's whereabouts could be accounted for. When CC became so offended by Bart's rude remark, she'd told her to take a thirty-minute break.

But I didn't care what Sandwich or anyone else said, CC was innocent, and I was going to prove that by going into this prison and making Ralph spill his guts.

"I don't care about the evidence against her. It still doesn't feel right, Dove," Win said, mirroring my thoughts.

"Which is exactly why I have to go in there. Do you want her to sit in jail, or do you want to get her out before she freezes her teeny-tiny acrobatic butt off in that leotard?"

Win laughed. "We'd better hurry."

"Then let's do this."

$\sim$

*a*s I sat across from Ralph in the rather cheerful visiting room of the prison, painted in cool blues and decorated with inspirational art, I couldn't help but notice how undisturbed he appeared about Bart's death.

While the guards looked on, their guns at their sides and the strict visitation rules posted, I was amazed Ralph had no idea who I was or why I was here. According to him, they didn't tell him anything other than Bart's stepdaughter wanted to speak with him.

Letting my chin rest in my hand, I looked at him long and hard. He was as nice to look at as Bart in a totally different way. Where Bart was classically handsome, Ralph was boyish and boy-next-door, despite his age. He had deep-blue eyes, crow's feet at either corner of them, yet they sparkled bright and clear.

Ralph's hair was gray now, too, but of the salt-and-pepper variety, slicked back from his face with a dashing swoop to it across his forehead. He even looked pretty good in orange, and he was tan—very tan. He didn't have handcuffs on and his body language said relaxed, as though he hadn't a care in the world.

"Dead, you say?" He paused and I thought it would be to gather his emotions. Instead, his jaw hardened for just a moment and then he sighed in a dramatic release of air, not quite meeting my eyes. "Ah, well."

Was there no camaraderie in grifting? No common thread that sewed two scam artists together? No remorse for grifting days gone by?

"So you're not upset Bart's dead?"

"Should I be?" He almost appeared appalled at the notion, but his blue eyes went dark for a moment. It was brief and as fleeting as youth, but it was there.

Still, I couldn't help but probe the dynamic of his relationship with Bart. "Weren't you friends? I mean, I found you in a bunch of pictures with him at all sorts of events. You guys looked pretty friendly."

"And what was the common denominator in those pictures, Miss Cartwright?" he asked in a deep, cultured timbre.

"Um, fancy parties? Diamonds?"

"Women," he said, his tone flat. "We were there for one reason only. The money. The women who *had* the money."

"Right, I get that. But I got the impression the two of you did this together. You know...wooed rich women. Sort of like a swindling tag team."

He surprised me again by barking a laugh. "No, dear. We weren't in anything together. We were each other's competition. I could never get that son of a gun off my tail. He came out of nowhere, charming, suave, seemingly educated. I might have liked him because his game was sharp, if I didn't hate his guts because his game was so sharp and he was snatching my leads up left and right. Every time I'd think I'd shaken him off, he'd show up at another event. It got to the point where we'd lay bets on who could win the attention of the richest woman in attendance before we ever stepped into the room."

Ugh. "So it was like a game?"

Gosh, that was horrible. How cruel to scope women out for their money. I know it happens all the time, but to hear it from the horse's mouth in such a matter-of-fact manner… Well, it was awful.

He grinned, suddenly and gleefully. "We didn't have anything official going, mind you. But before I was arrested, I was two up on Bart. I heard he slowed down after he met your mother. Maybe it was really love after all." Then he grinned again, likely at the absurdity of it all.

My eyes widened. "So he was doing this while he was married to my mother?"

"Men like us are always looking for the next scam,

Miss Cartwright. Some say that's horrible, but that's the truth."

I hated to admit it, but Ralph made me endlessly curious. "So you're here for tax evasion and fraud. How'd a crafty guy like you get caught?"

For the first time, Ralph gave me a surprised look. "I'd think you'd know that, being his stepdaughter. Bart turned state's evidence and got himself a get-out-of-jail-free card because of it."

I couldn't hide my surprise. "He turned you in? *Bart?*"

Ralph smiled as though he admired what Bart had done. There didn't appear to be any lingering hatred—if there ever was any. "He did. We were both involved in a scandal and in order to get himself out of the scandal, he handed me over. I'd have done the same, mind you. He was just quicker on the draw, and he saved his own hide."

So maybe Ralph could have ordered a hit from prison? Did swindlers use mob methods to rid themselves of their foes?

"Were you angry with him?"

"If you're suggesting I was angry enough to kill him, take a look around you. I think the night of your party I was otherwise engaged. On a rousing bathroom patrol, perhaps."

But that didn't mean he didn't have contacts who could kill Bart. But if he did, why would he wait three years to do it? He'd been tried and convicted a while ago now.

I knew this was a long shot, but I was going to ask anyway. "Do you have any idea who killed him? Who'd *want* to kill him?"

Ralph winked. "I'd say half the female population in the one-million-dollar-and-over club. I know that's a broad stroke, but there it is. Bart made many people angry, Miss Cartwright. It's the nature of our beast."

"You know what I don't get. How is it that none of these women ever told each other about the two of you? Like, have each other's backs, warned others like them away from the likes of you?"

Ralph didn't appear at all taken aback by my harsh tone. In fact, he seemed pretty unfettered by guises. He knew who he was. A cheat with no regrets.

Folding his hands in front of him, he shrugged nonchalantly. "The circle is small, no doubt, but when you're like Bart and I, you get in, you get what you want, and you get out. You don't linger. You swap out identities as fast as possible and you move on to the next mark. These women have reputations to protect. They don't want anyone knowing we did naughty, naughty things to them in order to win their hearts and purses. It's rather humiliating, wouldn't you say? Would you want the world to know you'd been had?"

I'd want to let the world see me punch him in the face because I'd been had. But I refrained from saying as much. "Fair enough. So one last question, if you don't mind. Did you call Bart or did Bart call you here at the prison?"

There it was again. A small flicker of discomfort,

but then he looked me directly in the eyes. "Why would we call each other, Miss Cartwright? We were, essentially, foes. Now, as lovely as you are, as much as I wish there was something I could *do* about how lovely you are, I'm bored with this conversation. I'm sorry for your loss. Have a lovely life."

And that was that. He rose from his chair with the grace of a gazelle, held out his wrists for the guards to take him away, and he was gone in a blur of orange jumpsuit and regal stature.

CHAPTER 16

"*B*oy, he was some smooth operator, huh?" I asked when we reached my car and I was tucked safely inside.

"Cool as the north of Wales in spring," Win agreed.

"He almost didn't blink an eye when he heard Bart was dead."

"*Almost* being the key word, Dove. He hid it well, but he glitched. It was in his tone, in the slight flicker of awareness in his eyes."

I leaned back against the car door, facing the passenger seat, and considered that. "So you think maybe he really cared about Bart? Considered him a friend?"

"No. Hardly. But I can't shake the feeling he knows something."

"Like? I couldn't get a feel on him one way or the other. I saw the glitch you're talking about. But I feel like it was more about his mortality than Bart's death."

"Maybe," Win murmured.

Sighing, I stretched my neck, the tension easing. I didn't realize how edgy I'd been in there, but there'd been a heaviness that lifted when I left and breathed in the air outside the prison walls.

I was becoming frustrated though. We needed answers if we hoped to get CC out of this jam. "Well, that was our last viable lead. I'm telling you, Win. I felt like I was onto something. It's like I'm this close, but the answer won't get off the tip of my tongue."

"Your theory that Ralph could have put a hit out isn't outrageous, Dove."

"But after all this time? He's been incarcerated for three years. And it didn't come off like he hated Bart at all. He might not have liked him encroaching on his turf, but I almost got a reluctant admiration vibe from him."

"Then we move on and revisit this later."

"So we probably should attack the list of staff at the party. We should start talking to some of them. All the wait staff, the chef, the sous chef, the linemen, the orchestra, the DJ. The list is endless. Remind me the next time you want to throw a party to run in the other direction. We'll be talking to potential suspects 'til this time next year. Next party we do Cheese Whiz and Triscuits. Got it?"

"Ugh, you're a heathen, Stevie Cartwright. I'll eat my shoe before I put canned cheese on my tongue. Now, how about we ride home with a little Beethoven to soothe our stalled investigation and battered egos. It's a bit of a drive, might as well enjoy it, yes?"

"My mother texted to tell me she and my father took Whiskey and the Bats on a day trip to Seattle. Apparently my dad's never been to the Space Needle and Mom's been cleared of any wrongdoing in Bart's death, so they're celebrating. She said they won't be back for dinner."

Win hummed "I'm In The Mood for Love" then chuckled. "Doest thou think your parents might rekindle their old flame?"

That made me pause. I wasn't sure how I felt about that. After I'd witnessed firsthand how my mother treated men, I wasn't sure I wanted her to sink her claws into my father. "Thou is going to put that on the back burner."

"How are you feeling about your father after last night, Dove? He truly rallied for you."

He sure had, and I'll admit, it made my insides all warm. I smiled. "He kinda did. I don't think he had anything to do with Bart's death anymore. But it's my mother and what *she* did that still has me feeling like I'm going to wake up and this will all have been a dream."

Win snorted. "I'll say. I mean, she did willingly take those filthy animals to the Space Needle. Surely she's turned over a new leaf."

"You should have seen her, Win. She was all fire and brimstone with the rain pouring down on her and sleet pecking at her perfect skin. She's never gone to bat for me before. No one ever has but you."

Win's warmth washed over me, his aura brightening. "I will always go to bat for you, Dove. However, I rather like knowing Mama Bear is right beside me. I can't tell you how pleased I am to find Dita has a redeeming quality and that you were the one who benefitted from such. I don't know what I would have done without her help."

"What exactly did she do? I've never heard the spell she used before. Could you see her? Hear her?"

"At that point, it was more a feeling than anything else, though I could hear you screaming in the distance…" Win paused then, his voice growing hoarse. "Yet, I knew with certainty it was Dita, or her power, that helped me survive."

"Are you ready to talk about what happened?"

Win's gruff sigh sounded tired. "I can only tell you it happened as quickly as the last time when he possessed the Bustamantes' *abuela*. One moment I managed to make myself appear to you, the next I was sucked into some sort of vortex. It was ugly, desperate, then it got hotter than Hades itself…and I felt his hatred for you, tasted it. The emotion was palpable and left me gagging. I didn't know what to do. The only thing I *did* know was I had to move toward whatever was pushing me into this black hole of despair. Call it instinct or whatever, but I'd have been and *will be* damned before I let that happen."

His words were so final, they frightened me. Shook me to my core. "How did you make yourself appear?"

"Lots and lots of practice behind your back. But here's something to chew on. You saw me, Dove. You, the ex-witch with no powers, *saw* me. And that isn't all you've had happen over the last couple of months. I firmly believe we can find a way to get your powers back."

I couldn't think about that right now. The notion was too fleeting. Too based in hope rather than reality. There was more to focus on anyway. Like Win and the chance he took trying to save me.

"Listen. I know being a big bad spy, you don't want to talk about this, but I need you to promise me something, Win. If Adam comes for you again, find the light. Just go into the light. Please. I'm begging you. If he steals your soul…" I had to swallow back my tears before I could finish. Gripping the steering wheel, I bit the inside of my cheek before I said, "If Adam can get his hands on your soul, it will be the worst hell you've ever known. Please, don't do that for me. I'd have to live with that, and I don't think I can."

"You won't have to, Dove. I won't allow it. Now, Beethoven, please."

I started the car and put on Beethoven, letting it flood my ears as the sun pierced my eyes, making them sting. I was pretty sure the golden rays weren't the only thing responsible, but I couldn't dwell on what could happen.

Not yet.

~

"*I*t's good to be home, huh, Spy Guy?"

"Indeed, Mini-Spy. There really is no place like home."

I sank down in the chair in the parlor. Apparently, while we'd made the trip to the Penn, the police had cleared the room and we could now use it as a living space again.

My father had taken great pains to clean it up and rearrange the furniture so I could hopefully forget it had been a crime scene. He said so in the note he'd left me with a box of blueberry Pop-Tarts on the counter, for which he left strict instructions they were to be eaten *after* my dinner.

Now, Win and I sat by the hearth, a small fire glowing. Me tucked into my jammies after a long hot shower, and Win in my ear as we looked over the list of wait staff in order to tackle questioning them first thing tomorrow morning.

"Do any of the names ring a bell, Dove?"

"Nope. Not one. I say we just tackle them alphabetically tomorrow. Sound good?"

"First thing," Win agreed.

Looking to the end table next to the chair, I grabbed the box I'd previously forgotten about Hardy dropping off and slit it free of tape with my letter opener.

That was odd. It was addressed to me in a lovely script scrawl, the lines of each letter billowy and precise. "No return address. Huh."

"Maybe you have a secret admirer, Dove. A gallant young man on a white steed who's sending you gifts to express his love."

I snorted sarcastically. "Or it's my stuff from Woot."

"Stuff?"

"I might have ordered Whiskey a little something…"

Win's chuckle was indulgent. He loved Whiskey as much as I did, and I'd caught him instructing Bel to order things online for him on more than one occasion. "More tennis balls, perchance? Honestly, I don't know where he hides them all."

"I'll tell you where he hides them all. In the backyard, where all the holes that are deep enough for bodies are." I stuffed the letter opener in the pocket of my bathrobe next to my phone and flipped open the box.

My hands stopped all motion as I recognized the vinyl blue squares in the box.

Passports?

There had to be a dozen or so at least. My first thought was they were Bart's. Maybe the aliases he'd traveled under, because there were a bunch of them. Possibly the man who'd leased the villa to him had gathered his things and sent them?

I looked at the postmark, but it wasn't from Greece. It was from Paris…

With shaking hands, I pulled one blue vinyl square

from the box and flipped it open, fully expecting to see Bart's handsome face staring back at me.

But that's not what I saw. That's not what I saw at all.

No. I'll tell you what I saw.

I saw Win's.

CHAPTER 17

I gasped, the echo harsh in my ears as it reached the raised ceiling. I dug into the box again and pulled out yet another passport and flipped it open.

And there was Win's face again.

And not one of them said Crispin Alistair Winterbottom. In fact, they had all sorts of names: Franz Henry, Marco Desalva, Leopold Arnold.

My mouth ran dry, my lips sticking together as I dug through the box with frantic fingers. It was just full of passports. Who would send these to me? Who knew of my connection to Win?

Why would they send them to me *now*?

"Shall I explain?" Win asked, his tone stiff.

"I think I can guess what they are, Win. They're your aliases when you were a spy, right?"

Please, please, please say that's what this is. For a crazy moment, I wondered if I'd been had just like all the women in Bart's and Ralph's lives.

"That's exactly what they are."

I let out a breath. Of course that's what they were. "Any thoughts on who would send them to me? *Why* they'd send them to me? Did you call up MI6 and tell them I was your earthly friend and all your belongings could be sent here?"

Win's silence deafened me, making my concern grow in leaps and bounds and my stomach rumble with discontent.

When he finally spoke, he said, "I don't know, Stevie. No one knows you exist or have any connection to me. I made sure of that. I made sure of that for a reason."

Now *I* was quiet while I tried to form a theory. "Do you think this has to do with Adam? Do you think he could contact someone you know and give them the head's up that I got all your money?"

"If I find that's the case, I'll—"

The doorbell rang, interrupting his words, but I knew what he was about to say anyway. I just wish he realized that even spies like him weren't a match for powerful warlocks like Adam.

"Hold that thought," I said, slipping from the chair to run to the door before they rang again. Win had insisted on an obnoxious gong as the sound the doorbell made. He said it had a regal air to it.

I said it sounded like we'd just entered the Temple Of Doom.

It was dark by now, but this time I was ready. I'd been caught off guard twice at my front door, once by a deranged killer, and once by someone who wasn't a deranged killer at all, but no one was catching me with my pants down this time.

So I grabbed my car keys from the basket on the entryway table and put them between my knuckles. Win had taught me keys in the bad guy's eyeball sockets could cause some severe damage.

The light was bright on the front porch for the reasons I listed above, but I didn't see anyone. If it was those kids who'd dropped by and ding-dong-ditched me because they were angry I'd stolen their super-secret hangout when I'd moved in, I was going to do some ear pulling while I called up their parents.

Pulling the door open, I looked outside, peering into the darkness to the edge of my lawn that fell off like a cliff right down to the beach below my property. The lights on the front lawn glowed, soft and dewy in the mist of rain, the stars and moon covered by the clouds moving in.

And nothing but crickets.

Slamming the door, I held up my fist in rage and gave it a mighty shake. "Swear it, Win. I don't care if those boys are just kids, I'm going to find those little wankers (I love that word. Win taught it to me. It made me feel very British) and steal their lunch money—"

"Stevie! Look out!"

Those were the last words I heard just as someone burst through the dining room window, the glass shattering into a million pieces all over the brand-new hardwood floors.

I was taken so utterly by surprise, I almost couldn't move until the person who'd crashed through the window came at me, full steam ahead. His face was filled with fury, his eyes bulging and wide.

"Stevie, get out! *Gooo!*" Win yelled.

For the briefest of fleeting moments, I cursed my predicament. Would I never learn to wear my work boots all the ding-dong-dang time? Even when I slept? I was never taking them off again. In fact, I was going to have them waterproofed so I could bathe in them, too.

Because my fuzzy slippers just weren't cutting the mustard when it came to fleeing the crazies. Just once, I'd like to be caught by a madman in my sneakers.

But upon instruction, I flung the door open and barreled down the steps, flying along the walkway as the beat of heavy footsteps followed me in close pursuit.

"Who the heck is that?" I squeaked in my panic.

"Forget that for now! Get to the car, Stevie! Get in the car!"

I mentally measured the distance to the car as I ran, my legs pumping so hard I thought they'd fall off. I clung to the keys, pressing the fob to unlock it, thankful I didn't park it in the garage tonight.

My feet began to sink into the softened lawn, my slippers becoming more of a detriment by the second. The lights flashed on my little Fiat, signaling she was ready for entry, so I made a lunge for it, deciding all those stupid kettle exercises Win made me suffer three times a week were actually paying off.

I stopped patting myself on the back when I felt a hand grab onto my hair and yank me backward, slamming me against a hard chest.

Argh! I needed to run more and build up my speed. Either that or get some bionics. Did I have enough money in the bank for bionics?

"Stevie! Hold on to those keys and thrust backward. Got that? Up and back. Nail him right in the eye!" Win yelled.

And I did just that. Reaching behind my head as he grabbed me around the throat with his arm, I thrust. I thrust so hard, I also had to give Win credit for the jousting sessions he forced me to take. Because wow, whoever this particular crazy was, he squealed like a pig, so it must have hurt.

"Jab to the ribs! Give it to him hard with your elbow. Do it!"

Again, I did as I was instructed. I uppercut him in the ribs with my elbow with everything I had in me. And then I was free, running the rest of the way to the car and flinging the door open.

"That's my girl! Now shut the door! Shut it and lock it and move it. Get to the police station *now*!"

I slammed the door shut, catching the edge of my bathrobe in it, to immediately find my attacker was right up against the window. His eye bleeding profusely, his face a mask of rage as he pounded on the glass over and over.

He began to step up his game, slamming his fist against the window even harder, and what came next was my downfall.

Getting a clear view of him as the motion sensor lights on the front of the garage flashed on, I gasped.

Just before the glass of the window broke, smashing to smithereens and flying into my eyes, I knew exactly whom I was facing.

There was no mistaking who he was. He looked just like him.

In fact, other than his height, he was a carbon copy of him.

~

"Stevie! No time to waste! Key in ignition *now!*"

My hands, shaking like two leaves battered in a rainstorm, fumbled as I tried to jam the key into the ignition while he screamed at me, pulling at my hair, trying to wrench me from the car.

"Why couldn't you keep your nose out of it, you stupid woman?" he screamed at me as he attempted to drag me through the window.

The glass cut into my shoulders, the force he used to yank at my hair making me dizzy.

"Stevie! Use your free hand and grip the steering wheel. Grip it hard! Use it as leverage and get that key in the ignition!"

I did as instructed, my cold, clammy hands slipping before I got a good grip and manage to yank myself far enough over to reach the ignition.

But then he yanked harder, wrapping the length of my hair around his wrist and pulling with such force, some of it began to pull from my scalp. "He deserved to die! That scum deserved to die for everything he put me through!"

Shrieking, I found myself enraged. "Let! Go!"

I was trying to grow my hair out, for Pete's sake! But that thought gave me the fuel I needed to jam the key in the ignition and twist. The sound of the engine turning over was the sweetest sound I'd ever heard.

But just one thing. I sort of forgot to put it in reverse. The second Win yelled, "Reverse, Stevie!" was the second I jolted forward after putting my sloppy slippered foot in the kitchen, resulting in my attacker letting go—and me crashing into the garage door.

Wood splintered in every direction, my heart slammed against my ribs painfully, and my attacker's roar of anguish as he ran toward me, his form flashing in my side-view mirror, almost made me freeze.

Except for Win, who was right there in my ear again. "Reverse, Stevie! Put this baby in reverse and put your foot to the floor!"

I put the car in reverse by feel, praying I'd done it right, grinding my foot to the floor. We zoomed backward so fast, everything around me flashed in a blur. I steamrolled down our long driveway, narrowly missing the gate to the left of it that led to the beach-front of our property.

There was a thump, a *loud* thump—a loud, sickening crack of body against metal when I realized he was on the roof. Somehow, he'd launched himself onto the roof!

"Drive, Stevie! Put the car in drive and go! Drive as fast as you can make the car go for the most impact. Don't think. Don't look at anything but the road ahead of you, just drive fast and then slam on the brakes and knock him off!"

I'd gotten quite good at following Win's directions in times of stress. He was almost like my boxing coach, directing me from an invisible sideline. So as the rains slashed at my face and the wind from the speed I was traveling froze my skin, I thought I had this one in the bag. I dug in my pocket and as I picked up speed, swerving and swaying the car to attempt to knock my attacker off, I found my phone and held it up, just about to dial 9-1-1.

That is, until the bad guy reached in the broken window and wrenched the steering wheel to the left, managing to gain control of it for just enough time to have us headed straight over the low guardrail and down the rocky path leading to the beach.

My tiny car took some licking, bucking, scraping, and rocking until I realized I hadn't taken my foot off the accelerator, and as my attacker clung, we were headed straight for the water.

"Stevie! Slam on the brakes!" Win roared.

But my reaction time was too late. We plowed into the freezing cold of the Puget, plunging nose first to its frigid depths.

The moment the water hit my skin, I lost all good sense and began to struggle not only to act, but to think.

As I sank into the water, my pulse racing, I got as stupid as a girl sitting on the bleachers waiting for some guy to ask her to dance at prom. I froze, the icy water enveloping me until I was under its black waves.

"Stevie! Open your eyes, Stevie! Open them, Dove!"

But I couldn't. I don't know *why* I couldn't, I just couldn't. My lungs began to burn, my limbs growing light and weightless as I rose to the ceiling of the car.

"Stevie Cartwright, you will open your eyes *now!*" Win bellowed, his tone angry and harsh with impatience. "Don't you chicken out on me! Open those baby blues!"

With everything I had in me, I forced my eyes to open, the water rushing into them, stinging, making me very aware. But I couldn't see anything! It was pitch black and murky.

And then Win, with calm, orderly instructions, said, "Listen to me, there's not much time, Dove. Feel to your left. That's it. Reach your hands out. That's the window. It's broken. You must swim through it, Stevie, and you must do it instantly! Don't hesitate, listen to me. Swim, Stevie, swim!"

I didn't think I had it in me, my arms feeling as sluggish as they did, my chest and ears about to burst from the pressure of the water, but I jetted forward, feeling my way to the frame of the window, the ragged opening cutting my hands.

"Use it, Stevie, use the frame to push out and up!"

My biceps ached and my legs threatened to seize up on me, but I pushed for all I was worth, pistoning upward.

"Push, Stevie! Puuush! You're almost there!" I heard Win encourage as the pounding of my heart matched the pounding in my head.

I broke the surface with a gasp, a harsh, water-filled, desperate breath for air until I found buoyancy. The water threatened to drag me back to its depths, but Win yelled, "Kick, Stevie! See the shore, the lights of the house? You're not that far. Kick harder. Use your arms! The water is too cold to linger!"

Okay, so here's the truth: I'm not the greatest swimmer, but add in the bulk of my clothing, a head rush to beat any drug-induced high, and the ice-cold temps of the water, and I was a recipe for a *Titanic*-like disaster. No one was ever going to invite me to join the swim team.

But I pounded that water with my hands like I *wanted* to be on the swim team. The lights grew closer, but my body grew more tired by the second.

"No, Stevie, no! Spies never give up! Push, Stevie, *push*!"

My limbs burned with the ache of such laborious physical activity, and just when I didn't think I could take another stroke, I felt the rocky bottom beneath my feet.

"Out, Stevie! Get out. You have to get out and get back to the house! You must warm up!"

Which was easy for Win to say, and if I lived to tell the tale, I'd bet swimming lessons were in my near future if my spy had anything to say about it.

Gasping for air, fighting to get as much into my lungs as I could, I stumbled and tripped the rest of the way to the shore. It was so dark, I almost couldn't see where I was going but for Win's instructions and the vague lights of our house.

"Get out, Stevie! Don't stop now. Move, Dove! Move!"

The shoreline appeared as though rising up to meet me. Either that or I was falling forward with exhaustion. As I hit the ground, the rocks scraped my face and palms, already bloody from my escape from the car.

So I wasn't expecting what came next. And I suspect neither was Win. Because he didn't fire off a warning.

A fist like iron struck me on the side of the head, knocking it back on my shoulders and leaving me seeing stars.

And then I was being dragged forward, over the rocks, over the debris, into the sand, where my attacker threw me like a dead fish.

CHAPTER 18

"Why wouldn't you just stay out of it?" my attacker screamed into the night. "You should have never gone to the prison. He told you, didn't he? He told you! He had the letter! He told you!"

The man fell down beside me, leaning over me, his eye still bleeding, salty water falling from his face onto mine.

"Stevie, don't freeze up! Catch him unaware. Don't listen to him prattle on. Wrap your arms around his neck and put him in a chokehold then snap his neck!"

But I think what Win wasn't quite grasping was the fact that I couldn't really feel my arms very well at the moment. In fact, I could only wiggle my fingers. But my eyes? They worked just fine as my attacker glared down at me.

So I whispered, "*Why?*" It was all I could manage.

Gripping the lapels of my sodden bathrobe, he hauled me up so our faces were mere inches apart.

"Because you interfered! You were at that prison today, asking all kinds of questions of that stupid Ralph! Why else would you be there? He told you about me, didn't he?"

"*How?*" I spat the word, using all my energy. "How did you know I was there?"

Gripping me harder, his hands shook with his rage. "You know how!" he bellowed. "I saw you! All my life I didn't understand these visions. All my life I was afraid of what they meant. I was alone. Always alone!"

Visions? Sweet Jean. Was it *his* magic my mother had smelled that night?

"Admit it! He told you, didn't he?"

Told me about *him*? "*Who are you?*" I asked on a gasped breath.

He shook me like a ragdoll, my whole body limp as a wet noodle. "You *know* who I am! I'm that shyster's son! The son whose mother locked him away in boarding school after boarding school because she was ashamed of me! Because she was too far along to abort me when she realized she was pregnant! I'm the one with the mom who thought I was 'weird' because I see things. I'm the son whose existence was filled with nothing but misery and pain! The son they were *ashamed* of. The son they tortured with his illegitimacy and made him feel dirty just for existing! All because that scumbag knocked her up and ran off with my grandfather's money!"

Seeing him so closely, I knew what I'd thought earlier was spot on. There was no denying it.

This was Bart Hathaway's son.

And if he was Bart's son, he was, at the very least, half warlock. Aw, hell on a stick.

"Visions?" I croaked, my lips cold and stiff. That word stuck out in my mind like a sore thumb. Still, I wasn't sure I was hearing right.

"Yes, *visions*!" he spat at me, water spraying from his twisted mouth. "I can see the future, you idiot! I had a vision today of you going to the prison to see Ralph!"

As he gave me another hard shake to emphasize his point, I managed to respond. "You're a warlock?" I was still astonished. This man had spent his entire lifetime without any guidance at all. Without anyone from the coven to aid him.

He stopped as suddenly as he'd begun, his grip loosening ever so slightly. "I don't know what I am!" he cried, hoarse and raw. "I don't understand any of it and no one will help me!"

"Stevie! I need you to dig deep, Dove! Stop sympathizing with the poor bad guy and do something! Dig as deep as you can and *do something*! Reach beside you, there are rocks. Large rocks. Hit him with one. Warlocks can die, too! Don't mess around with this one, Stevie, *please*!" Win hollered, his tone pleading.

But I just couldn't move. My arms would not connect with the signal my brain was sending. So I kept talking, attempting to distract. "Are you *sure* Bart fathered a son?" I sputtered, my words gurgling as water began to rush its way out of my mouth and I was racked with a coughing spell, the rattle of my labored attempts strong in my ears.

I don't know why I was repeating myself, but I just couldn't fully wrap my head around this information.

"Yeah, he fathered a son, if that's what you want to call it!" he sneered, his eyes wild and glazed, his teeth clenched. "Me! He fathered *me*, and then he abandoned me just like he did that sorry excuse for a mother I have. But I made him pay! I spent years trying to figure out who he was. *Years!* But I found him, didn't I? And then I tracked him here. I got a job as a mime at your shallow party just so I could get up close and personal with him and then I confronted him—and he wouldn't even acknowledge me! Refused to call me his son. But I showed him what denying my existence is all about! I'm sick of being denied like I'm some piece of garbage! All I wanted was for him to confirm it. To acknowledge I was his son!"

There it was. A small rush of heat in my left leg. And if one leg was enough to take out this twisted sister, I'd be in good stead, but he was strong. So darn strong.

"You went to the prison?"

"I called the prison. I called and tried to see the scumbag my father used to turn tricks with. But he wouldn't see me! I sent him letters and they were sent back. I know my father must have told him who I am! But *you* saw him, didn't you? He told you about me, and now you have to die, too!"

"Stevie! Move, *please*, do something! If you don't

move, I can't help you!" Win's warning held desperation, but I couldn't even blink at this point, let alone fight this madman off.

"Belfry," I whispered finally. "Find Belfry..."

"*Who?*" the man screeched as rain beat down on us.

Win's voice was getting smaller. "I can't find him, Stevie! I can't take time to leave you to find him. *You* have to do this. You must move. I will not allow you to die! You will not die while I watch! You will not leave me!"

"He didn't tell me," I sputtered and wheezed on another cough, my chest heaving and sore from the fight for air. It was the only thing I could think of to say. But I wanted him to know—this was all for naught. Ralph had never said a word about Bart having a son.

Pulling me closer, he looked me right in the eye and I was convinced, evil truly did walk this plane. His lips twisted in disgust. "I don't care. I don't care about *anything* anymore. You know now. I have to kill you," he said with eerie calm, just before he slammed my head against the ground.

"Stevie! Bloody hell! Get your hands up in the air and hit him where it hurts! Push your thumbs into his eyes, drive them to the back of his skull if you must, but do it!"

As my vision blurred, my hearing didn't. I heard Win, I even saw him in my mind's eye. A rush of images of the things we'd done these past months flooded my brain. Laughing, talking, sharing meals together, performing séances, him saving my hide on more than one occasion.

Us sitting in the parlor…

The parlor!

I don't know what happened. If it was divine intervention, Win's will for me to live, or just an adrenaline rush at the right time, but as Bart's son lifted me once more by the lapel of my bathrobe, preparing to smash my head into the ground, my fingers sprang into action

Reaching into the pocket of my robe, I almost cheered in relief when my hands touched the letter opener I remembered stuffing into my pocket before I went to answer the door.

With a scream of terror, I plunged it into his shoulder with the hardest jab I could summon, pushing it deep into his flesh.

"That's my girl, Dove!" Win cheered.

The man's roar of anger reverberated through the night but it was enough to make him let go of me. I slammed back to the rocky ground, prepared to try to roll over and get on my feet, when I heard Dana Nelson call out, "Stop! Police! Hands in the air!"

"Thank God!" Win said in a gasping breath.

I heard Whiskey's familiar bark and the rush of several pairs of feet as they thundered past me, but one pair stopped right beside my head. Out of the corner of my eye, I saw they were shiny and perfect.

"Daughter!" my father cried, his voice full of horror. He kneeled beside me and gathered me in his arms, hauling me up into his warm embrace. He smelled of the ocean and his signature spicy cologne. And he was warm. So warm. "Answer me, Stevie! Tell me you're all right!"

I only remember blips of getting to the house. There was a lot of shouting, and of course, Bart's son screaming his hatred at the police as they cuffed him and led him away while Whiskey tugged viciously at the hem of his pants.

But there is one thing I remember clearly as they hauled Bart's son away. His chilling last words to me. "He's coming for you! *I saw him!*" he'd screamed, his face a twisted mask of agony. *"He's coming for you, Stevie, and he's going to make your death a living hell!"*

Then I remember my father carried me back, all the way down the beach and all the way up our long driveway.

I remember my mother's face. Just a quick glimpse of shock and fear as she ran to my dad and met him halfway across the lawn. I remember her peeling my soaking-wet pajamas off, wrapping heated towels around me, sitting me in front of the fire.

Now, almost two hours later, as Sandwich sat on the opposite couch, he explained who Bart's son was. "You went to that prison, didn't you, Stevie."

"Guilty. You itchin' to use those cuffs on me for it?" I responded wearily as my father handed me a cup of steaming coffee.

Sandwich's sigh was ragged, but still, his lips lifted upward. "Stevie, when are you gonna learn to let *us* do the police work? This is the third time, it almost got you killed."

"You want the truth, or a pretty lie?"

He shook his head and made a face. "That's what I thought. Listen, that Ralph up in the Penn? The guards there say he got suspicious after he got a slew of anonymous mail from who we found out tonight is your stepfather's son. His name is Charles Rawlings, by the way."

I almost sat up, but I could only manage to stir in my surprise. "*Clara Rawlings?* That's his mother, isn't it?"

"Yep. And I'm not even gonna ask how you knew that."

"I know how she knew that," my favorite Officer Unicorns and Rainbows said. "She was sticking her nose in it again, that's how." Only this time, he didn't glare at me. He winked.

"Hardy told me about her," I said with a perverse sense of superiority. "He said he told *you*, too. I can't help it if I just ask all the right questions, but I'd be happy to impart the tricks of my nosiness if you'd like."

Sandwich shook a finger at me, but still he smiled. "Anyway, Charles found out about Ralph probably the same way you did, by digging up pictures of him online. He tried to get in to see ol' Ralph, but was denied. Guards say Ralph tried to get in touch with your stepfather, Bart, or whatever his real name is, when he got the letters, to tell him someone was poking around about Clara, but never heard back from him. So he sent all but the one letter he'd already opened back, thinking maybe the sender was just some prison groupie who'd looked up his history online."

"So you're basically telling me that con artist saved my hide? The irony," I said on a laugh.

Sandwich popped his lips. "In a way, yep. When you paid Ralph a visit earlier today, asking all those questions and told him Bart was dead, the con artist managed to put two and two together. After you left, Ralph reread the letter he'd kept, where this kid Charles asked if Bart knew Clara, and then he notified the prison officials, who contacted *us*. The prison officials said Ralph thought it might be Clara who'd killed Bart. We got in touch with Clara Rawlings, who admitted her involvement with Bart all those years ago and their subsequent child. But when asked, she also admitted she hadn't seen her son in days."

I almost felt sorry for Charles. Likely, Clara hadn't even known he was missing from her life at all, and worse, she probably had no idea the kind of power he possessed.

"So Ralph knew Bart had gotten someone pregnant?"

"He didn't know for sure who the kid was because the Rawlingses took great pains to keep him hidden, claimed he's mentally unstable and they've had problems with him from the start. It's almost like Charles didn't exist. But he said Bart had grumbled about something to that effect a long time ago, and then he never mentioned it again."

That explained what Charles meant about all those boarding schools and being hidden away. How sad for him. How different his life could have turned out, had someone just given him the attention he so clearly needed.

How different it could have been if he'd been taught to use his visions properly. How different it could have been if his mother had taken the time to listen to Charles, to try to understand what she considered mental instability.

When Baba got wind of this, Bart would probably be glad he was dead.

"So the Rawlingses didn't want anyone to know about him because he was born out of wedlock. I think I get the rest," I said in disgust. "But why did he come after *me*? I had no clue it was him. I didn't even know he existed until he had me on the beach and I really saw him. He looks just like Bart."

I knew I had to ask that question in order to keep suspicion to a minimum. I'm famous for snooping. If I failed to wonder out loud something as basic as why Charles had come for me, Officer Astute would wonder why I hadn't. I couldn't very well tell them Charles had a vision of me.

I had a vision of my own just then. The one where I tell the police Charles hunted me down because he saw me go into the prison in the future. Office Nelson would laugh and laugh.

"He's a crafty one, that kid. He tracked your stepfather to Greece and then to Seattle, got himself a job at your party, confronted Bart...and you know the story."

"Right. But that still doesn't explain why he'd come after me."

I knew I was pushing, but I was curious to know how Charles explained what he knew without making everyone think he was a tenth-level nutter.

But Sandwich threw up a finger. Uh-oh. I felt a sermon coming on, about how I should keep my nose out of police investigations.

"He had himself a hot police scanner and heard we put out an APB on him tonight. He knew we were looking for him. But what gave *you* away was his mother and your trip to the prison, Stevie. He says he *saw* you go into the prison. We figure Charles must have been staking the place out. Once he'd killed Bart, he was especially worried your mother might pay Ralph a visit, and find out about that letter. What cinched the idea Ralph might have told *you* about him was the phone call he got from Clara."

I nodded in total understanding, as though I was letting everything fall into place. "She called him and wanted to know why he was sending letters to Ralph, didn't she? Because she just wanted to keep sweeping this all under the carpet. So, I'm guessing she also told him you'd been in touch with her and were looking for him?"

"She did. And then he got really antsy. Especially after we put the APB out on him. Said he couldn't take the chance Ralph had told you something. He swears up and down he didn't mean to kill Bart. He said things just got out of hand when Bart told him to go to hell. He gave us all kinds of heat-of-the-moment stuff, but in the end..."

My mother shuddered, but I smiled and grabbed her hand, tucking it next to me.

"So that's why Bart had the number for the prison I found in his money clip? Because Ralph tried to reach out to him?" I asked.

"So when you told me about the evidence you saw in the parlor that we'd missed, you already knew what it was, didn't you?" he asked with that look that said he obviously already knew the answer.

I gave him a guilty look. "Yes. I knew what it was, but I didn't touch it, I swear. So did Ralph call Bart?"

Sandwich pursed his lips. "That's the best we can figure. Maybe Ralph left him a message and he jotted down the number for later use. We're still checking phone records from the prison. Could be Ralph got a hot phone from some unknown source and it won't show up anyway. Gotta tell ya, though. I feel sorry for the kid. He's been spouting some of the craziest stuff I think I've ever heard after almost ten years on the force. He's sure messed up."

I felt sorry for him, too. I had a hunch Bart did know about Charles. I also had a hunch he knew about his son's attempt to contact Ralph, and he knew because he'd used his magic to find out. Though, I'd probably never be able to prove it. Maybe Bart could see the future, too. Right now, I was too tired to delve deeper into that particular mystery.

"I hope he gets the help he needs. All I can say is, thank goodness you all showed up when you did," I said. "Thank you for saving me once again."

Officer Nelson pointed at my father. "That was all because of your father. He's the one who saw your car take a dive into the Sound. He's the one who called 9-1-1."

"I had no idea it was you, Daughter, but when I saw your car missing, someone from above— Er, something inside me told me I had to get to the beach. Thank God you're all right." He pressed a kiss to my hand and squeezed it before he rose.

I shivered, still chilled to the bone despite the blankets. "So are you guys releasing CC? What about the fibers of her bathing suit on Bart's jacket?"

"Yep. She's free as a bird. Not that it matters much, now that Charles confessed and we all heard it, but we have two theories. Either Bart *did* get frisky with her…" Sandwich stopped for a moment out of respect for my mother, but she waved a hand to signal he could continue. "Or when she hugged Charles that night—or he hugged her—when she showed him how to tie his bow tie, fibers transferred to *him*. Could have rubbed off on Bart's suit when Charles… Well, you know the rest."

I rubbed my eyes, still stinging from the water. "I'm glad she can go home."

"Gentlemen," Hugh said, tucking a heating blanket

under my chin. "My daughter's exhausted, as you can see. Are we through here? She needs her rest. However, I'd be happy to take selfies with you and sign autographs if that will encourage you to speak to her in the morning. You can tell all your friends how you met the famous Hugh Granite."

Sandwich and Officer Nelson both looked at me, their brows furrowed, but I could only giggle, which then made me cough.

Officer Nelson was the first to tuck his notepad away. "I think we have everything for now, Mr. er, Granite. Stevie? You rest." Then he crouched beside me and grinned, patting my arm. "From here on out, all bets are off now. Even-steven, Detective Cartwright? Say it out loud or I can't leave."

I shook my head but I grinned, holding out my hand to shake on it. "Even-steven, Officer Rigid. For now, anyway," I agreed on a chuckle.

But I crossed the fingers on my other hand—you know, just in case (wink-wink).

EPILOGUE

Later That Week...

I dropped a kiss on each of the Bats's heads, giving Uncle Ding an extra nuzzle. "You guys be safe on the way home, huh? And keep your sonar to yourself, mister," I teased.

Deloris steamrolled Belfry on the kitchen table. "C'mere, my squishy face, and give your mother a kiss before she goes."

"Ma! Quit!" But he was giggling when he protested. "Make sure you call when you get home, and you two, don't give Mom any more trouble. We've had enough of that around here."

Wom and Com chuckled before flying to the open window to prepare to take flight.

I scooped Bel up and put him on my shoulder. "Bye, guys, safe trip!"

As each of the Bats took off, soaring upward, their

tiny wings but specks in the setting sun, my chest grew tight. I was actually sad to see them go.

"Phew," Belfry said. "Can't believe we only lost one vase and a cabinet door handle during that entire visit. I think we just set a record."

I giggled. "We lived to tell the tale, buddy."

"Stephania?" my mother called to me from the entryway. She was leaving, too. Not alone, mind you, but in better hands this time.

I'd done some research on this Raul, and if he was nothing else, he was incredibly charitable, philanthropic, and most of the articles we'd read on him said he was a decent enough guy—which was why I'd privately warned him about my mother. It was the least he deserved.

"You're off, I guess?"

She smiled at me, beautiful in her flowing lavender dress and big dark sunglasses. She held out her hand, and I took it and squeezed. I was actually sad to see her go, too. We'd spent a lot of time talking this week, trying to work through our issues; we'd cried a little, but we'd laughed, too, and during that time, I'd set firm boundaries about my life and the way she treated me.

None of that erased my childhood, but we had a good starting point for my adulthood, and a solid future.

She'd promised me she'd speak to Baba Yaga about Charles, too. Yes, he'd killed Bart, but he'd end up in a human jail with human prisoners. Who knew what he was capable of? He was out of control and in desperate need of containment. If Charles really could see the future —something my mother assured me, if Bart was capable of, she hadn't known—this poor kid was a loose cannon. A chance like that was a risk Baba wouldn't want to take.

We'd also had a small memorial for Bart. Just Win, Bel, Mom and me. I'd said a few words and my mother had apologized to him for her deceptions. I don't know if Bart can hear, wherever he is, but her words actually sounded quite genuine. I left it at that and we scattered his ashes over the Puget.

"I wish you could stay longer, Mom." I never thought I'd say those words, but there they were.

"I need to tell you something, Stephania... *Stevie*," she enunciated, finally calling me by my preferred nickname.

I cocked my head in question. "Sure, Mom. Anything."

Mom's fingers let go of mine as she gripped my upper arms, almost pinching my flesh. "Something changed in me that night with Adam Westfield, Stephania. I thought I knew who I was. I thought I had it all figured out. But seeing you in so much danger, hearing that bastard warlock threaten your life..." She paused, lifting her chin, her gaze faraway. "Well, I've never felt such rage. Such uncontrollable anguish and pure hatred...such *fear*. I wanted him dead. I wanted him to hurt the way he was hurting you. I wanted to hurt him ten thousand times *more* than he hurt you. And it frightened me to my core, but it also gave me quite the wake-up call."

Whatever had happened that night with Adam, whatever it was that had unlocked something inside of Dita, it truly had changed her. It was like watching someone turn over a completely new leaf. I have no explanation for this change, and I'm not questioning it. Not now, anyway.

"Do you think maybe you have the mom gene after all? Maybe it just took time to mutate or something," I teased, trying to keep things light because I'd never seen her like this. I'd never seen her so rattled.

Her grip lightened and she rubbed my upper arms with her hands and smiled. "I don't know what I have. I *do* know that moment, that single second where I thought he'd kill you, shredded me, and I need to reevaluate my life, Stevie, your childhood. The things I did so wrong when you were growing up. The things I ignored in favor of my own needs. But I'll be back, Stephania. I'll be back often and we'll talk more. I hope you'll let me come back so we can do that."

As she looked at me, her blue-gray eyes so like mine were hopeful and warm, and that was shredding *me*.

"Do you promise to clean up after yourself and keep your dead husbands under lock and key?"

She laughed then. We laughed together. Then we hugged. For a long time before she hopped into Raul's smart Mercedes convertible and drove away, her long scarf streaming behind her, the last vestiges of the sun glinting on her beautiful chestnut hair, just like in the movies.

"Daughter?" Hugh popped in from nowhere in a cloud of emerald-green smoke, his movie-star smile in place.

"Hey!" I said on a return grin, falling into one of his hugs as if I'd done so all my life.

We'd spent a great deal of time together this week, too. I'd looked up his website, where he'd shown me all the amazing experiences he'd had over the course of his career. We looked at the list of his movies—movies I'd never heard of—but most of all, we'd bonded.

Big time. I told him everything that had happened with Adam Westfield, with Win and the house and Madam Zoltar. And I didn't care that he talked about himself most of the conversation. When it counted, he'd been there. Rock solid.

Hugh and my mother hadn't talked much during their stay—they didn't hate on each other or argue, either. In fact, they didn't often acknowledge each other one way or the other.

I guess my childhood dream of Hugh whisking her off her feet and riding off into the sunset with all three of us on his horse wasn't ever going to come true.

Hugh was beholden to no one woman except me, he'd told me, and I was okay with that as long as he was happy.

"Are you leaving me, too?" I made a sad face at him.

"Never," he whispered dramatically from above my head. "Not permanently, anyway. But my fans call,

Stevie. I have another movie I'm shooting and I must prepare. Though, I do hate to leave you after all you've told me."

A tear stung my eye, but I scrunched them shut and said against his jacket, "I hate it, too. But I understand. So you'll poke around for me, about what Charles said?"

"I'll do more than poke, beautiful daughter. I'll make it my mission," he said in his game-show announcer's voice. "Win, I expect you'll watch out for my daughter as though your spirit depends upon it?"

"You have my word, sir."

My father had also heard what Charles said before he was taken away, and he'd shown genuine concern. He'd promised to contact the council about Charles, and to have the spirits he communicated with on the reg watch over me in his stead.

"Thanks...*Dad*..." The word slipped off my tongue with great ease.

Hugh set me from him then and chucked me under the chin. "You are the best gift I could have ever given myself. Well, unless the gift was me, of course," he said on a cheesy wink. "Now, you stay safe, and if you need me, anytime, no matter where I am, just use the amulet I left you. It's heavy with magic, Daughter. Wear it always, and I'll always be with you."

I held up the thin gold chain with the sapphire amulet my father had given me. He said it reminded him of the color of my eyes. "Got it. But come back soon, okay? Thanksgiving? Christmas? I'm going to miss you."

"And I you, Daughter. Now no sad goodbyes. They create pesky wrinkles you'll never be rid of. Aunt Imelda is keeping tabs on you from the great beyond, and if all else fails, tweet me." With that, he dropped a kiss on my cheek and snapped his fingers, leaving as quickly as he'd come.

Rubbing my arms, I sighed a happy sigh.

"You were lovely with your mother today. You are the kindest person I know, Stephania."

"Or the most gullible, Winterbutt." But I paused for a moment, one long one as I reflected on my mother's words. "Do you think she meant what she said?"

Win cleared his throat. "I do, Dove. I truly do. Your narrow escape from death was jarring, no doubt. I can't say she didn't deserve a good wakeup call."

Sticking my hand in my pocket, I pulled out what felt like a piece of thin cardboard. "I forgot all about this," I said, holding up Petula's chewed business card. "Did we ever find out who wrote Bart's name on the back?"

"Nothing concrete, but I'd bet my Aston Martin it was Charles. Why he'd do it escapes me, though."

I shook the card in the air and laughed. "Your Aston Martin, huh? Might be worth the expense of a hand-writing analysis."

"You'll never get your hands on that car, Stevie. Never!" Win teased, then sobered. "Also, more intel from the afterlife this morning."

I groaned. "Do I want to know so soon after this last mess?"

"It has to do with this last mess. Remember the lovely southern spirit who contacted us while we were at the store?"

I nodded. "Oh, yeah. Did she come back?"

"She did. Her name is Beth Ann and she was referring to Bart when she said he did it, and he wasn't what he seemed. Meaning he was a con artist. Beth Ann was one of Bart's many conquests. We rather overlooked the picture at the shop of Bart and your mother on the shelf next to your hoard of snow globes—which was what she was referring to when she imploded it. She apologized profusely for breaking it in her attempt to share her information."

"So I blamed my totally innocent father. That'll teach me to make assumptions when I'm so emotionally involved in an investigation. Poor Beth Ann. But tell her I said thanks for trying to help."

Win barked a laugh. "I wouldn't feel sorry for Beth Ann. According to her, she finally had the chance to give Bart a piece of her mind before he crossed over. She seemed quite pleased with herself."

Smiling, I chuckled. "Then all's well that ends well, huh?"

Win's tone was dark when he said, "Not all has ended well, Dove. We must discuss our plans for the words Charles spoke."

The ominous dread those words evoked washed over me again with spidery fingers. "Like a plan of attack? I'm sort of defenseless, Win. I have no powers to fight that sort of threat."

And that notion terrified me.

"Do you think Charles really can see into the future, Dove?"

I shrugged. "There's no record of him anywhere in our archives, according to my dad. But that's because his mother didn't want anyone to know about him, and the impression I got from Charles was that his mother thought he was weird. Maybe he shared visions when he was frightened by them and Clara labeled him crazy?"

"Poor chap. To be so misunderstood all his life."

It made my stomach turn to think of how he must have suffered. "I blame Bart for that. I can't shake the feeling he knew about Charles, and if he knew, then he should have realized Charles was at least half warlock."

"Do you think your mother was telling us the truth when she said she didn't think Bart had visions? That he was just your average, every day warlock?"

"I don't think she'd lie now. Not after everything that happened. But maybe that's what kept Bart from getting caught by Baba all these years? He knew when she was coming because he could see it?"

Shaking my head, I felt nothing but dark and cold when I examined Charles and his life, so easily swept under the carpet by his family and their wealth. He had a rare gift and it had been stifled and misunderstood.

Charles was someone I'd keep tabs on, because I

couldn't bear that he wouldn't at least be given a chance to understand what he was—would be.

"Either way, his words are still an issue, but I don't believe we can't fight fire with fire if we can just obtain your powers," Win remarked. "In fact, I refuse to believe such. *Refuse*. Your powers have flickered. They remain somewhere inside you. We need to find out how to reactivate them."

"It's not like I can drink a magic potion or that I have a switch I can just turn back on, Win. It doesn't work that way."

"But they *have* reappeared. I won't stop until we rediscover how to obtain them once more."

Right. Just like he wasn't going to stop trying to get back to this plane. For the moment, I needed some downtime from threats and the afterlife and Adam Westfield.

"Can we revisit this discussion at a later date?"

"We can. *We will*."

Closing my eyes, I let go of the past days and cocked an ear. "Hear that?"

"What?"

"The sound of silence, my friend." I inhaled and smiled as seagulls soared, the motorboat engines hummed, but no one was buzzing about my head—or in my nightgown. Once more, peace was restored at Mansion Mayhem and Madness.

"'Tis quite lovely indeed."

"C'mon, International Man of Mystery, let's go have some Cheese Whiz and Triscuits. I'll introduce you to the culinary delights of processed, glutinous gobs of deliciousness from a spray can."

"You have the most immature palate I've ever encountered, Stephania Cartwright. How can you eat such atrocities when there are leftover goat cheese and fig wraps?"

I made a gagging noise, making Whiskey plow down the stairs to meet me at the foot of them as Bel snored softly from my shoulder.

"I'd rather lick a toilet bowl, Spy Guy."

"That's vile, Stephania Cartwright—"

The gong of the doorbell thwarted Win reading me the riot act about my taste buds.

My finger shot up in the air. "Save the foodie sermon just a minute more. Maybe Mom forgot something. Like the spare husband she had stashed away in the closet."

Win's laughter rang in my ear as I grabbed the door handle and looked out the stained-glass window.

As you all know, I have really bad luck when answering my door, but I was pretty sure it was Sandwich who said he'd drop off Bart's personal effects around this time.

Popping it open, I felt the warm breeze blow in, but Sandwich wasn't who was on my doorstep. A very handsome gentleman in a crisp suit, probably in his early thirties, with dark hair and even darker eyes, looked back at me.

"Stevie Cartwright?" he asked in a cultured British accent.

I smiled and nodded. "In the flesh. You are?"

He paused for only a minute, his eyes intensely scanning mine, before he said, "My name is Winterbottom. Crispin Alistair Winterbottom…"

The End

(For now, but don't miss the first chapter below for book four of the Witchless in Seattle Cozy Mysteries, titled *The Ol' Witcheroo*—coming in August of 2016! I so hope you'll join me to find out who this man claiming to be Stevie's beloved Winterbottom is, discover more clues about Win's mysterious life and death, and help the gang solve another murder! Until then, happy reading!)

PREVIEW ANOTHER BOOK BY
DAKOTA CASSIDY

Chapter 1

I remember the moment like it was yesterday. The day
I met the man who claimed to be Crispin Alistair

Winterbottom, my dead British spy gone ghost. Which was impossible, because Win wasn't just dead; my British spy specter had been right in my ear, calling this handsome man a liar.

We'd just wrapped up a particularly crazy week in our unconventional lives. I use the word "unconventional" because, hello, how many people do you know who have a ghost always yapping in their ear with a sexy British accent? (Truth. Swear it on my secondhand Carolina Herrera pantsuit.)

For that matter, how many people do you know whom, after losing their witch powers (that's me. Little Lost Ex-Witch) and being shunned from their coven, end up broke and a little battered in their old hometown of Ebenezer Falls, WA, with a saucy and eternally hungry bat familiar to feed?

To make things really outlandish, how many broke ex-witch's do you know who not only stumble onto a dead body, but make contact with a dead British Spy who has a house straight out of an episode of *The Munster's* and a zillion dollars he wants to give you, if you'll help him solve the murder of his beloved medium (the dead body), Madam Zoltar?

That's what I mean by unconventional.

Add in the fact that I've taken over Win's favorite medium's business and reinvented myself as Madam Zoltar 2.0, and we now basically live together in this monstrosity turned majestic mini-mansion with my bat familiar, Belfry, and our rescue dog, Whiskey, in a town made up entirely of humans—a town where you'd think murder was the least likely event to occur yet seems to happen every month or so—and you have my unconventional life in a nutshell.

Anyway, we'd just finished up a grueling week when this imposter, as Win calls him, shows up at our door. We'd hosted a housewarming party earlier that week because my uppity British Man of Mystery thought I needed to make more friends and reconnect with my old and new fellow Ebenezers. And in the midst of this amazing party with mimes and Cirque Du Soleil acrobats, my stepfather, Bart Hathaway, was murdered.

Also in the middle of this big, fancy party chock full of the most disgusting goat-cheese-and-fig appetizers I've ever tasted, the father I didn't know about, international star of stage, screen and film in Japan, Hugh Granite, showed up and announced, well, that he was my father.

Crazy, right? After almost thirty-three years of a fatherless existence, I have this man—handsome, incredibly egotistical, yet still charming and as charismatic as one of those TV preachers—show up and claim ownership of parental duties like he'd always been my dad.

Now, dig if you will the picture (Prince forever!), the other half of my gene pool—my mother, Dita. As vain as my father, but not quite (read: not even close) as charming in her own brand of vanity, with dead husband number five on her hands. I think he was number five. I've lost count (apologies).

Mom's husband is dead, right? Murdered at the height of our housewarming party. To be precise, he was strangled with one of the acrobats' silky sheet thingies. Outwardly, she does all the right things. Cries, wails, grieves when prying eyes are upon her. But behind my back, while I'm still digesting the death of my stepfather, a man I didn't even know, she's scoping out the lay of the land for her next husband.

During all this upheaval, my familiar Belfry's family arrived and wreaked havoc on our beautiful new home, while Win and I attempted to catch a killer amidst complete chaos.

So one more surprise on the very day we'd cleared the house of any and all manner of bananapants after solving said murder—wherein I almost drowned in Puget Sound in my cute little Fiat (currently swimming with the fishes. Sad panda)—this guy claiming to be the man I've been solving mysteries with shows up.

He says he's the man I've had inhabiting my ear for since February. The man I still know very little about…

Anyway, on this day, I was in the middle of making jokes about how awful some of the appetizers at the party were, and Win was bashing my ill-refined palate. That was when the gong of the doorbell thwarted him reading me the riot act about my taste buds…

My finger shot up in the air. "Save the foodie sermon, Iron Chef Winterbottom, just a minute more. I don't know who this could be." Then I laughed. "Maybe Mom forgot something. Like the spare husband she had stashed away in the closet."

Win's laughter rang in my ear as I grabbed the door handle and looked out the stained-glass window at the warped figure.

I've had really bad luck when answering my door in the recent past, but I was pretty sure it was Sandwich, who'd said he'd drop off my stepfather Bart's personal effects around this time. So I wasn't at all prepared for what—or rather *who*—greeted me.

Popping the door open, I felt a warm breeze blow in, but Sandwich wasn't on my doorstep. A very handsome gentleman in a crisp suit, probably in his early thirties, with dark hair and even darker eyes, looked back at me. Or at least I think he did. The sun was a blazing hot ball of flames, glaring me in the eye, so it was hard to tell.

Either way, he definitely wasn't Sandwich. Sandwich smelled of old school Old Spice and peanut butter. This man didn't smell like peanut butter.

"Stevie Cartwright?" he asked in a cultured British accent.

I smiled and nodded, still unable to clearly see his face in detail. I squinted. "In the flesh. You are?"

He paused for only a minute, his eyes scanning mine. Again, I couldn't *see* his eyes, per se. Rather, I felt them on me—felt their intensity, felt their scrutiny.

Then he moved in closer, smelling of subtly expensive cologne, before he said, "My name is Winterbottom. Crispin Alistair Winterbottom."

I frowned at this stranger, cupping my hand over my eyes to block the sharp rays. "Say again?"

"I said, I'm Crispin Alistair Winterbottom. You *are* Stevie Cartwright, correct?"

"Maybe..." I offered, my eyes trying desperately to adjust to the harsh glint of sunlight. What in sweet Pete was going on?

"Cat's out of the bag, Dove. You already told him who you were, Stephania," Win chastised in my ear. "Always remember what I've taught you. Never reveal vital information unless forced by jumper cables or, heaven forbid, water torture."

"Might I come in and ask you some questions?" he inquired, almost pushing me out of the way as he stepped into our wide foyer. And yes, now I could see his eyes penetrating mine.

Yep, they were definitely penetrating.

So I took a step back and blinked away the white spots floating in my vision. "How do you know who I am?"

"You were easy enough to find," he said affably, the breeze lifting his hair and ruffling it in ripples of deep chocolate. Which I could see as my eyesight adjusted. His hair was as thick and lush as the real Winterbottom's.

And then the sun moved. Moved so far right, I got an unobstructed view of this man who'd called himself Winterbottom.

I'm sure right at that moment, I gaped at him. Openly, awkwardly gaped.

First, let me say, I've only seen Win once, and that was during the mess while we were investigating my stepfather death. Somehow, he'd managed to make himself appear to me from his afterlife haven.

The incident had been brief, but I'd seen him as clear as day. Recalling that moment still makes my heart pound harder than horse hooves racing in the Kentucky Derby. It isn't because I've never seen a ghost. On the contrary. I've seen many. But since I'd lost my witch powers, I hadn't seen a one.

Second, I only have one picture of Win. I've looked at it a thousand times since he'd admitted it was, in fact, a photo of him. It's older and faded, a shot taken with his ex-lover, Miranda. They were at the Eiffel Tower, and from the way they looked at each other, they'd been nuts in love.

Until she'd killed him. Or at least that's what *my* Win claims she did, anyway.

So as this man audaciously entered my house and looked me square in the eye as though I owed him money, my mouth fell open. Unhinged completely.

Because I gotta say, he really did look exactly like my picture of Winterbottom in Paris.

When I was finally able to put words together, I wiped my sweaty palms on my thighs and asked, "Who did you say you were again?" Maybe I'd heard wrong, or maybe he'd been making some kind of sick joke.

A thought occurred to me then: Could this be one of Winterbottom's spy friends, playing some elaborate hoax.

Who looks exactly like him, Stevie? What episode of the Twilight Zone *are you reenacting?*

He smiled pleasantly, a gorgeous, toothpaste-commercial-worthy smile that didn't quite reach his eyes and repeated his words. "I said, I'm Crispin Alistair Winterbottom."

"Stevie!" Win finally spewed in my ear. I'm not sure what took him so long to react, but by the sounds of it, he surely had a grip on the gist of things now. "That is absolutely *not* me. Do you hear me? He's an imposter. I repeat, an imposter!"

Yeah, yeah. I heard Win. But here was a guy standing in my foyer, wanting to talk to me, claiming he was *my* Spy Guy and he was, without a doubt, the spitting image of my Spy Guy. Not a chance in the deep blue sea I was passing up this newest mystery.

"But he looks exactly like you," I muttered under my breath.

"Say again?" Fake Winterbottom requested in a pleasant tone, his head cocked as though he were intently listening to me.

"Well, that I can't deny, Dove. I don't know how or why, but he does uncannily resemble me."

"Uh-huh," I whispered.

"Aha!" Win declared with a tone suggesting he'd figured things out. "Maybe Arkady Bagrov sent him? Though why, I can't begin to guess. Surely that crafty wank Arkady's long over our last little disagreement, wherein I bested him in a rousing game of Disarm the Nuclear Missile, Save Istanbul? But to go to this extreme? Bah." Win dismissed the notion. "Arkady's a vengeful man, but I don't recall him ever using plastic surgery as part of his criminal portfolio—it's too extreme even for him."

I turned my back on Phony Win and whispered, "You knew criminals who used plastic surgery for disguises? Like, that was really a thing?"

"If you only knew how much of a thing," Win confirmed.

Faux Winterbottom was growing impatient. I saw it in his gorgeous face when I turned back around, still astounded a spy tactic like plastic surgery, a tactic so James Bond-ish, did indeed really exist. "You were saying, Miss Cartwright?"

"Um, sorry. Nothing. I'm just…"

What was I? Stunned was too small a word. I was verklempt. Flabbergasted. Gobsmacked, as Win would say.

I lifted my shoulders in helplessness. "Um, I'm just…"

"Just in my house?" he asked, driving his hands into the pockets of his expensive suit. I knew it was expensive. I'd know Armani blind and without benefit of the gift of scent.

"I'm in *your what*?" I spit the words out, frowning.

"Oh, tell this numpty to move along, Dove! He's handing you a load of bollocks," Win groused, totally dismissing the man who looked exactly like him.

Leaning in, Phony Win kept that irritating smile on his face as he dropped the bomb. "I said, you're in my house, Miss Cartwright. I purchased this house, and somehow, *you've* managed to end up the one living in it. How did that happen, do you suppose? Are you an identity thief?"

Now *I* was getting impatient. Who the heck was this guy and how dare he claim our house was *his* house? If this was some sort of convoluted joke—though again, I stress, plastic surgery just to prank someone is far and away well beyond elaborate—someone was going to have to pay for stirring me up like this.

So I crossed my arms over my chest and looked this crackpot right in the eye with my best stern face. "Look, I don't know who you are or what kind of sick game you're playing, but Crispin Alistair Winterbottom is dead, and this is *my* house. It's easy enough to look up at the Department of Land Records right here in town. So why don't you go do that and get back to me when you have some solid proof of alleged ownership?"

He sucked in his cheeks, and oddly, when he did, it was exactly how I imagined my Win would look when he grew impatient with me. "Oh, I assure you, this is no game, Stevie Cartwright. I *am* Crispin Alistair Winterbottom, and this is *my* home, and I fully intend to prove such. Until then, take notice, I don't know how you got your hands on *my* house, *my* money, but prepare to pay back every dime you've stolen from me —including the cost of these borderline garish renovations you've perpetrated!"

"Garish?" Win squealed with indignant outrage.

"Box this nutter's ears, Stevie! Box 'em but good then send him on his way!"

I waved a hand at Win, trying to get him out of my ear, but I didn't need to bother shooing him away. Phony Winterbottom pivoted on his heel, barreled back down the steps and made a graceful exit to his car.

An Aston Martin, I might add—a black one with yellow rims.

"That's my car! Did that son of a backside scratcher steal my *car*?" Win yelped in utter outrage.

There was lots of very inappropriate language at that point. Words I didn't even consider my cultured Spy Guy knew. But he used them, and he continued to use them in the ensuing days.

But since that day, we hadn't heard from Fakebottom, as I'd begun to call him. Not a peep. And I was glad. I had no explanation for his existence. I almost think his uncanny resemblance to my Win was too creepy for my head to wrap around.

Nothing about his showing up out of the blue made sense. Nor did his claim he could prove he was Winterbottom. Even if something as outlandish as plastic surgery was involved to make himself look exactly like Win (and let's be realistic here, folks. That kind of plastic surgery only exists on soap operas), there was DNA and fingerprints to consider.

So while it lingered heavily in the backs of our minds, we went right on living, and from time to time discussed the absurdity of it all—neither of us able to come up with a feasible explanation as to why he looked so much like Win. We speculated that Fakebottom had likely gone away because he really couldn't prove he *was* Win. Doing that would mean he'd have to come up with some DNA, and that was simply ludicrous, given Win's background at MI6.

He assured me MI6 had not only his fingerprints but plenty of DNA to spare, should push come to shove. So we filed it in our Impossible folder and moved right along.

Though I admit, I've secretly stared at that picture of Miranda and Win in the privacy of my bedroom a hundred times since Fakebottom showed up, and it freaks me to the ends of the earth and back how identical he is to my Spy Guy.

But we were in the midst of enjoying a lovely summer, with plenty of tourism at Madam Zoltar's, picnics on the water every weekend, nights spent with a bottle of wine on the back patio, now totally renovated and sparkling with Chinese lanterns, Bel buzzing about in the evening sky and Whiskey at my feet.

Life was really good and I was pretty content. Probably more so than I had been my entire life—even as a witch.

Which brings us to today—two months later.

When life got very, very ugly-complicated, and there was plenty of discontent to spare...

NOTE FROM DAKOTA

I do hope you enjoyed this book, I'd so appreciate it if you'd help others enjoy it, too.

Recommend it. Please help other readers find this book by recommending it.

Review it. Please tell other readers why you liked this book by reviewing it at online retailers or your blog. Reader reviews help my books continue to be valued by distributors/resellers. I adore each and every reader who takes the time to write one!

If you love the book or leave a review, please email **dakota@dakotacassidy.com** so I can thank you with a personal email. Your support means more than you'll ever know! Thank you!"

ABOUT THE AUTHOR

Dakota Cassidy is a USA Today bestselling author with over thirty books. She writes laugh-out-loud cozy mysteries, romantic comedy, grab-some-ice erotic romance, hot and sexy alpha males, paranormal shifters, contemporary kick-ass women, and more.

Dakota was invited by Bravo TV to be the Bravo-holic for a week, wherein she snarked the hell out of all the Bravo shows. She received a starred review from Publishers Weekly for Talk Dirty to Me, won a Romantic Times Reviewers' Choice Award for Kiss and Hell, along with many review site recommended reads and reviewer top pick awards.

Dakota lives in the gorgeous state of Oregon with her real-life hero and her dogs, and she loves hearing from readers!

OTHER BOOKS BY DAKOTA CASSIDY

Visit Dakota's website at
http://www.dakotacassidy.com for more information.

*A Lemon Layne Mystery, a Contemporary Cozy Mystery
Series*
    1. Prawn of the Dead
    2. Play That Funky Music White Koi
    3. Total Eclipse of the Carp
*Witchless In Seattle Mysteries, a Paranormal Cozy
Mystery series*
    1. Witch Slapped
    2. Quit Your Witchin'
    3. Dewitched
    4. The Old Witcheroo
    5. How the Witch Stole Christmas
    6. Ain't Love a Witch
    7. Good Witch Hunting

Nun of Your Business Mysteries, a Paranormal Cozy Mystery series

1. Then There Were Nun
2. Hit and Nun

Wolf Mates, a Paranormal Romantic Comedy series

1. An American Werewolf In Hoboken
2. What's New, Pussycat?
3. Gotta Have Faith
4. Moves Like Jagger
5. Bad Case of Loving You

A Paris, Texas Romance, a Paranormal Romantic Comedy series

1. Witched At Birth
2. What Not to Were
3. Witch Is the New Black
4. White Witchmas

Non-Series

Whose Bride Is She Anyway?

Polanski Brothers: Home of Eternal Rest

Sexy Lips 66

Accidentally Paranormal, a Paranormal Romantic Comedy series

Interview With an Accidental—a free introductory guide to the girls of the Accidentals!

1. The Accidental Werewolf
2. Accidentally Dead
3. The Accidental Human
4. Accidentally Demonic
5. Accidentally Catty
6. Accidentally Dead, Again

7. The Accidental Genie

8. The Accidental Werewolf 2: Something About Harry

9. The Accidental Dragon

10. Accidentally Aphrodite

11. Accidentally Ever After

12. Bearly Accidental

13. How Nina Got Her Fang Back

14. The Accidental Familiar

15. Then Came Wanda

16. The Accidental Mermaid

The Hell, a Paranormal Romantic Comedy series

1. Kiss and Hell

2. My Way to Hell

The Plum Orchard, a Contemporary Romantic Comedy series

1. Talk This Way

2. Talk Dirty to Me

3. Something to Talk About

4. Talking After Midnight

The Ex-Trophy Wives, a Contemporary Romantic Comedy series

1. You Dropped a Blonde On Me

2. Burning Down the Spouse

3. Waltz This Way

Fangs of Anarchy, a Paranormal Urban Fantasy series

1. Forbidden Alpha

2. Outlaw Alpha

Made in the USA
Monee, IL
15 July 2022